YOU W

The insect's he...
cocoon imprisoning Alaire. Then the Bard saw that it was not a head, but only one of its eyes. As he gaped at the creature, it dumped him inelegantly onto the stone floor. The two giant insects regarded him for a moment before one of them spoke in broken Althean.

"You will come with us, prisoner," he said. "If you try to escape, we will cut you in half."

To demonstrate, the Arachnian reached down with a claw and clamped around Alaire at the waist, exerting just enough pressure to let him know the creature meant business. Alaire was convinced that they could snip him in two with very little effort.

"You will obey," the Arachnia said.

Alaire nodded, but apparently the Arachnian wanted a more substantial reply.

"You will obey!" the Arachnian said, and with a wave of the massive claw knocked Alaire to the floor.

"Yes, I will obey."

THE BARD'S TALE NOVELS

Castle of Deception
by Mercedes Lackey & Josepha Sherman

Fortress of Frost & Fire
by Mercedes Lackey and Ru Emerson

Prison of Souls
by Mercedes Lackey & Mark Shepherd

Thunder of the Captains
by Holly Lisle & Aaron Allston

Wrath of the Princes
by Holly Lisle & Aaron Allson

Escape from Roksamur
by Mark Shepherd

ALSO BY MARK SHEPHERD

Wheels of Fire
(with Mercedes Lackey)

Elvendude

Spiritride

A BARD'S TALE
ESCAPE FROM ROKSAMUR

MARK SHEPHERD

BAEN

Escape from Roksamur

A Baen Books Original

The Bard's Tale characters and descriptions are the sole property of Electronic Arts and are used by permission. *The Bard's Tale* is a registered trademark of Electronic Arts.

Baen Publishing Enterprises
P.O. Box 1403
Riverdale, NY 10471

ISBN: 0-671-87797-6

Cover art by Darrell K. Sweet

First printing, August 1997

Distributed by Simon & Schuster
1230 Avenue of the Americas
New York, NY 10020

Typeset by Windhaven Press, Auburn, NH
Printed in the United States of America

Chapter One

Home, at last, Bard Alaire thought as he rode his mare through the open gates of Silver City. The searing summer heat wrapped its arms around him even now, as the sun set behind the great capital of Althea. Despite the bandana wrapped around his head, sweat dripped onto his already perspiration-drenched clothing.

Shade and water will come soon enough, he thought, as the closing gate's shadow passed over him.

Exhausted and thirsty, as was his mare, he made for the nearest well. Alaire shared a bucket of water with her before proceeding to the palace, wishing the news he'd gathered for his brother, King Derek of Althea, had been more helpful than it was. It did little for his spirits to deliver more evidence of the Althean drought, as the kingdom already had other problems.

Better to present my report now and get it over with, Alaire thought grimly.

The Bard led his mare to a stable and started off towards the palace, an ominous, square structure dominating the horizon. Merchants and tradesmen waved greetings but did not attempt conversation.

1

The guards at the front door bowed as they recognized him, allowing him to enter the palace unchallenged. But, as Alaire had feared, King Derek was in conference with someone. His temper short and his patience fragile, he might have barged in unannounced if he'd known who the king was speaking with. But to do so would only have embarrassed himself; familiarity with the king, even when he was your big brother, was something better expressed in private.

He sat on a lumpy, padded bench in the gallery and tried to relax. The summer heat had seized the palace and a hot, muggy blast blew through the gallery's open windows. This was not the sort of summer Alaire or anyone else in Althea had expected, and it was certainly not one the Bard enjoyed.

"King Derek will see you now," a young servant said from the open doors of the royal chambers. "Please forgive the wait," the boy said. "With the situation as it is, we have been rather busy today."

Bard Alaire nodded. He understood fully. "That is quite all right," he replied, starting for the door. "I've seen firsthand what the problem is."

Alaire recognized the two noblemen, representatives of the Farmer's Guild, as they left the king's chambers. Their long faces tilted toward Alaire respectfully before they took their leave of the gallery.

And I am nowhere close to finding a solution to the problem, Alaire thought morosely as he entered his brother's chambers.

Two years of rule had added lines to Derek's face. When their father, King Reynard, had died after a long illness, Derek was well prepared mentally for taking over the duties of the King, as he had been in training since he was thirteen. Emotionally, as Alaire recalled, Derek took more time in adjusting to the loss of their second parent; Grania, their mother, had died a year earlier. Alaire's seven brothers had all assumed the roles they'd been trained for, including war lord, seneschal and priest. Of these positions and others, Alaire reasoned, the role of king would have to be the most difficult. Derek's sudden aging, and a new swath of gray in his hair supported this.

"Dear brother," Derek said warmly, turning from the open window of his chambers, along which was a long marble table with a pewter pitcher and tankards. "I was expecting you back a fortnight from now," he added, with an audible touch of anxiety. Unsurprisingly, his ermine cloak hung from the gilded throne, and he wore only a tan silk shirt, light breeches and boots. The king's beard, usually trimmed neatly, had grown bushy lately, and Alaire suspected he might even consider shaving it off altogether if this heat kept up. Derek's smile seemed forced as he embraced Alaire; the Bard had heard, since arriving in this part of Althea, that the king had been up at all hours lately, calming his staff and placating the nobles. Alaire had assumed this had been a rumor, but seeing his brother in person confirmed it.

And the news I bear will not improve the situation, Alaire thought, forcing a smile of his own.

"I saw what I needed to, on the Fox River," Alaire said, though what he had found was no river, but a trickle of water running across a long bed of mud. "The situation is as reported. The eastern region, around the Fox in particular, has seen little rainfall since spring. The few crops that managed to sprout are dying." Alaire paused, wondering how much detail he should go into. "The harvest will be very bleak, if there is one at all."

Derek's face fell more, which Alaire would not have believed possible a moment before.

Alaire took a seat on a long marble bench, which was not as cool as he'd hoped. Derek looked forlornly out the window, as if the intensity of his gaze would bring the much-needed rain to Althea.

"I found twenty abandoned farms on the way," Alaire continued, knowing that however negative the report was, the king needed to know precisely what was going on in his land. "Dead cattle, withered crops. Some farms are managing with wells, but these are growing shallower with each passing day. Springs are drying up. The Fox River itself was a mere stream." He left out the part about the dying, rotting fish, with a notion to mention it later if it turned out to be important.

"So unless we see rain soon, there *will* be a famine," King Derek said softly. He turned slowly and fixed his brother with a hopeful, pleading look. "Can you do *anything* about it?"

Which meant, could his Bardic magic bring the rain?

"I don't know," Alaire said, though he really did. "Famine is not inevitable. We do have Suinomen to the north. News from their traders indicates their harvests have been bountiful this year."

Derek shook his head, as Alaire expected. *When will he learn there is no disgrace in seeking help?* "I don't want to depend on Suinomen to keep Althea alive, dear brother."

"For one season?" Alaire countered. "If not that, then what?"

"What will we trade?" the King argued. "Our coin does not spend very well in Suinomen markets!"

"Barter, of course," Alaire countered. "Our gems from our mines . . ."

Derek groaned. "You know as well as I do that spending gems on the market devalues them. No, brother, there must be another way. We still have a hope for a crop, if rain comes soon."

Alaire avoided meeting his eyes. *How do I tell him that what he asks is next to impossible?*

The Bard took the harp off his shoulder and regarded it as if it were an oracle. This was his older harp, the one with which he trained under his Bardic master, Naitachal. It was sturdier and more suitable for travel than his newer harp, which he'd left in his quarters. *What would the Dark Elf do in this situation? Would his opinion be so colored by familial ties as mine seems to be right now?*

Alaire shook his head slowly, but resolutely. "Derek, I don't know how to tell you this," he began hesitantly. "Bardic magic has its place in healing, in spellcasting, in other things as well. I am good, but I am not a master, and may never be one. What you are asking is nothing less than the total upheaval of the world's climate." He paused, regarded his harp briefly, as his own spark of hope came and went. *Can Bardic magic bring rain?*

"You don't have to tailor your words for me," Derek said. "I know that what I ask is probably impossible. But we must try something." He yawned expressively, and rubbed his eyes. "It need not be major. Just a light rain at *least,* to break up this oppressive heat."

Alaire relented. "I will try, brother. But not now. I need water, a bath and rest, in that order. Tomorrow I might be able to attempt something."

"Why didn't you say so?" Derek said, reaching for the pewter pitcher and pouring clear water into a tankard.

"I thought it was wine," Alaire said, taking the tankard of water thankfully.

The king chuckled. "Not this afternoon, little brother. We're thirsty enough today without the spirits."

A knock sounded at the chamber's door. Alaire drained the tankard, grateful for the water, paying only slight attention to the interruption.

"Enter," Derek said, in a deep baritone voice.

The young servant who had admitted Alaire entered sheepishly, evidently under orders to interrupt only when necessary.

"Your Majesty," the servant said. "There is a mes-

senger from Suinomen. Just arrived, sir. He claims to
have urgent news for you, which he must deliver
personally."

The King frowned, but didn't hesitate to say, "Show
him in, then."

The servant mumbled something unintelligible to
someone in the gallery, then a rider, wearing the uniform of the Suinomen army, entered and bowed graciously. He clutched a flat leather pouch and had
evidently shed certain parts of his uniform, no doubt
because of the heat, giving him a disheveled, road-
weary appearance. The Suinomese generally enjoyed
cool temperatures, even in the summer, and no doubt
the messenger had been sent without regard to dress.

"I beg forgiveness for my ignorance of your language," the rider said, in a heavy, Suinomese drawl
that sounded rehearsed. "King Kainemonen has sent
word to you about your ambassador."

Derek's eyebrows raised. "Is that so," he said, taking
the pouch, but the rider only bowed. Apparently, these
were all the Althean words the messenger had memo-
rized; his look was blank as he handed the message
over.

King Derek carefully unfolded the parchment and
gazed down at it as if it were tinged with poison.

"Dear gods," Derek said softly, as his complexion
turned a horrid shade of gray.

Alaire was too tired to react; he remained seated,
holding the tankard, as the messenger remained standing, however nervously. The Bard recalled another time,
with another messenger, in another place far to the north,
when a message had led himself and his master,
Naitachal, on a rather eventful trip to the country of
Suinomen.

A trip I very nearly didn't return from, he reminded
himself, *when I spent those terrible days, or weeks,
or moments, in the Prison of Souls.* Alaire shuddered

at the memory. *My dear mother, gods rest her soul, is the only reason I escaped.*

"Our ambassador to Suinomen, Sir Erikson, has been *assassinated*," the King said woodenly as he collapsed on his throne.

Alaire stood up, the tankard clattering to the tiled floor. The messenger jumped at the sudden noise, then bowed to Alaire in embarrassment. The Bard waited several long moments for his brother to continue. "He was stabbed to death in his sleep," Derek continued. "What they have sent," he said, holding up the parchment, "is an apology, as well as a statement that the Suinomen government had nothing to do with it."

Then who did? Alaire wondered, but waited for Derek to recover from the news.

"Is the message from Kainemonen himself?" Alaire asked.

"Yes," Derek replied. "It bears his seal. But who would want to see our ambassador dead?" The hand holding the message dropped limply to one side, and Derek stared forward at nothing Alaire could see.

"May I read it?" Alaire ventured, and Derek absently handed the parchment over to him. The note had been composed by a scribe, complete with all the fancy calligraphy and seals mandated by a royal message. The information was brief, and to the point.

Your Majesty, King Derek of Althea,

We so very much regret to inform you that your Ambassador to Suinomen, Sir Erikson of Gnarwald, was found stabbed to death in his chambers at mid morning. We cannot express the grief we feel today, and we fear this message will not convey sufficient apology. I can say with absolute certainty that none in the Suinomen government is responsible for this ghastly deed, and we will spare no expense or resource to get to the bottom of this crime. As King of Suinomen, I respectfully request that you send two most capable emissaries, Bard Alaire and Master Bard Naitachal. I am acquainted with them both and would be honored by their presence, even under these less than favorable circumstances.

> *Yours Sincerely, and most regretfully,*
> *King Kainemonen*
> *Ruler of Suinomen*

Alaire's gaze wavered from the message to the man who brought it. *Not much older than the messenger who brought the other news to Naitachal and myself, six years ago. And he looks worse off than I do.*

"Come with me," Alaire said, and led the young messenger to the gallery where the servant was waiting with obvious anxiety.

"Give him the best guest room in the palace," Alaire said quickly. "And a bath and a meal."

"Yes, sir," he replied quickly. "Yes, indeed." He bowed and excused himself, leading the messenger quickly down the hallway.

Alaire returned to his brother's chambers and collected the tankard he'd dropped to the floor, and poured himself more water. The King hadn't moved from the throne and continued to stare vacantly.

"I believe," Alaire said slowly, "that the King of Suinomen is telling us the truth." The Bard pulled a chair up near the throne, to better speak with his brother, who did not look very well at the moment. He also didn't look as though he was hearing anything Alaire said, but the Bard knew better. *He's listening, and thinking.*

"You know Kainemonen," Derek said after a lengthy pause. "And you've been to Suinomen before. What do you think might have happened?"

Alaire studied the tankard, the water sloshing around

inside. "Kai's government is not to blame," Alaire said with certainty. "He *might* know, or suspect who did it, but he wouldn't have included that information in the message."

Derek roused himself from the slouch he'd descended into and rubbed his temples. "Any chance this note is a forgery?"

Alaire looked at the parchment. "Possible, but doubtful. The only reason for anyone to send a forgery would be to incite a war between our two countries, or at the very least strain our relationship. But it would take more than a mere forgery to accomplish that."

"Aie, it would," Derek agreed. "Then we should assume the worst. He asked for you and Naitachal. If I recall, both of you went up there to straighten something out."

"Yes, we did, and we very nearly didn't return," Alaire replied. "Up until then, Althea barely acknowledged Suinomen."

"Well, we never traded with them," Derek said. "And they don't have nearly the population we do."

"You might be surprised," Alaire said, remembering the size of Rozinki, the capital city. "Rozinki was a major port before we even began trading. For centuries we missed the boat, as it were, in trade with them. Anyway, I was training under Naitachal in Fenrich, which wasn't far from the border."

The memory of the enigmatic Dark Elf brought a smile to Alaire's features.

"You miss him, don't you?" Derek said, with a smile of his own.

"Of course I do," Alaire replied. "Ever since I became a Bard, he's been off wandering by himself. Occasionally traders coming through Silver City tell stories about him. He's been all over Althea and Suinomen, two or three times over."

Alaire wondered what Naitachal found so interest-

ing about travel—but then, trying to figure out any
Dark Elf usually led to frustration. That this particular elf had become a Bard only added to the confusion—Necromancers tended to remain Necromancers,
and Naitachal had done a radical about face in his ca-
reer when he became a Bard. "Kai, of course, probably wouldn't know that Naitachal is off doing Bardic
things on his own."

But evidently Derek's mind had wondered off, as
he stared off into nothing again. "When you and
Naitachal were up there, you interrupted a coup of
sorts."

"That is correct."

"Carlotta had attempted to seize the throne . . . again.
And you destroyed her, I believe."

Alaire nodded, "When we left for Suinomen, I had
already assumed Carlotta was dead. The stories passed
around the family, as well as the overheard conversations, had suggested as much. Yet, the sister of our
long ago king proved to be more resilient than we
thought. Not only had she survived the original attack from bardling Kevin, she disappeared for many
years. Later, she surfaced in Suinomen and began
manipulating Sir Jehan, a nobleman of the Suinomen
court."

The king took a long drink of water. "We had wondered what happened to you up there." Derek set the
tankard down, and fixed Alaire with a direct, somewhat
accusing look. "Are you certain Carlotta is dead?"

Alaire might have taken offense at this question, which
cast doubt on his own abilities. But Derek was king,
and Alaire himself had wondered whether or not the fairy-
human hybrid had survived Naitachal's attack.

"It was a horrible thing to behold," Alaire said softly,
remembering the unmaking spell Naitachal had woven.
When the Dark Elf finished, there was nothing left
of her except the limp remains of her clothes. "But

yes, I am certain of her demise. And no, I don't think she is behind Sir Erikson's assassination."

"What of . . . certain elements, left over from the previous coup attempt?"

Alaire had to think about that one for a moment. "The political struggle resulted in Archenomen's overwhelming victory. The only thing holding the opposition forces together was Carlotta's magic, and once she was dead, the coup dissolved. All that was left was the resultant mess, which consisted of a confused rabble of Carlotta's pawns, who hadn't fully realized they were being used."

"Possible then, but unlikely," the king supplied. Alaire nodded.

"We won't know anything until we go up there ourselves," Alaire said, but even as he uttered the words he dreaded the prospect of more travel. Particularly across the parched countryside of Althea. *Gods, not again, not already* . . .

His distaste evidently showed on his face. "Perhaps a seagoing vessel, to take you there. There are regular routes between Silver City and Rozinki," the king suggested.

He hadn't considered going by ship; the prospect changed the complexion of things altogether.

"The weather would be much more agreeable," the King pointed out. "Plenty of water. You could even use the time to rest up."

"That is a splendid idea," Alaire said, though he questioned how well he could sleep on a moving ship.

"In view of the fact that you were nearly subdued the last time you traveled to Suinomen, how many troops would you like to take as bodyguards?"

"Soldiers? Don't be silly," Alaire said, but even as he replied, he noticed a sly smirk on the king's tired features. "I know Kainemonen quite well," he continued. Perhaps too well; he was a little embarrassed

at the familiarity he had with the King of Suinomen.
Is he really the king now? he thought, remembering
the drunken crown prince he'd met while pretending
to be Naitachal's "secretary," and the sudden and dramatic change in him when they were both nearly killed.
*Becoming the king was the last thing Kai wanted, and
he found himself on the throne sooner than anyone had
expected.*

"It would be very troubling, brother, if any rem-
nants from the coup attempt remained," Alaire said.
"If such folk had been lying low for this long, that would
suggest a true dedication to stirring up trouble."

"So you'll go, then," Derek said. "I mean, if I ask . . ."

"Of course I'll go," Alaire replied. *Did he think I
would refuse?* "I need to get out of this stifling heat
somehow, and what better way than to go north,
where it's *cold.*"

"Excellent," Derek replied. "Who then, will you take
with you?"

Alaire didn't have to consider this for long. "Reykir,
my apprentice, of course."

"May I make a suggestion?" The king's tone hinted
that Alaire might not like the suggestion. To Alaire's
hesitant nod, the king continued. "Do you think brother
Craig would be a suitable traveling companion?"

The question, at first, stunned him. *That drunk? But
why would Derek even suggest . . .*

"I know, I know. Irresponsible, even if he is your
older brother."

"All my brothers are older brothers. I'm the baby,
remember?"

Derek shrugged. "He hasn't been doing much really.
I'm embarrassed to have him on the council, as he
usually shows up drunk. And the women . . ."

Alaire held a hand up. "You don't have to tell me.
I know that he is a bit . . . free, I might say, with
the womenfolk. Of all classes." He frowned, consid-

ering an unpleasant possibility. "If he went, would we not be running the chance of embarrassing Althea?"

The king looked ready to disagree vehemently, then sighed. "It has occurred to me. But the possible benefit of his going along may outweigh that risk."

The Bard was confused. "What benefit?"

The words came with visible difficulty. "The king of Suinomen was once a bit of wastrel, wasn't he? And now . . ."

So that was it. *Teach by example. Particularly when everything else has failed.*

The king continued, as if to fill the air with words, to prevent Alaire from objecting. "I can see to it that the ship does not stock wine. So at least he will be sober when you reach Rozinki."

"At least," Alaire said, liking the idea of taking Craig along, if not altogether certain *why*. "I see a good deal of merit in the plan. Kai, if anyone, will understand what it's like to be a royal drunkard. He might even have some suggestions." *Even though it took a near-death experience to get Kai's attention six years ago.*

"Craig is not very dependable, true, but he is your brother," Derek said. Alaire heard the anxiety behind his voice. "I will extract a solemn oath from him that he will do nothing to humiliate the family, the crown, or Althea."

"*And?*"

"I will direct him specifically to keep his hands off the native girls."

"*And?*" Alaire was enjoying this.

Derek held his hands up in frustration. "What, keep his manhood locked away in a box while he's away?"

"Hmmm," Alaire said. He hadn't considered that. "That would eliminate about half our problem. But no, I think that would be a bit extreme."

Derek tried to bite back a grin, but was unable to

hold it in, and he broke down in a fit of laughter. "We can always threaten him with that later, if he doesn't behave."

"And speaking of not behaving . . . " Derek said, his tone indicating a clear change of subject. "Your student, Reykir. The lad is not well bred, that is true, but do you think you can get him to leave the kitchen girls alone? There have been . . . complaints."

"Oh? From the girls or jealous boyfriends?" Alaire said, trying to sound innocent. *Yes, Reykir. I should have known he would find some sort of mischief while I was surveying muddy rivers.*

"Are you certain you don't want to take a foot soldier or two along . . . ?" Derek was serious again.

"To what, deal with a couple of rowdy boys?" Alaire sniffed. "I think I can manage."

"I certainly hope so," the king said. His lack of faith was disturbing to Alaire.

After all, it hasn't been all that long since I was a randy youth. As he considered this, he frowned. *Has it?*

Chapter Two

But I can't swim! the bardling thought, alarmed at the prospect of going to sea. He forced his expression into neutrality as Alaire, his master, watched him with growing curiosity.

"Yes, Reykir?" Alaire asked as he opened a wardrobe, a piece of heavy, wooden furniture that looked as though it was a part of the palace. "Is there something wrong with traveling north by ship?"

Damn, Reykir thought. *Alaire either read my face or my mind. I can never figure out which!*

"Oh, nothing," the bardling said, and wondered if he should sit to make himself look less nervous. "It's just that it's been so long since I've been on a ship. I've had my land legs for quite a time now."

"Hmmm," Alaire replied, not looking, or sounding, convinced.

Reykir was appalled at taking passage aboard a sailing ship, but he was not about to let his mentor know it. He had grown up in the streets of Silver City, first as a hustler and a thief, then as a hustler and freelance musician. At no time did he learn how to swim.

"You'll be getting out of this stifling city," Alaire pointed out as he went through his wardrobe and tossed clothing into a large wooden chest. "And you'll be seeing a new land."

15

"Oh, that I know," Reykir said. As Alaire's bardling trainee, he had a smaller room adjoining Alaire's quarters. The suite had originally been designed for a master and a personal servant. Not that Reykir minded his mentor or his quarters; Alaire was a good teacher and friend, and living in the palace, *anywhere* in the palace, beat living on the street.

"Then why," Alaire asked, as he tossed a pair of breeches into the chest, "do you look so reluctant?"

Think fast, Reykir thought to himself. *Tell him the truth, or tell him something far more interesting?*

"Its just th-that," Reykir stammered, a terrible habit he fell into when he was about to lie. "I wanted to . . . Can I . . . ?"

"What?" Alaire asked.

"Take Rak along?" *Of course. Why didn't I think of her right away?*

"I don't see why not," Alaire said, after a maddening pause. "It's only a one week trip, at the most. There are ports along the way. I suspect we'll be going ashore at least once during the trip, if you want to let her hunt fresh food."

Reykir made a point of looking relieved. "Oh, she can get by for days on jerky, if needed," the boy said, patting his waterproof leather pack. "I've got enough for both of us." When Alaire had mentioned a voyage, food was the first thing Reykir had packed. As it was daytime, Reykir knew that Rak, his hunting owl and closest friend, human or non, was probably asleep in the rafters of the King's stables. He knew she was safe there; since becoming Alaire's student, Rak had become a welcome fixture. Rats and mice had become only a minor nuisance, and no longer fouled the grain supply. Knowing his owl could come along did indeed make the trip more palatable. *As long as I don't fall overboard, everything will be just fine.*

Despite having soothed his apprentice, Alaire looked

troubled, perhaps by something other than the assassination of Althea's ambassador. Reykir had a mild talent for telepathy, and a slightly stronger one for empathy; but reading the signs in his teacher required neither. *He must be tired, or else there's more about this journey he's not telling me,* Reykir thought.

"Who will be traveling with us?" Reykir inquired. Alaire had mentioned nothing of traveling companions, but he had a hunch this might be part of the problem.

"My brother. Craig," he said, with a sigh. "Derek seems to think this trip might do him some good." His tone, however, indicated that he didn't agree.

"Do *you* think so?" Reykir asked. It still felt odd to be talking about the King of Althea in such familiar terms. To do so with Alaire was acceptable, but he had to watch his tongue around everyone else, particularly the servant boys. They were jealous enough of his sudden, dramatic rise in social position. In one day he had gone from living the life of a gutter child, culling the street's garbage for food, to becoming a formal student of Bardic magic, with the king's own *brother* as his teacher.

Reykir knew better than to shove the other boys' noses in his amazing stroke of fortune. He might be rubbing elbows with Althean royalty, but he was still outnumbered and small for his age. He'd learned long ago the hard lessons of the street, and avoided trouble whenever possible.

The bardling stopped short of referring to Craig's drinking habits, which were well known in the kingdom. Then he began to see why Alaire was so concerned.

"Craig might find a positive influence in Kai," Alaire said. "I think that's what Derek thinks."

"Who's Kai?"

"Prince, I mean *King* Kainemonen. We became

acquainted before he ascended to the throne of Suinomen. He was a bit of a drinker himself, getting into trouble, getting *me* into trouble, while all around him his subjects were conspiring against him."

Alaire opened a drawer filled with fancy objects Reykir couldn't begin to identify, and looked over the contents. "The two of us walked right into a plot. It took Naitachal and me a while to figure out what was happening, but it took Kai longer, and he was on home ground. He was so drunk most of the time that he didn't know what was going on around him."

"So what changed him?" Reykir said, sitting on an odd chair that didn't match any of the other gaudy furniture in the bedroom.

"A close brush with death," Alaire replied. "I hope Craig does not have to go through that as well. Perhaps some of Kai will rub off on him."

Ordinarily, Reykir would have pressed his master for details of the story, but Reykir's gift let him see that Alaire was unwilling to go into further detail.

"At any rate, we set sail at dawn. I strongly suggest that you get plenty of rest. I have a feeling this voyage is not going to be easy."

Just after daybreak, Alaire and Reykir arrived by carriage at the port of Silver City, which was a short distance from the palace. Alaire had grumbled something about Craig being along later, but again, didn't seem to want to talk. Shortly after awakening Reykir recalled hearing raised voices, one of them Alaire's, but he didn't pry. Instead he found himself getting excited about the trip; his first concern about swimming had evaporated when he remembered hearing that there were sailors who had been to sea for years who couldn't swim either.

At Alaire's suggestion he had chosen simple, comfortable clothes for embarkation. Over his breeches he wore the shortest, briefest tunic he owned, with the intention of going shirtless if the heat became what it promised to be. Alaire, on the other hand, apparently having to keep some royal face, wore a short, high-neck houppelande with baggy sleeves. Reykir noticed that the fabric was sheer, giving the illusion of thickness while being quite airy. Alaire also wore a jeweled dagger which, the Bard explained, was for good luck; it had accompanied him on his last journey to Suinomen.

Rak sat perched on Reykir's shoulder as he climbed out of the carriage, stirring from foot to foot whenever the boy moved. As the owl was a nocturnal bird, she was rather groggy whenever the sun came out and would normally be settling down to sleep at this time.

:Hood. Now.: Rak whispered in his mind. *:Bright.:* Earlier, Reykir had offered the owl a light hood to shield some of the sun out, but Rak had declined. Now, in the direct morning sunlight, she'd apparently reconsidered.

"Sure, sure, Rak," Reykir soothed out loud. He reached for his belt pouch and fished out a soft, suede hood. Meanwhile, dockworkers scurried to pick up their bags. Alaire had his chest and a single canvas bag, and over his shoulder hung his harp. Reykir had only his pouch and leather pack, and his wooden flute hung from a thong around his neck. With some trepidation he regarded the dock, a long foundation of rock, shale and timbers that stretched into the bay like a long oak branch, from which hung a small armada of tall sailing ships. Instead of the usual beehive of activity Reykir was used to here, he found an eerie silence, punctuated with idle sailors talk. With the drought, there was little produce to export, and whatever had been imported must have evaporated from the docks the moment it arrived. The spice and tea trade with the western coast of Althea seemed to be the only market making good this season.

The nearest ship was small, with two masts bearing triangular sails, but men were loading nets on it.

There didn't look as though there would be enough room to even stand, much less find a place to sleep. The ship behind it was even smaller, and beyond that one Reykir saw the outline of a vast sailing ship by peering through the masts and lines of the other, lesser vessels.

"Our ship will be the only one crewed by Arachnia," Alaire said, peering across the dock.

"What's the name of our ship?" Reykir asked.

"It's an Arachnian vessel," Alaire said evenly. "They don't name their ships. They're . . . superstitious about that."

"Oh," Reykir said. Then he saw an Arachnia on the dock. He'd seen the humanoid insects before, doing everything from bookkeeping for counts to farming land, but he had never dealt with one. The huge praying mantis made its way towards them, ambling in a lopsided gait on one good leg and a wooden peg leg. It was as tall as a man, and its shell looked as tough as armor. The two huge forelegs had three jointed sections, and were attached to the top of a very long thorax. The two front sections of the forelegs were spiked, and looked uncomfortably as though they were useful for grabbing—or killing. Both forelegs were partially tucked up close to its body, but Reykir guessed that, fully extended, they had quite a reach. He knew that flecks of white appeared on Arachnians' chitinous shells as they reached advanced age, and this one was covered with them. He certainly would not toy with this creature; in fact, he would go out of his way to avoid it in a dark alley.

Alaire ventured a few steps in the Arachnia's direction. The insect looked up with its orblike, black eyes.

"Greetings," the Arachnia said, in a scratchy, whispering voice. Its head cocked to one side as it regarded them. "You must be our passengers," it said after a few moments of study.

"Aye, and you must be our captain. I am Bard

Alaire." He extended his hand cautiously, and the Arachnia took it gently with a hooked claw. "And this is my apprentice, Reykir."

The Arachnia gave him a passing glance, which sent chills down the boy's spine. "And I am Su'Beltor, captain of our vessel, " the Arachnia replied. "She's docked at the far end. The only one going to sea today." The captain glanced back up the dock. "Did you not have a third passenger as well?"

Alaire expelled a long sigh. Reykir didn't know if Craig was coming or not, after the row he'd overheard earlier that morning in the palace.

"He will be along shortly," Alaire said. "But we will not wait."

Reykir peered down the dock, but the ship in question was the large one behind the other two and not easily seen, except for the front of the hull which protruded over the dock. On the nose of the bow was a wooden carving of an Arachnia.

"We are bound for Rozinki," Alaire said. "How calm are the waters?"

The Arachnia eyed him strangely, the oval head rotating gracefully on a thin neck, its eyes large and rounded, but definitely insectoid. "They are calm enough. Further north, who's to say? We won't be far from shore, whatever happens."

The assurance was more disturbing to Reykir than comforting; he doubted he would be able to make it to shore if his life depended on it. But now was not the time to bring that up. His pride would not allow him to reveal his weakness to this seasoned, nonhuman sailor, or to his master and teacher.

"And what manner of creature have you there?" the captain asked, directing his attention to Reykir's owl. "A bird? A parrot?"

"An owl," Reykir said proudly, but nervously. "She's not, how should I say, a mongrel or pest, either. Sir."

"Oh, that I believe. A well-trained pet, eh?" the Arachnia said.

The dockworkers hurried on ahead of them with their luggage, and the captain guided them towards the vessel. "We spent all of yesterday loading wares for trade in Rozinki," the captain said. "Had your emissary not contacted us late last night, we might have already embarked. He's paid us good coin. You have a guaranteed passage to Rozinki and back, provided you don't stay more than a fortnight."

"Then it's a good thing we moved when we did," Alaire said, and Reykir noticed that he kept his stride even with the captain's. "I've been traveling for some weeks now and I wasn't looking forward to another overland trip."

"I see," the captain said, leaving it at that.

When they reached their ship, a change in mood was clear. Unlike the rest of the sleepy dock, this part bustled with activity. A dozen Arachnia scrambled up the masts, checking rigging and sails, which were still furled on the booms and yards. Reykir saw why the Arachnia made excellent seamen, at least on a ship that was still docked; the insectlike beings crawled and skittered up and down the masts with ease, in a fraction of the time it would be likely to take a human.

"She is a secure ship," the Arachnia chittered as they crossed the boarding plank. "A hundred years old, and as watertight as an iron kettle. She's been around Althea more times than I can remember, and has transported a kingdom's worth of goods."

"A hundred years?" Reykir breathed, but Alaire didn't seem too concerned about the ship's age.

The human workers stood by their luggage, which they'd set on the deck. Alaire gave them each a copper, and they scurried off, apparently wanting to spend as little time as possible on the Arachnian vessel.

"Your quarters will be on the poop deck, near the

mizzenmast," the captain continued, pointing with a clawed hand towards the rear of the ship, on which was built a gallery of three decks. "We can be underway soon, if the other passenger . . ."

As if on cue, a small carriage pulled up at the end of the dock. A sullen fellow, wearing dark clothes and a wide brimmed hat, sulked off the carriage. He too carried a single bag and regarded the dock and ships with visible distaste.

"Looks like Craig decided to join us after all," Alaire said softly. "Captain, where did you say we were going to be berthed?"

"Follow me," the captain said, and led them to a tiny, cramped room with three beds, one being a pulldown. The place smelled of fish, saltwater and sweat, but even Reykir knew these were plush accommodations for a sea-going vessel of any size. "We will set sail promptly," the captain added, leaving them to get settled.

"Would you show Prince Craig where we are?" Alaire asked. "I have a feeling he's going to want a bed soon."

"Aye, Bard," the captain said. "Oh, and would it be imposing," the large Arachnia added, pausing at the door, "to ask you to play a few tunes for us, once we are underway? It is not often that we have Bards for passengers."

"No imposition at all," Alaire said as he tossed his bag on one of the beds. "It will be my honor."

The captain closed the cabin door behind him, and Reykir heard his wooden leg thumping down the gallery.

Reykir reached up and pulled down the top bunk, which squeaked loudly from hinges badly in need of grease. The bed was little more than a wooden box with a canvas sack of straw. *Oh well,* Reykir thought. *I've slept on worse. As long as the straw isn't moldy.*

As he poked through the sack, something small and furry skittered away.

Rousing from her slumber, Rak arched her body in response to the sound. Reykir quickly removed her hood and watched.

:Mouse!: Rak's thoughts echoed in his head. Rak hopped onto the bed and quickly cornered and subdued the rodent in a talon. With two quick thrusts of her beak, the mouse was dead.

"Doesn't look like food's going to be a problem for your owl," Alaire said as he examined his straw mattress. "Wonder where that damn fool brother of mine is?"

Reykir leaned over and peered out of a small wooden hole in the wall of the cabin, a simple opening with a small set of shutters which also squeaked loudly when he opened them. Gulls kited lazily just off the edge of the dock, and a sudden blast of salty air surged in through the porthole. A crewman's shadow passed briefly across the opening, and Reykir saw that the window opened onto a walkway. Above them he heard skittering feet and shouted Arachnian orders.

"Sounds like we're getting underway," Alaire said. "I'd like to see this."

They were headed for the cabin door when it opened and Craig appeared. As fitted his apparent mood, he was wearing all black. His clothing was rumpled, as if he'd slept in it.

"Is this *it*?" Craig snorted, glancing down at the beds. His skin was pale, his eyes sunken and bloodshot. "I have to sleep on those? I'd rather sleep with the horses in their stables!"

Reykir caught a strong whiff of Craig's breath, which smelled like bad wine.

"Which could probably be arranged," Alaire pointed out. "There's still time to change your mind." The floor lurched violently beneath them, and Reykir and Alaire exchanged looks. "If you change it quickly."

Craig came into the cabin and tossed his bag on the nearest bed. The leather sack clinked when it fell.

"So when did you go to bed last night, anyway?" Alaire said.

Craig wheeled around and glared at his brother. "Who said I've *been* to bed?"

The ship lurched again, and Craig toppled over on the bunk. "If you don't mind, I think I'll stay here for a while," he said. A moment later, he was snoring.

"The best thing for him," Alaire said, his disgust evident. "Come, let's go watch this beast set sail."

They left Craig to sleep off his drink. Rak, still devouring the mouse, remained with him in the cabin. Down a narrow corridor they found an even narrower ladder leading to the upper deck. When they emerged into daylight, the ship's crew was in full motion. In front of the ship, down in the water, were two long rowboats. In each boat about ten Arachnia rowed feverishly, pulling taut the long line connecting the rowboats to the bow of the ship. With great effort the Arachnia towed the great ship away from the docks; the progress was slow but steady, and with each pull of the oars the boy felt a distinctive lurch under his feet.

Those rowboats are pulling a thousand times their weight, Reykir guessed.

The rowboats struggled to pull the ship's bow to the left, and moments later Reykir saw why. The wind was coming up hard from the starboard, and as the ship crept its way into the bay, the wind struck it broadside. The deck began to tilt, much to Reykir's alarm, but the crew didn't seem concerned, so the boy made do with grabbing a rail on the deck and holding on tight.

Arachnia skittered towards lines tied to huge pegs on the main deck, untied them, and pulled the huge booms around at a shallow angle.

The captain barked an order and four sailors began pulling the rowboats in. Beneath them, the ship creaked and protested, reminding Reykir of its advanced age. The boy didn't realize it at first, but his heart was pounding hard at his ribs, and he was grinning from ear to ear. In that moment he had a flash of insight, answering his own long-asked question of why sailors did what they did, why they married the sea.

And the sails weren't even out yet. The Arachnia who had been rowing the boats climbed aboard with ease, using the skimpiest of rope ladders to reach the deck. The crew winched the boats up the sides of the ship and stowed the oars. The captain barked more orders and the masts blossomed to life.

Arachnia scrambled down from the three main masts as the sails unfurled. One by one, the sails popped taut with the wind, and Reykir felt the ship leap forward beneath him.

Behind them, on the deck close to the stern, was an Arachnian steersman operating a lever protruding from the deck. As he moved this lever, which was as tall as he was and swung like an inverted pendulum, the ship moved. The steersman watched the sails change shape and tension, and with the lever trimmed the direction of the ship to make up for it. *That must be attached to the rudder,* Reykir thought. *And the rudder for this ship must be huge.*

Alaire put a hand on his shoulder, and when Reykir glanced up at his master, Alaire looked as though he was in heaven.

"Breathe that air," Alaire said, and Reykir did. Fresh air, without the stink of the city, cooled the sweat on his back, giving him goose bumps. *I think I'm going to like this trip.*

"Too bad Craig isn't up here to see this," Alaire said, but Reykir heard resignation, not regret, in his master's voice.

I had no idea Craig was such a drunkard, he thought, but caught himself before he uttered the words. *Craig is a prince, and I cannot speak ill of him. Alaire can do that for me. For the both of us.*

"If we explore the ship, we must be careful," Alaire said. "See that rope over there?" he asked, pointing to a pile of rope neatly coiled on the deck. "If you step in that, you might end up suspended from the top of the mast."

"I'll keep that in mind," Reykir said uneasily. *Aie, yes, there were probably quite a few dangers on this ship.*

He looked back towards land, and felt a bit of early homesickness as he watched the dock grow smaller. Silver City spread across the horizon, the spires of the palace glinting in the morning sun. The boy looked over the side, watching the water whoosh past as the waves lapped against the hull.

"We're going straight out to sea," Reykir said. "Weren't we going to stay near the coast?"

Alaire shook himself from a distant thought. "We'll be near the coast, but we must be far enough in the open sea to avoid hitting reefs. Also, the winds are better further from land." He glanced over with a smile. "You're not getting nervous about this trip, are you?"

"Oh, no," Reykir said, but he knew some of his fears probably showed.

After giving a series of cryptic orders, the captain climbed up to their deck and stood with the steersman, watching the sails and the water. Apparently satisfied with the ship's trim, the captain joined them at the rail.

"Aye, we've got a good strong wind this morning," the Arachnia said, sounding as if he was having trouble shifting from his own language to the humans'. "If we can avoid storms, we might even arrive in Rozinki before schedule."

"That would be a great help," Alaire replied. "As

much as I'm enjoying the voyage so far, the sooner we arrive to conduct our business the better."

The captain studied something out at sea, then idly scratched behind his right eye with a claw, an amazingly delicate task for a foreleg that large. "I suppose then, Bard, that you wouldn't remember the last time you nearly set sail with us? We were crewed by humans then, as I was having trouble at home finding hands, and had to rely on what I could find at Silver City."

Alaire looked puzzled. "The last time?" He thought this over a moment. "I've sailed three times before, but not on a vessel this large, I'm certain of it."

The Arachnia turned his head at a curious angle; though his features were essentially unmoving, the mandibles angled in a close approximation of a smile.

"I said nearly. You were interrupted before you boarded."

Alaire looked the vessel up and down, then regarded the captain with cool bemusement. "Of course. Rozinki."

The Arachnia nodded. "My men were in the water, ready to row us out. At the Rozinki port there was a stiff current a stone's throw from the dock, and we would have been off like the wind if we'd had the chance."

Alaire shook his head, his expression not especially pleasant. "Then Sir Jehan jumped us."

"Master, what are you talking about?" Reykir asked, unable to hold his curiosity in anymore. *Was this when Alaire and his master, Naitachal, got involved with that power struggle in Suinomen?*

"So *this* was the ship," Alaire said, sounding as if he didn't believe he was standing on her. "Reykir, I told you about my first encounter with Suinomen. My master and I stumbled into a plot to overthrow the king, but by the time he knew we were in trouble, I was away in the tavern district pretending to have a good time with Kai. Two assassins jumped us, tried to kill me, and struck a fatal blow to the prince. I had to use Bardic magic to bring him back. The spell worked, but in so doing I managed to break a serious law of Suinomen. To make a long story shorter, Kai went back to the palace to tell the king about the plot, but was thrown into the dungeon for his trouble. Naitachal escaped with the help of the captain of the guard, who had also arranged passage for us. On this very ship, it seems."

"I remember it all," the captain bragged. "Would have had you out of here in no time. The dock was buttoned down tight, but we would have gotten you out of there, we would."

"What happened?" Reykir asked. He had a pretty good idea, but the story was too good to let pass.

"Sir Jehan, the noble who was trying to seize the throne—and did, for a short time—had a little welcoming committee for us. His men were all over the place, on other ships, on shore, everywhere. We didn't have a chance."

The captain made a rude snorting noise that passed for a retort. "If I'd had my men . . ."

"If you'd gotten involved you would have all been killed," Alaire said simply. The casual words chilled Reykir; it sounded like an insult, in a way, though he obviously spoke the truth. "They had arrows, bows and crossbows. True, your Arachnia would have won handily if it had come down to hand-to-hand combat. Doubtful it would have gotten that far, if you want to know the truth. The crossbows would have taken you out the moment you advanced."

The Arachnia shrugged. "Long time ago, that was. Things have changed in Rozinki since then. That new king, Kainemonen, he knows what he's doing. We've been trading with Suinomen for years, and everyone has prospered. If not for this thrice damned-drought."

"Yes, indeed," Alaire said thoughtfully. "In the very near future, that trade might well increase." But he didn't get any more specific than that.

The captain looked as though he was about to ask for elaboration, but apparently thought better of it. Reykir looked back at the shore, now a thin line on the horizon.

Chapter Three

The captain didn't ask about Craig. Good, I'm not in the mood to discuss my drunken brother with anyone, much less with the captain of this ship! Alaire thought, hoping the captain wasn't keeping them company on deck out of politeness; there were probably a hundred things the Arachnia needed to attend to.

One of the seamen was lowering a rope, with knots tied several paces apart, over the side of the ship.

Alaire inquired about this, and the captain replied, "That's how we measure the ship's speed." He paused, glancing upwards into the sky, then down at the waterline. "I know we're traveling around ten knots right now. I can tell from just looking. But the line will tell us for certain."

Alaire wasn't familiar with the unit of measure, but he did know they were traveling rather swiftly for a large merchant ship. A moment later the seaman called up in the Arachnian tongue. The captain shrugged. "Eleven knots, is it?" The Arachnia seemed disappointed. "I'm starting to slip in my old age."

The captain offered Alaire and his student a tour of the ship. Reykir seemed eager to explore, and that he was willing to do this under the direction of the captain was a good sign that the boy intended to stay out of trouble. At least, for the time being. The Bard

31

had to admit that he was curious about the ship's workings belowdecks.

Beneath the poop deck, the captain showed them the stern, where the ship's rudder extended into the sea. Here a bar from above, where the steersman had been, connected with the tiller, which turned the rudder. The captain explained how this new invention, the whipstaff, made steering much easier. Before the whipstaff, the steersman was below decks, guiding the tiller without being able to see the sails, responding to shouted commands from above.

One of the sailors came over to the captain and told him something, then scurried off. The captain turned to them and said, "I am needed above decks," he said. "Feel free to explore the ship, but wherever you go be careful."

Alaire nodded towards the captain, but he was already following the seaman above.

These Arachnia move quickly, he thought, with awe. *I wonder why we've never employed them in numbers to be mercenaries? They would be quite formidable in a war.*

"Let's go see what's down here," Reykir said, and started towards the bow of the ship. The place was dark except for a few places where the ports were open. Alaire followed him, with half an eye wary for any trouble the boy might get into. *He acts just like me when I was that age,* he thought with a sigh. *That's probably what worries me the most about this voyage.*

They found large stacks of cargo, barrels of what was probably water, and something they weren't expecting. While most of the crew was above decks getting the ship underway, a half dozen or so Arachnia were berthed down with the cargo. *Well, the sailors for the night watch have to sleep sometime,* Alaire thought, wondering if they'd inadvertently wakened them. But with all the creaking and rattling of the ship's timbers, he doubted anything short of a hurricane would wake these crewmen. A row of several hammocks, some occupied, some not, hung from the deck above.

"Whoops," Reykir whispered. "Maybe we'd better go back."

"Perhaps you're right," Alaire said, but when he stepped back he spied an Arachnia gazing at them from a hammock. Their eyes met and locked. The Bard had trouble reading him; even in the dim surroundings, this Arachnia looked darker and somehow different from the others. *But Arachnia are only one breed, one race,* he thought. *Aren't they?*

The Arachnia chittered something in his native tongue that sounded uncomfortably like annoyance. Alaire and his apprentice withdrew faster, the Bard sensing they had violated someone's space.

Before they had gone more than a few paces, the Arachnia skittered about in the darkness behind them, then appeared in front of them. He wasn't exactly blocking their way, but it wasn't easy to get past him, either. Alaire eyed the crewman's claws uncomfortably, acutely aware they could snap his neck with ease.

Reykir looked as though he was going to dart off in another direction, but Alaire gently touched his shoulder, signaling him that this would be a mistake.

:You,: the Arachnia's voice thundered in Alaire's head. The unexpected psychic contact surprised him so much the Bard staggered backwards. *:You are the singer, the one who is going North,:* the Arachnia said. Reykir glanced quickly from his master to the Arachnia, then back again.

"What is—" Reykir started to say. Alaire held a palm up, silencing him.

:Yes, I am,: Alaire said, attempting the same mode of communication in return, hoping he wasn't shouting in the crewman's mind. They stood in a swath of light cast from a port, and Alaire saw the Arachnia clearly.

He was indeed black instead of the usual gray-green, with an odd pattern of dots on his chitinous shell. But none of this was as nearly out of place, and out of character, as the crewman's ability to communicate *telepathically*. This was simply not something Arachnia were known for being able to do.

:I will not harm you,: the Arachnia said. *:But my brothers to the north may.:*

Alaire shrugged, trying to grasp the visual image he sensed coming from the crewman. *:What brothers? Of your family, or your race?:*

The Arachnia looked around furtively, as if he were afraid someone might overhear him.

:I come from a different hive: the crewman said, *:than the others on this ship. The hive mother guards the ocean, and I am here by mistake. My kind know this, but make little of it.:*

Alaire knew the Arachnians hatched from eggs, which incubated in protected hives, but beyond this he knew little.

:Guards the ocean?: Alaire asked. *:Explain.:*

The Arachnia hesitated, acting as if he'd said too much already. *:My family grew up with the water,:* the crewman continued. He seemed to have difficulty defining life on land as opposed to life on the sea. *:We live on the sea. We—:*

A clatter from above distracted them as another Arachnia came below. The new arrival looked around the deck for a moment before picking up a small barrel of fibrous material, and stopped dead when he saw the two humans and the Arachnia.

:Another time, singer: the Arachnia said, and turned away, moving towards his hammock. *:I am weary, and we must speak in private.:*

:Another time, then,: Alaire agreed. "Reykir, let's see how Craig's getting on," he said. Reykir took the hint and followed his master to the nearest ladder.

✧   ✧   ✧

"Now *that* was weird," Alaire said softly as soon as their cabin door shut behind them. "Did you pick up any of that?"

Reykir checked on Rak, who looked contented, dozing with a full stomach. "You were speaking telepathically," Reykir said. "But I could not listen in. What was he saying?"

Suddenly weary from the day's activities, Alaire sat on the bunk opposite his brother's. Craig continued to sleep soundly, not having so much as stirred when they entered. "That I'm still trying to figure out. But there seem to be two races of Arachnia."

"Two? But there's only one race." He hesitated, then continued with less conviction. "Isn't there?"

Alaire lay back on the lumpy hay mattress and put his hands behind his head. "That's what we thought. But didn't you notice his color? And he had different markings."

"Well, in the dark it was hard to make anything out. I must admit, I'm not that familiar with Arachnia, of whatever race." Reykir withdrew his flute from his tunic. Alaire frowned, since he preferred his student to concentrate on the harp. But Reykir had steadfastly refused to relinquish his flute, since it had provided so much companionship, and busking income, when he was running loose in the ghettos of Silver City. Besides, Reykir had pointed out convincingly, what was wrong with learning two instruments?

"The Arachnia we know cannot communicate telepathically, for one thing," Alaire said. "This one did, and quite well. He managed to block you out, which is difficult for *any* being to do." Alaire closed his eyes, reviewing the entire exchange all over again. *It was a warning, but against what? His own kind?*

"Whatever it was, he didn't look too comfortable discussing it around that other crewman, even telepathically," Reykir said, in between practice scales on the flute. "Do you think he's an outlaw?"

"Perhaps, but unlikely," Alaire replied. "Maybe on another ship, but not this one. My brother had this ship checked out thoroughly before making any deals with Captain Su'Beltor. He knew who I was. That I was a Bard."

"Is that so odd? Is your identity a secret on this ship?" Reykir said, then launched into a complicated, lively tune on the flute.

. "I suppose not," Alaire replied. *What did he say, exactly? His brothers to the north may harm me. What in the seven hells was that supposed to mean?* He glanced over at Reykir, and a disturbing thought came to him. *Was the Arachnia mistaking me for Reykir?* "You don't have any Arachnian enemies, do you?"

The music stopped. "Me, master? Certainly not. I've never met an Arachnia until today." He returned to his song, looking a bit disturbed nonetheless.

"Just a thought," Alaire said. *Only asking. You have a shady past, young one, but that doesn't mean I don't trust you. Those who lead such a life tend to accumulate enemies whether they want to or not.*

Craig rolled over and opened a single eye, gazing at his brother in evident pain. "I wasn't asleep long enough," Craig said, looking and sounding much older than his twenty-nine years. "When do we eat around here, anyway?"

"Good question," Alaire replied. "I would think that after last night, your hunger would be a bit subdued today."

Reykir continued to play the flute, a little softer now, a technique Alaire knew he used to listen in on conversations.

Craig sat up, looking pale and gaunt as ever, still smelling strongly of wine, but with a little more energy. "Don't start with me, brother," Craig said. "Only drunks get hangovers. I've never had a hangover in my life, and I'm not about to get one now."

That's because you've never sobered up long enough to have one, thought Alaire, keeping the jibe to himself. *No need to start a fight here in front of Reykir. He probably got an earful already, after our row this morning.*

"I have an appetite," Craig insisted. Alaire said nothing, wishing the conversation would change to another topic, or cease altogether. "When *do* we dine?"

"The captain never mentioned the eating schedule, so I assume around sunset." He glanced out the porthole, noting the shadows outside. "It's not even noon yet."

"Here," Reykir said, tossing a pouch over. "Have some jerky."

"I guess it will have to do," Craig said, but when he opened the bag he recoiled in disgust. "Aaargh!" he said, throwing the bag to the floor.

"Ooops," Reykir said, reaching for another bag. "I gave you the bag of fresh quail. Here, *this* is the jerky." As if to prove it, he pulled out a few strips and tossed them over.

"Thanks," Craig said, without much enthusiasm, and began gnawing.

Alaire realized he'd managed to get very comfortable even on this rather lumpy mattress, and found drowsiness overcoming him. Even this early in the day a nap sounded good; he hadn't quite recovered from his long overland voyage, and the king *had* promised him an opportunity to rest up. So he closed his eyes and took advantage of the soothing movement of the sea.

A young, small Arachnia came to their cabin some time later and informed them that dinner would be served in the captain's cabin, one deck up. Alaire didn't know how long he'd slept, but noticed the shadows had lengthened substantially. A few hours, at the very least, he figured. Besides feeling renewed from the nap, he now had an appetite which must have matched his brother's earlier one.

As they climbed up the ladder to the next deck, the Bard also observed that the ship was pitching and rolling more than when they'd left; after one particularly heavy lurch sideways, Reykir gave him a worried look.

"I suspect we're far at sea," Alaire said, in answer to Reykir's unspoken question. "Where the sea's a little rougher," he guessed.

Craig remained rather quiet as they ascended to the captain's cabin. When he passed by an open porthole, Alaire saw a greenish color in his brother's face. He did not look well, and the Bard wondered if this was the beginning of seasickness. *If so, then all the better,* Alaire thought, with bit of satisfaction. *If he gets ill on this voyage, he'll have to sober up. This might even be the best way to do it.*

The captain's cabin was a lavish gallery, with a long table down the center with settings for sixteen. The table itself was anchored firmly to the floor with wooden pegs. Even so a servant was cleaning up a broken dish that had fallen to the floor. Ten or so Arachnia had already seated themselves, each dressed for a formal dinner. Alaire noted wryly that the Arachnia had tried to imitate human dress, having donned elegant robes and doublets trimmed with fur and lace. The effect was comical on the gathering of insects, particularly when he noticed a codpiece on one. The Arachnian sex organs remained a mystery to Alaire, but he knew there was nothing where the codpiece was. Perhaps, he guessed, they dressed in this fashion in deference to their human guests, and wiped off whatever trace of a smirk had appeared on his face.

"Bard Alaire," the captain said, seated at the far end

of the table. "Please, be seated, honored guests." As they sat the ship pitched again, and Reykir stumbled.

"You should have your sea legs by the end of the day," the captain offered. "Until you do, I suggest that you use rails whenever possible." The captain glanced at Craig, who had managed to seat himself without incident, but said nothing. In the full light of the gallery Craig's queasiness was visible, and Alaire wondered if it had been a mistake for him to come to dinner at all.

"The seas seem to be a bit rough this afternoon," Alaire said conversationally as the servant poured wine in wooden tankards. The tankards were bottom heavy, apparently to make them stable on moving surfaces. "We're not anticipating a storm, are we?"

"Storms are always possible at sea," the captain said solemnly. "But yes, we've hit some rough water. In the distance we see the beginnings of a storm, but our navigator believes it is moving away from us."

"It isss what'ss leaving the rough seass behind," an Arachnia sitting across from Alaire said. His grasp of the human language was not as deft as the captain's, but the words came through clearly, in spite of his curious lisp. "It'ss nothing to worry about."

"We should be past it tonight," the captain said curtly, but even though he was an Arachnia, with difficult-to-read intonations, Alaire sensed some tension in his words. The Bard recalled that Arachnia were very sensitive to criticism, so he decided not to mention the weather again. *He might read that as a comment on his nautical abilities. Better not to rock the boat, as it were,* he thought.

The servant appeared with the appetizers, shrimp and clams, with a plate of black goo Alaire didn't identify at first. But when he saw the Arachnia reach for it immediately, he remembered this was a favorite delicacy of theirs: a light sauce made from beetles.

Tasty, I'm sure, Alaire thought, holding back his own revulsion. *For Arachnia. I wonder if Craig would like some?*

One glance at his brother suggested this would not be a good time to offer it. His shade of green had deepened, and he reached for his tankard with a shaking hand.

During the first course, thunder rolled across the sea but the Arachnia seemed to ignore it. Reykir hungrily consumed the shrimp, but fortunately didn't make a nuisance of himself. Alaire had Craig, who was downing tankard after tankard of wine to rely on for that.

I should have told the stewards not to keep filling his mug, Alaire thought, distressed. *Oh well, too late now. If I say anything now, Craig will cause a scene, and with this storm coming up I'd much rather not create any distractions for the crew.* At any rate, the wine seemed to be helping Craig's queasiness, at least on the surface. He looked less green now, and even managed a smile or two.

When the servant brought the main course in, a long tray of big, red lobsters, he whispered something to the captain in the Arachnian tongue.

"If you will excuse me," the captain said, standing. "A matter has arisen that needs my personal attention." The navigator and one other Arachnia stood halfway, before the captain spoke a brief sentence to them in Arachnian, and waved them back to their seats.

"Nothing to worry about," the captain said. "Please, continue dining. We should be through the storm soon."

The captain moved quickly through the gallery. Alaire glanced over at Reykir, who was heartily devouring a lobster. The Bard glanced at his own shellfish, wondering where to begin. He'd never had lobster before and didn't know how to get through the shell, and the

remains of Reykir's lobster did not offer many helpful clues. With the knife he began prying pieces of
the shell back, and forked at the tender meat inside.

"Aye, tis good wine, this is," Craig said, with a rosy
glow resonating behind his voice that Alaire recognized
all too readily. "Servant, would you pour me another?"

Alaire cringed. He'd barely touched his own wine,
finding it a bit coarse for his tastes, and much to the
Bard's approval, neither had Reykir. The boy had
never been one for drinking, at least not in front of
Alaire, and for this he was grateful. As rowdy and
mischievous as Reykir already was, he did not need
the extra encouragement of spirits.

It would be like pouring lamp oil on a fire.

They finished supper quietly without the captain,
and one by one the Arachnians excused themselves.
Thunder boomed through the ship, rattling the walls,
shaking the lanterns, sounding as though it was getting
closer.

"I'm off to go see what's going on above decks,"
Alaire said, standing.

"I'm going with you," Reykir said, joining him. Both
he and Alaire turned back at the same time, first
glancing at the full carafe of wine on the table, and
then at Craig, still whittling away at his lobster. Alaire
didn't much like leaving the carafe and his brother alone,
as he knew the wine would be gone in moments, but
he saw no effective way of getting it away from him
without fuss.

"You all go on," Craig said, his voice booming as
loudly as the thunder. "I'll be along."

"Aie, yes," Alaire said with a resigned sigh, as another
blast of thunder rocked the boat. They climbed a ladder
to the next deck up, and a trickle of water came down
over them.

"Good gods," Alaire said, when he looked above
the deck. Rain was coming down in a fine mist, but

directly ahead of them he saw the fiercest, blackest thunderstorm he'd ever seen in his life. It was a wall of cloud, reaching from the sky all the way to the sea, pierced by frequent lances of lightning.

"I want to see," Reykir said, scurrying up beside Alaire. "Oh, no I don't," he said, when he saw what was confronting the ship.

"This doesn't look good, young friend," Alaire said. "Maybe we should go back below."

Around them the Arachnian crew scrambled to adjust the sails. It looked to Alaire's untrained eye as though they were trying to turn the ship towards the starboard, where off in the distance he saw a patch of clear sky. But the storm continued to grow. The thunder became louder, and followed the lightning in ever shorter intervals. The dampness of the air bore down on him like a bad cold, and his ears popped with a sudden change of air pressure. The Arachnian crew called out in their native language, and while Alaire spoke none of it, he heard the urgency behind the Arachnian words. For the first time during the voyage he thought that maybe, just maybe, this might be dangerous.

Their cabin was down the corridor from them, and Reykir said something about Rak and started in that direction. The corridor was dark, but Reykir found their room with no trouble and opened the door. Weak light sliced into the corridor. Reykir went to Rak, who was standing rigid at the far corner of the upper bunk, fluffed up like a scared chicken.

"There, there," Reykir cooed as Rak stepped delicately up on the boy's hand. The bardling held the owl close to him, opening up his coat and sheltering the bird inside. "It's only a storm," the boy said, but even Alaire heard uncertainty in his voice. "Gods, *what* a storm," Reykir said, his voice trembling now as he cuddled his bird. "This ship can take it, can't she?"

"Of course she can," Alaire said, peering at the

storm through the porthole. "Stay here," Alaire said, suddenly concerned for his brother. "Craig will probably need help getting back here."

Only after Alaire left the cabin again and started up a ladder did the storm truly hit.

Rain pounded at the deck over him, and what had to have been a wall of wind slammed against the side of the ship. Timbers groaned and creaked around him, and the sudden roll threw Alaire against the corridor wall. Above him an Arachnian crewman screamed as something heavy dropped on the deck, splintering the planks above the Bard's head. He struggled to his feet and started back towards the gallery, where he had last seen Craig.

When he reached the dining room he found it a shambles. The table had overturned, having shaken free of the pegs holding it down, and the few lamps that were lit when he left had blown out. Rain was spraying into the gallery from open ports, so Alaire quickly closed the shutters against the storm. Before closing the last one he noted that the storm had blotted out the evening sun, shrouding the ship with gray, and rain which, in the brief flashes of lightning, blew horizontally. By design or accident, the ship was now pointed downwind, with the sea churning past at a dizzying rate of speed.

Alaire staggered out of the gallery, along a floor which refused to hold still, and dodged three Arachnian crewman who skittered past. Two carried buckets of thick fibrous material, the other a set of simple carpenter's tools.

I hope that damn fool child stays where he is, Alaire thought, briefly wondering if he meant Craig or Reykir. Craig and a carafe of wine was a dangerous combination, and he prayed only that his brother stayed out of the way of the crew, and remained out of danger himself.

Then the captain came below, and looked like he would have walked past Alaire without speaking if he hadn't stopped him.

"Captain, tell me, what is going on?" Alaire asked, feeling rather stupid. *Of course I know what's going on, we're in a bloody storm, that's what's going on!*

"Found a bit of weather, we have," the captain said sourly. "Nothing to worry about. Go on to your cabin now."

"But captain, this storm . . ."

"Never you mind. Think of it this way. With a wind to our stern like this, consider the time we'll save getting to Rozinki! Now, off with you!" the captain snapped, and followed a crewman down another ladder to the deck beneath them.

Something about this situation disturbed Alaire immensely. First, the crewmen with the hammer, saw and nails, and the bucket of other stuff, had gone below. Then the captain had followed them down for a look, when now, of all times, he should have been supervising the sailing of his vessel through the storm.

Against his better judgment, Alaire waited a moment longer, then followed the captain down, to see what *was* wrong down there.

I'm going to regret this, he thought frantically, as water splashed over his head, prompting a moment of panic. But no, the water stopped before flooding the entire deck, managing only to soak him completely. What's more, the water was ice cold, chilling him to the bone.

Carefully seeking sound footing as he descended to the lower level, he dropped into wet, dank darkness. Then he saw what the problem was.

Yes, I regret coming down here, all right, he thought dismally. Something had pierced the hull of the ship, making a hole big enough to put two fists in. Crewmen tried desperately to patch it with wood, straw, anything that was available. By itself, this probably wouldn't sink the ship; even so, he was standing ankle deep in water that became noticeably deeper as he watched.

The captain called out orders in Arachnian, and proceeded down the length of the ship, splashing inelegantly through the lake that had formed. The creaking and groaning was more pronounced down here, and with some alarm the Bard realized he was well below sea level, with only a few inches of wood separating him from the chaotic waters.

Wasting no time, he decided he wanted to be above sea level right then, even if it would mean little if the ship sank.

I've got to find out where Craig is, he thought. *He might have made it back to the cabin. . . .*

But he hadn't. In the cabin Reykir sat with his owl, shivering in the cold that had fallen on them.

"Alaire, what's going on?" Reykir said thinly, but his tone suggested he didn't really expect an answer.

"We've hit a hell of a storm," Alaire replied anyway. "I'm going to keep looking for Craig."

He left the cabin, swearing beneath his breath at his brother. *Now, of all times, he decides to get drunk and wander off! Leave it to him to find a secret place to get soused in the middle of an ocean!*

He went back up to the hatch again, only this time rain hammered against it. Cautiously, he opened the hatch and climbed to the deck.

Wind and rain stung against him as he found his footing on the poop deck, the raised platform at the rear of the ship where two more crewmen had joined the steersmen in wrestling the whipstaff. The bar fought them as the ship jammed through the waves, but the crewman struggled to keep an even keel. The ship pitched violently to port, and Alaire grabbed onto a rail to keep from falling over. One of the crew scrambled over to the hatch, closed it, and shouted something at Alaire in Arachnian.

Where the hell is Craig? Alaire thought. If he had come up here he certainly would have gone overboard by now. Great waves of green swept over the bow, for a frightening moment appearing to submerge the ship altogether, blanketing the deck with foam. An instant later the ship rose from the sea as it rode another massive wave, which seemed to carry it all the way to the sky; Alaire was soaked and chilled to the bone, and he shivered from cold and fear as he watched their vessel bob around in the sea like a cork. He felt powerless, truly insignificant in an ocean that seemed to be toying with them.

I'm getting below, Alaire thought, looking for the hatch that had admitted him to the deck. He had to wait as another huge wave surged past, while Arachnian hands clutched lifelines as the sea rolled above them. Before he reached the hatch he heard a commotion, a dozen Arachnian voices shouting over the storm, coming from the bow of the ship.

On the foremast, which supported the first main sail, a boom had broken clean off, and the sail was fluttering helplessly in the wind. Crewmen scrambled to secure the renegade sail, but it seemed all they could do was to keep from being washed overboard. The Bard saw one brave Arachnia climbing up the mast, but the great wind that surged up forced the foresail even further back.

Alaire watched the ship fall apart, amazed at his complete lack of emotion. Then, with a mighty crack as loud as a cannon, the foremast broke off with the Arachnia on it, falling backwards into the second sail, then collapsing in a tangle of ropes. The falling sail had jarred the main sail, ripping a row of belaying pins from the deck. The ship careened out of control, spinning in wide, nauseating arcs in the sea.

This ship isn't going to make it, he thought with sickening clarity. He scrambled for the hatch, but another wave came over the deck, washing him over to the main deck below, where the sails had fallen. Alaire struggled out of the spider webbing of rigging he'd fallen into as the ship rolled far to port. Alaire thought she was going to capsize, but then she righted herself.

The horrible sound of splintering wood reached his ears. The smaller mizzenmast which rose from the poop deck snapped like a stick, sweeping the steersmen into the sea with it. Beneath him the ship trembled, as its hull screamed at the sea. A jagged fissure of planks and frame opened near him.

The ship is breaking in two! his mind screamed, once he comprehended what he was seeing. The ship had impaled herself on a rocky reef, Alaire saw as the waves rolled past, and the keel was straddling it like a scale. All was lost, Alaire knew, but before he could think another massive wave rolled across the deck, capsizing what was left of the great ship.

Then the water closed in over him.

Chapter Four

Reykir held his owl closer to him, but Rak began to struggle. The bardling tried to let the bird fly about in the pitching, rolling cabin, but Rak clung painfully to the boy's left fist, gasping and panting. He had never seen his bird so frightened before.

This ship is falling apart, Reykir kept thinking. *The ship is falling apart, and when it does, I will drown.* He held Rak closer. *Rak will fly away before I die, at least.*

It was easier for him to concentrate on the bird's fear than his own. Since Alaire had left to go searching for his brother, the ship's motion had become even more violent, if such a thing were possible without capsizing.

The ship rolled hard to the right side; fear gripped him, and Rak hopped off his fist to perch on the highest point in the cabin, the upper bunk.

Without breathing, without thinking, Reykir waited for the ship to roll back, as it had to. For a perilous moment it held position then, maddeningly, it continued the roll in the same direction.

Rak squawked as they both fell off the bunks and landed against the opposite wall, beneath the porthole. Granted, it was a short journey but an unexpected one, and the boy grunted as his shoulder struck the wall.

Sea water poured into the porthole in torrents.

Biting back a scream, Reykir struggled to reach the porthole, splashing his way through salty water which stung his eyes. With trembling hands he shut the shutters, ending the flood. The ship had finally begun to sway back in the other direction, and in the semidarkness he saw the owl fluttering around the cabin in panic. He tried to reach her with his mind, but the bird's terror shut him out.

And his own terror was starting to surface as well. The cabin remained flooded, although the ship had stabilized for a moment. Water lapped at his knees, and somewhere in the darkness, something swam.

Reykir held still, terrified that if he moved, that *something* swimming might take a big chunk out of his leg or other vital portions of his anatomy. Drowning, now, seemed a distant threat. The *something* splashed about in the water. Frozen in place, Reykir considered his next move.

The storm still raged outside, by far the primary threat to his well-being, but he knew that the storm was a storm, and he still had no idea what *it* was.

Then it brushed against his leg, something sharp and spiked.

A moment later the cabin's door flew back on its hinges as Reykir charged through it. Water poured into the corridor from his cabin and drained towards the rear. Soaked, Rak fluttered out of the cabin after him, having great trouble flying with wet feathers.

Reykir looked down at the *something* which had rubbed against his leg. He only saw a vague dark shape, flapping and writhing on the floor.

He ran in the opposite direction, towards the belly of the ship, then stopped again at a new noise.

Rak plummeted into his back, and let out a sharp squawk. But other sounds were echoing through the vast body of the ship, sounds which were far more frightening to him than a sea monster tickling his ankles.

Two sharp snaps reverberated through the craft, followed by muffled Arachnian shouts. Then the ship's hull screamed out beneath him. As he watched, the deck buckled, as if a great earthquake was splitting the ship in two. He didn't know which way to run, and he was beginning to wonder if it mattered anymore.

There must be a way out of here! he thought. *The lifeboats. There must be . . .*

But he knew he would never have time to reach them. The crack in the ship's deck continued to spread, and suddenly he was looking up into open sky, with the front half of the ship tumbling off into the sea.

:Fly out of here, Rak!: Reykir mindshouted as he flung his owl up through the opening. Rak struggled against the rain, gaining altitude with a sudden gust of wind. Then she was out of sight.

For a moment he stood there, on the edge of the splintered deck; as the waves rolled away, he saw the Arachnian crew struggling in the water by a rocky reef, now completely at the sea's mercy.

Reykir considered praying, then remembered that during his transient life he had never learned how.

I'll just stay here, he thought, but immediately saw a problem with that plan. He stood on a deck held together by little more than friction, and another big wave would probably sweep the ship's remains into the surging ocean. He thought he had caught a glimpse of Alaire swimming past, but the waves were too violent for him to be certain.

The bardling was looking around madly for something buoyant when another huge wave pushed the ship off the reef. Without thinking he started climbing to the highest point on the wreck. The hull did a slow turn, like a dead fish going belly up.

Please, don't let me drown, he thought, crazed,

unsure who exactly he was talking to. Then he looked up and screamed as a huge wave rolled over him and the wreckage, sweeping him into the dark ocean.

Icy water chilled his body quickly, but the panic brought on when he started to sink jolted him into action. He clawed his way to the surface, took in a deep gulp of air, and grabbed onto a piece of floating debris which looked suspiciously like the remains of one of the longboats. The ship's wreckage, what remained above water, made a slow spiral as it sank, and Reykir prayed he was far enough away from it that the undertow wouldn't pull him down with it.

He clung to his makeshift raft, bobbing roughly with the waves. Rain continued to fall in torrents, limiting his view of the disaster, and he had no idea how far they were from land. He saw nothing but angry sea, the flash of lightning, and the continuous downpour. Cold spread through him, and feeling soon left his hands and arms.

Reykir closed his eyes and held on tighter, savoring each breath of air he took in. He did not know how long he drifted on the wreckage; time passed slowly for him as the storm above diminished, but the storm within the sea, the rolling waves which seemed to take forever to pass, continued. Eventually on the horizon a long, rocky cliff appeared, but it seemed incredibly far away. With relief, he saw that it was getting closer, that perhaps he might live through this after all.

An Arachnia floated past him, its body stiff in the icy saltwater. The sight reminded him that he might yet die in these cold waters. They must have traveled some distance north in order to find this frigid sea. Reykir suspected that the rocky cliff he drifted closer to was Suinomen, and not Althea.

I can't feel my legs, he thought. *I can't feel . . . much of anything.*

For what seemed like years, the waves swept him towards the coast. He closed his eyes for a moment, and felt himself falling into an endless, dark tunnel. When he came to what felt like a century later, salt-water was burning the back of his throat, but his feet were touching sand. He rode the last few waves onto the beach and staggered ashore, too exhausted to think, much less feel grateful that he'd made it to firm ground.

Reykir woke from a nightmare of drowning. He had fallen into the sea and the waves had covered his head, but instead of floating to the top something grabbed him from below, something that stabbed his leg as it pulled him into darkness.

The darkness turned to light, and he awakened in the prison of his flesh. His body was a mass of aches. Lungs burned, and when he coughed, water gurgled out. As his lungs kicked out the saltwater, he thought he would lose his dinner. Eventually his stomach settled down as he lay on the sand, chest heaving.

Good gods, I'm alive, he thought, with more surprise than was comfortable. The piece of wreckage he had used as a raft lay nearby. By the angle of the sun he guessed it was midmorning, and the sky blazed with a hot, naked sun. No sign of the storm remained, except a lingering scent of rain. He tried to sit up, but his body simply would not allow him. Reykir was so exhausted he was ill, and he lay back on a patch of white sand warmed by the sun, and closed his eyes. The flute still hung around his neck, and he touched its familar roundness.

He reached out to Rak with his mind, but no one replied.

She's either too far away, or sleeping, he thought. *Or she didn't make it.*

Pushing this last thought away, he felt his body for injury, finding a particularly nasty bruise on his right knee, and a throbbing in his right ankle. Sprained or broken, he did not know, and for the moment, didn't care. All he wanted to do was to sleep the day away, and wake up in a nice, warm bed.

A shadow passed over his closed eyelids. Somewhere between sleep and wakefulness, he sensed someone standing over him.

With a start he opened his eyes; for a moment all he saw was a huge blob silhouetted against the blinding sun. It moved a bit, shutting the sun out completely, and Reykir got his first good look at the visitor.

It was not a man, but an animal. From the size of it he guessed at first that it was a horse, but there was something rodentlike about its skull, and it had large growths visible over its shoulders. Its head was certainly as big as a horse's, but longer and more narrow with whiskers sprouting from its snout.

The thing opened its mouth in a fair approximation of a snarl, revealing long, ratlike incisors.

This is no horse, Reykir thought, forcing himself to stay calm, but his heart raced out of control anyway. He scrambled away from it, crawling backwards like a crab, and found temporary refuge behind the remains of a rowboat.

Even though he was stiff and sore, he moved with agility that amazed even himself. His right leg hurt like hell, but at least the ankle wasn't broken, or he doubted he'd be able to walk on it.

"Good gods from above," he said, leaning against the wreckage and peering over it. "What *is* this thing?"

Whatever it was, at least it didn't seem to be in any hurry to turn him into a meal. The beast was big, larger than any stallion he'd ever seen, and gazed at him with a hard expression that managed to convey intelligence.

Reykir had no idea what classification of beast this

was until it started moving, slowly at first, with brief but quick ratlike scampers sideways to keep Reykir in view.

The creature regarded the boy; the boy regarded the creature, wondering just how fast the thing could run. Then he saw clearly for the first time the growths on its back, and decided they must be wings, folded up like a bat's. It had no feathers, just a fine layer of fur over the thin membrane that draped over the bony frame. It held them tucked in, so he couldn't tell what kind of wingspan it had, but if it used them to fly they would have to be *enormous*.

Reykir didn't know whether to run or stay put. The thing looked fearsome but was making no move to attack; it was watching him as warily and cautiously as he was watching it. When their eyes met, Reykir sensed that this creature was much smarter than the average sewer rat.

Then images and feelings popped into his head, an unclear message with a clear emotion behind it. The words came as images and feelings, a general inquiry as to who Reykir was, what he was.

"I'm . . . Reykir. From the south," the boy verbalized. The creature did not look like it understood, tilting its head in a strangely human gesture of incomprehension.

Reykir replied again, this time by putting the words into thoughts. He imagined an image of himself and Alaire, with his master teaching him the harp. This seemed to interest the rat immensely. The boy summoned all the emotions connected to being a student, the frustration, the humility, as well as the joy in mastering a new song, and the relief of receiving praise from his master.

The rat's eyes softened, as if it understood what it was like to be a student. *No, not a student. A servant.* Reykir thought, as the images blurred. The connection broke off, and the rat looked away, as if contemplating a thought too painful to share.

Reykir walked closer to it, but not *too* close, and phrased another question with images.

:*Where did you come from?*: Reykir asked.

The rat paused, looked past Reykir, then raised a front paw. With a single digit, it pointed at the sea behind him.

:*From over there. A long distance,*: the rat replied. :*Did the storm bring you also?*:

As their communication continued, Reykir relaxed, confident now that his new friend was not going to try to eat him.

"I must be in Suinomen," Alaire said to the cliffs towering above the beach. "Althea's beaches are smooth, with no great barrier in the way." The cliffs did little to shield the sun, which was fine with Alaire, as he was still chilled to the bone. Though his clothes were mostly dry, the sea clung to him in a gritty veil.

He hadn't really thought he would live through the ordeal, and when the waves closed in over him half a hundred times, he had thought he was done for. At some point, he'd passed out. Moments later, he'd rolled onto a beach, where he had struggled to crawl through the huge waves that threatened to pull him back into the sea. Then he had collapsed, uncertain if he was safe but too exhausted to move if he wasn't.

The sun greeted him when his eyes fluttered open again. For the first few moments he wasn't certain what had happened; then he heard the waves lapping at the beach, miniature versions of the monsters that had wrecked the ship, and he remembered everything. Nothing remained of the ship except for debris strewn in both directions on the beach.

Then he saw a portion of the once mighty ship far out to sea, perched on what had to be a submerged reef. There was no sign of life on the wreck, which looked as if the next big wave would sweep it off its temporary foundation.

No sign of Craig. No sign of Reykir. They must have . . . He stopped short of assuming they'd drowned. True, their chances didn't look good, particularly Craig's, who was drunk at the time of the wreck. But Reykir was a young, strong lad.

If I lived, certainly Reykir made it, but the totality of the ship's destruction did not provide much hope. Tired, exhausted, and saddened by the disaster, Alaire picked a direction, north, and started walking. As he trudged through the sand around a collection of boulders, he felt a soreness throughout his entire being.

There must be survivors.

Once he made it around the boulders, he saw another vast expanse of sand and a still, human form lying facedown. As he drew closer, he saw that it was Craig, and he didn't look as though he had survived the ordeal very well.

Alaire knelt down and gently turned his brother over, expecting the worst. But as soon as he was moved Craig started coughing and spitting out water. He still wore his dark attire, complete with cloak and boots. Next to him was a still-wet chunk of timber. It looked as though he'd only recently washed ashore.

"Seven hells," Craig muttered as he sat up. "Where'd the ship go off to?"

Alaire helped him to sit up, and plopped down next to him. "Well, brother, it's here, and there," he said, gesturing towards the debris. "And a big chunk of it is still out there, at sea."

Craig squinted to see the wreckage. "That's what's left?" He started feeling his chest and shoulders, as if to make sure he was still attached to them. "Did we *die?*"

"Not quite," Alaire said. "You're the first survivor I've found."

Craig coughed up more seawater. "Then what the bloody hell happened to us?"

Gods, he probably doesn't remember any of it, Alaire thought, checking his anger. He had very little patience left, and Craig was stretching it.

"We need water. And food," Alaire said, while hoping water was the only potable that had washed ashore. The last thing they needed to find on the beach was a keg of wine.

"Aye," Craig said, then leaned back on the sand and promptly went to sleep.

Just as well, Alaire thought. *He needs to sleep the drink off before he'll be any help, and now is just as good a time as any. We're not going anywhere soon. And if a keg did wash ashore, it will give me a chance to dump it before brother dear finds it.*

Alaire started off towards the north again. After his last trip he hadn't thought he would ever pray for sun, but the sea wind that rose chilled him. He walked some distance before he encountered another rocky barrier, seeing nothing on the beach that looked remotely usable. The sand ended at the base of several boulders. He would either have to swim or climb over them. Since he was just starting to get warm, he began climbing.

Halfway up the mound, he came to an abrupt stop.

There's something magical on the other side of these boulders. Something magical, and evil. He sent a tentative probe in the general direction of the magical source, to see what, if any, threat it was. In addition to the magical source, he sensed someone else. *Reykir! Thank the gods you made it.* The boy, however, was clearly frightened.

The Bard cautiously peered over the top of the boulders.

What he saw on the beach was nothing he would have ever guessed or imagined, even in his wildest nightmares. His exhausted condition made it more difficult to comprehend what his eyes were telling him; for a time he even thought he'd hit his head on something, very hard. He shook his head, cleared his eyes, and looked again. The giant winged creature was as it had been, only this time it was looking at him.

Their eyes met. Alaire felt himself pulled into them, and saw right away that this was no mere rodent. The thing was intelligent, perhaps as smart as a human. Then he noticed the leather collar around its neck, stones and crystals attached to it. He felt the power emanating from them: the ornaments were not a decoration, they were on the collar for magical reasons.

Ah, not the beast himself, he thought, relieved, though he had no logical reason to relax. *This creature is a servant or slave for whoever is harnessing the power of those stones and crystals.* He looked again at the collar, trying to identify the stones as best he could. At that distance, he could only tell that they were powerful, and must be the tool of a wizard or wizards with a staggering grasp of the magical arts.

The two continued to gaze at each other. Reykir waved, but made no move to reach his master. While Alaire considered approaching the beast, since it didn't seem to be preparing to attack either of them, the creature spoke.

Not verbally, but directly to Alaire's mind, with images and feelings, not words. The message became an assault on the Bard's senses, a message of fear and a bit of rage. Alaire had to filter out some of the more intense feelings to understand what the creature was trying to tell him. The images came quickly at first, but then the creature must have sensed he was going too fast, and the images slowed, the emotion dimmed, the anger faded.

Alaire saw a tunnel, through which he saw the creature flying through the sky. Rain stung its hide, and Alaire sensed panic, a familiar fear of drowning. Finding land was the most important thing to the creature, for without solid ground it would have nowhere to land, and would plummet into the ocean when the exhaustion became too much.

Alaire caught sight of the ocean, very far below. He flew through clouds, strong wings beating against thin air, and two other winged rats flew alongside. They too wore the collars with the stones and crystals. The tunnel widened, the images shifted, and he felt the scene changing to an earlier time, before the wingrats began their voyage over the ocean. Hordes of dark Arachnia with strange markings corralled large herds of the flying rats in pens. The collars kept them from flying away, from disobeying, from rebelling against the Arachnia in any way. Alaire took note of this new breed of Arachnia: they were larger, darker, and had a pattern of white dots on their pincers. They wielded magic in ways Alaire had never imagined possible by the insects, using it to bend the will and spirits of the wingrats. When the magic failed, the Arachnia beat and tortured the wingrats. In extreme cases their wings were ripped from their bodies in a massive tug-of-war by a dozen or so Arachnia. They bled to death quickly while the others watched, their last function serving as a grim reminder to the rest, if they ever forgot their place, as to who was the master, and who was the slave. . . .

Alaire felt a great rage, turning to sadness. He felt this happening in a daily cycle. The wingrats knew nothing else.

As he became aware again of his own surroundings, he saw that he now stood on the beach, several paces from the wingrat. Its expression was as sad as the story it had conveyed.

As his contact with the wingrat faded, Alaire ventured to send a question in the same way the creature had contacted him.

:What is your name, and why are you here?: Alaire sent. For a moment, the wingrat looked confused, then it replied with a set of images. In a night sky, a moon rose from the horizon. *:Your name is Moon . . . no, Low Moon,:* Alaire corrected himself, and he received an affirmative emotion from the wingrat.

Then, evidently as an answer to the second part of his question, he saw the image of three wingrats rising from a large island. Alaire figured this island was far out to sea, as no other land mass appeared in the image. With sudden clarity, he saw what their task was.

They are reconnaissance for the Arachnia, he thought. *But why? What interest do these other Arachnia have in Suinomen?* In the image he found not only the magical collars, but a series of reinforcement spells used to keep them under control at long distances, and to insure that they returned to their masters once they'd accomplished their mission.

The storm, Alaire saw, and he knew it was the same storm that sank their ship. The storm had disoriented them, and the other two wingrats fell to the ocean, unable to handle the terrible downdrafts they encountered. Low Moon survived by changing direction and going with the downdraft, instead of fighting it; though it lost altitude, it survived where its brethren had not. By changing direction, it found its way out, and rose on equally violent updrafts. Otherwise, it would have perished.

Exhausted all over again, Alaire dropped to his knees. The sand had warmed considerably in the time he'd spent in contact with Low Moon. He felt someone at his side, and when he looked up, he saw Reykir.

"Master, you're alive," Reykir said, giving him a

hand up from the sand. They embraced each other like lost friends, with surprising intensity. Alaire hadn't realized how glad he was to see him until their palms touched, and his presence became tangible.

"Thank the gods you made it," Alaire said before they separated. "Are you hurt?"

"Not enough to matter," Reykir replied, looking up at Alaire. "Master, you don't look well," he added, casting nervous glances from his master to the wingrat. "What in the seven hells *is* this creature?"

"This is new to me, too," Alaire whispered. "Are you picking anything up from him, anything at all?"

At the use of the male pronoun, Alaire felt an urgent tugging at his mind. He looked up at Low Moon.

:*I am not a he, I am a she,:* Low Moon sent.

"Forgive me. *She.*" Alaire said. "It—she communicates with thoughts. Images."

Reykir looked at the wingrat, then at the horizon of the sea. "Like that Arachnian on the ship?"

Alaire didn't know what he was talking about at first. Then he remembered the crewman they had encountered belowdecks. The memory flooded back with all the subtlety of a bucket of ice water.

"Good gods, of course," Alaire said. *The Arachnia on the ship. The species of the island. They were the same. What was that poor creature trying to tell me?* Alaire looked up and down the beach to see if there were any other survivors. He saw none. Then he remembered that the Arachnia, with their hard, chitinous shells, didn't swim very well.

"Precisely," Alaire said, and turned to his apprentice. "These winged rats, they are from an island, far off to the east. Another species of Arachnia, like the one we saw on the ship, lives there as well, and has been breeding these creatures for . . ." It occurred to Alaire he didn't know what their purpose was, so he asked.

:Unclear,: Low Moon replied. *:We learn to fly with masters riding us,:* the wingrat continued. Alaire saw an image of Arachnia riding a herd of wingrats, twenty or so, but it seemed to be a sort of training exercise. The method of riding them didn't appear to be perfected yet, but it looked as if they were well on their way.

:Are your masters trying to fly to this land?: Alaire asked. He received an affirmative.

:Fly to, or invade?: the Bard continued. *:Seeking war with us?:*

The wingrat looked ready to reply, but a pained, tortured expression came over her face. Alaire sensed that she wanted to tell him, but something, a spell from the collar, was keeping her from it.

"The storm must have weakened their magic," Alaire said to Reykir as he regarded the now-clear sky. "A storm like the one that brought us here would be difficult to penetrate with any magic, particularly at the distance this creature appears to have flown." He looked into Low Moon's mind again, and perused the images she offered. The storm had weakened the spell, but in addition to its lingering effect, there were also psychological bindings to her masters. She didn't seem to know what to do now that she was without orders. The strangeness of the new land frightened her, although she had taken time out to roll around in the warm sand, something she didn't have at her island home.

There is a struggle here, a desire to return because she doesn't really know how to take care of herself, and a stronger urge to put as much distance between her and her captors as possible. It looks like the urge to be free is winning. But for how long?

"We must get rid of that spell," Alaire said. "Eventually I think it will draw her back to her home. And I don't think the Arachnia have our best interests in mind."

"How do you mean?" Reykir asked, fingering his flute still hanging on its cord from his neck.

"I think there is an invasion in the works, and our new friend here was part of the reconnaissance team," Alaire said. "We must raise some Bardic magic." He caught himself hesitating, without really realizing it; he was still accustomed to magic being off-limits in Suinomen. Indeed, breaking that law had nearly cost him his life. But those days were far behind, and magic was now welcomed in this kingdom.

"Shouldn't we be looking for food and water?" Reykir asked.

"If we free our friend here of her magical bindings, she can help us in that endeavor. More efficiently than we can," Alaire pointed out.

"I have my flute," Reykir said hopefully. Alaire frowned, admitting to himself that his prejudices against the instrument were unreasonable. He knew he had a definite bias towards the harp; after all, it was what he had learned his Bardic skills on, and it was the musical instrument with which he'd performed his first Bardic spell—the one which saved the life of the present ruler of Suinomen.

Reykir looked over the strewn ship's wreckage on the beach. "I think I lost my harp in the shipwreck," he said. "By the way, master, where did *your* harp go?"

Even though Reykir had his back turned to his master, Alaire knew he was smiling at him. The Bard grumbled a reply.

"What?" Reykir said, turning to face him, with an expression of innocence. "What did you say?"

"I said," Alaire said, checking his anger, "I must have lost my harp, too." He shrugged. "It looks like we must make do with what we have. We'll try voices alone first, then your flute, Reykir, if we must to raise what we need."

Alaire turned to the wingrat, who now seemed to understand something was up. The Bard conveyed to her what he intended to do; it must have taken a moment for her to realize what this meant.

:*Yes, freedom,*: Alaire said. :*We can free you of this spell. If that is what you want.*:

The wingrat took on a contemplative, human expression, as if she were considering what life would be like without the spell. She seemed to hesitate, and Alaire detected feelings of loneliness.

:*After all, there are no others like me here. The others perished, out there, at sea,*: she told Alaire, pointing a clawed hand towards the ocean. :*I am by myself.*:

Alaire understood. He considered working the spell anyway, so as to deprive the enemy of one of their trained creatures. But there was something inherently unethical about the move. The choice must be made by the one most effected, Alaire's inner voice told him. Low Moon would have to give her permission for him to proceed.

"What's the problem?" Reykir said, apparently sensing the hesitation.

"She's not certain," Alaire said. "Give her a moment."

It didn't even take that long. :*Remove it. The collar. The spell. Everything.*:

Reykir offered his flute, but Alaire politely declined. *My voice will work for this,* he thought, noting his own frayed nerves. *The last thing I want to hear is that thrice-damned flute piercing my head.*

Alaire began a simple spell of dismissal, finding the deep, lower range of his voice easier to invoke in his state of near exhaustion. He wove the spell around a housecleaning ritual, one he'd used to purify newly-built houses, or refurbished rooms in the palace; only with this one he added protection on top of the cleansing. Going on the fly like this, he knew his chances for success were slim. If he failed, he'd simply try again later, when some of his energy had returned.

Despite his doubts the spell seemed to be working. The collar fell to the sand. The wingrat jumped back in surprise; apparently, there had been something magical keeping it in place.

Alaire touched the spell with his naked mind and recoiled at the bitter, evil flavor it had, then extinguished it with his own magic.

The wingrat did not seem to know how to react. First she felt her neck and shoulder area, rubbing the fur with her claws. With gestures that looked almost human, she massaged her long, horselike jaw, vigorously scratching the hairless band where the collar had been. Then she began rolling around in the sand, frolicking in the sun.

"She looks rather pleased that the thing is off her," Reykir said, standing next to his Master. "Do you think she's ever been without it?"

"I don't think so," Alaire replied. "She certainly acts like this is the first time she's been free."

Soon Low Moon stopped her antics long enough to send Alaire a message. :*I've never known what it's like to be without the bindings,*: Low Moon sent. :*I don't know how to thank you.*: She regarded the beach, the wreckage, and the sea, her joyful mood quickly subdued. :*How might I help you return to your home?*:

"Well," Alaire said, more to Reykir than to his new friend, feeling as though he'd been shaken from a dream. "We do have our responsibilities in Suinomen to tend to." Then, remembering how he had to communicate with Low Moon, he sent, :*We need food and water. As do you, I suppose. Will you help us?*:

Low Moon sent an eager affirmative, spread her wings and began beating at the air. Alaire and Reykir stepped back, more to avoid the sand that her wings hurled up than the sudden gust of wind. Then she was off, with the grace of a seagull.

"Looks like this creature is going to come in handy

after all," Reykir said. "Perhaps we should start looking for survivors," the boy added, though little hope showed in his words.

"Craig's over there, sleeping," Alaire said. "I don't have much faith anyone else made it. We would have seen the survivors by now." Alaire scratched his arm, which, along with the rest of his body, was becoming itchy with the drying salt water. "What of your owl?"

Reykir turned away, saying nothing, and started walking forlornly down the beach. His fallen shoulders told the Bard everything.

There's always a chance, Alaire thought, turning his attention to the winged rat that circled in the sky. *Anything can happen in this land.*

Chapter Five

They found Craig still sleeping soundly, a gull pecking at his boot. The bird flew off at their approach, kiting away on the cool, ocean breeze. Alaire leaned down and shook Craig's shoulder. Craig sat up awkwardly in the rough sand as a fit of coughing seized him.

"Damn," Craig said, when he was able to speak. "That was either a giant bat or a cow with wings I saw a minute ago."

Alaire and Reykir exchanged looks.

"You're seeing things," Alaire said. *Yes, he is seeing things. Things that, this time, are really there.* "We need to find out where we are, so we can decide which direction to travel. I suspect that storm carried us a good distance towards Rozinki."

Reykir was snickering, and Alaire had a pretty good idea why. "Low Moon might be able to help us. Since we did her the service of removing that collar."

"Who?" Craig said, as he struggled to get up.

The question remained unanswered, and Craig didn't push for a reply. Once Craig was on his feet, they searched the beach one last time, this time finding an oilskin bag that Alaire recognized. "I don't believe it," he said, pulling out his harp, still damp from the sea, but potentially salvageable. "I may be able to put this to use again."

Craig grunted something unintelligible as he poked at a smashed barrel with a piece of driftwood. "I don't suppose any of our shipmates made it, brother?"

"Doubt it. The Arachnians can't swim too well," Alaire replied.

They spent a brief time looking for survivors along the beach, but when the wreckage ended, so did their hopes. *We're alone out here,* Alaire thought. *Perhaps, if we find that road Naitachal and I took on our last trip to Suinomen we might find some help.*

The Bard watched Low Moon flying in the distance; if Craig saw her, he pretended otherwise. *Okay, enough is enough,* Alaire thought. "Craig, we have something to tell you."

Reykir gave his master a disgusted look. "Oh, why spoil it?"

"This is no game," Alaire said. "We are in a little bit of a pickle, in case you didn't notice. But we have a friend, Low Moon, who is in a very good position to help us find our way around here."

The three had made their way from the beach up a gradual slope, where they could see the edge of a forest. Craig had begun to perspire, Alaire noticed, and probably needed a drink.

"Who is *Low Moon?*" Craig asked impatiently. "Is this a ghost or something that we've acquired while I wasn't looking?"

"In a manner of speaking," Reykir replied evenly.

Craig opened his mouth to reply, but as a shadow fell over them all, the sentence froze in his throat.

The wingrat had silently glided into a position above them, passing across the sun as she descended. Two strong beats of her broad wings cushioned her landing a mere five paces in front of them. She stood up, tucked her wings, and regarded Craig cautiously.

:*Who is?*: she asked Alaire.

"Craig, let me introduce you to our new traveling

companion. This is Low Moon, and she is friendly," Alaire said. Craig stared, open mouthed.

:*This is Craig,*: Alaire sent. :*He's on our side.*:

Reykir seemed to be enjoying the situation immensely, but thankfully said nothing. *Anything to get his mind off his lost pet,* Alaire thought. *Losing Rak must be bothering him more than he's admitting.* Over the course of their friendship Alaire had noticed a tendency in the lad to hide his feelings, or cloak them in some other emotion, like amusement. *If he wants to make fun of my brother, who so justly deserves it, then so be it.*

A long moment passed before Craig shook himself and asked, "Wha-what in hell's name *is* that thing?"

"What . . . thing, Craig? I don't see anything," Reykir said, before Alaire gave him a warning look.

"This is a creature that blew in on the same storm that, well, blew us *over,*" Alaire began. "She is quite friendly, and can communicate with us. She's telepathic."

"I suppose I've seen it all, now," Craig said, a crooked smile creasing his otherwise sour expression. "It's a rat the size of a cow. How charming." He bowed extravagantly, but he staggered a little. "Rat, nice to meet you. I'm Prince Craig."

It was the first time in many months that Alaire had heard him use his title. Alaire directed a message to Low Moon. :*What did you see while you were flying?*: he asked. :*Is there a city nearby?*:

The wingrat wrinkled her nose at Craig before turning her attention to Alaire. :*He should stay away from me,*: Low Moon warned. :*I get a very bad feeling from him.*:

Alaire sighed, resigned to her reaction. Everyone got a bad feeling around Craig, it seemed, and he didn't know what to do about it. :*He is my brother. We are . . . related.*: Alaire sent, trying to frame the image with a minimum of description. *:He can be trusted.:*

Low Moon did not answer, and Alaire assumed this to mean skepticism. *Not the least of our troubles, anyway,* the Bard thought.

:There is a dwelling nearby,: she sent, and Alaire saw from a viewpoint far above the ground, a thatched roof with smoke coming from a chimney. He caught a glimpse of what might be a field or pasture next to it, but he wasn't certain. *:That way. Some distance,:* she said without being too specific, pointing with a paw off to her right. Then, *:I haven't found much food. I must forage more.:*

Alaire sent an affirmative, then replied, *:We will approach the house first, and if we proceed, we will head north.:* Then he added, *:Good luck.:*

Low Moon spread her wide wings again, this time flapping with greater intensity. The great thrusts sent forceful walls of wind their direction. Craig teetered backwards, nearly falling.

Once Low Moon had gained some altitude and disappeared behind a line of trees, Reykir uttered a low whistle. "I wonder if you could ride something like that," he wondered out loud.

After regaining his lost footing, Craig exclaimed, "I wouldn't trust that thing for a second."

Alaire started walking in the direction indicated by the wingrat. *And the feeling is mutual, Craig,* Alaire thought to himself.

Until Alaire mentioned Low Moon's report on the house, Reykir hadn't known they had a destination. When Alaire had started off into the woods by himself, clearly annoyed with Craig, he thought they were just going to start walking until they found something interesting.

Rak's disappearance still tore at him. He didn't want

to believe the owl had died, though he'd seen no evidence that she had survived. *If that wastrel can survive the storm, Rak must have as well,* he thought. Again, for the hundredth or thousandth time, he sent out the loudest message he could muster in his present exhausted state; chagrined at his own desperation, he listened to the psychic echo of his mindshout, which returned as a bare murmur. He felt his shoulders slouch in disappointment and consciously straightened his posture, then plastered a smile across his face.

They trudged through the sand, which gradually gave way to real, sturdy soil and vegetation. The sand did not relinquish its hold willingly, the boy noted as they stepped through scrub brush and frail grass. *If Rak survived, where would she go?* he wondered. Ahead was a line of trees, which might mean small game. *Perhaps in there,* he thought hopefully. *Perhaps, perhaps.*

"You're not picking any of that up, then, are you?" Alaire asked. "Low Moon's communications, that is."

Reykir shook himself from his own thoughts. *Those images I saw earlier, that must be how Low Moon communicates,* he considered. *That's how the beast has been speaking with Alaire. But the images, they're muddled. As if the wingrat didn't want anyone listening in.*

"Nothing I recognize," he admitted finally, a little peeved that the creature chose to take its cues from his master instead of himself. Not that he would have done any better job diplomatically; it was just an automatic reaction he had when ignored. *I've been ignored all my life,* he thought. *There's no reason for that to change now.*

Then, he caught himself. *I'm tired and cranky, and I know it. Would I want to be the leader of this group?* He glanced over at Craig, who was walking with a limp, and whose face had turned an unpleasant shade of green. Reykir answered himself with a resounding *NO*.

"I'm only picking up pieces of what she's saying to you," Reykir clarified.

Alaire paused and then sniffed the air. "I smell civilization."

Reykir wasn't certain what Alaire was talking about until they reached the top of a rise. Here he saw a chimney atop a thatch roof, and smoke coiling from it. *A fire*. He sniffed. *And baking bread, it must be!*

At the scent of fresh bread, his stomach roared, loud enough to turn Alaire's head. Despite his best efforts to restrain himself, his pace quickened at the sight of the cottage.

"Careful, Reykir," Alaire cautioned. "Before we go storming up to the front door of that house, think of how we must appear. Not the kind of company good country folk would expect."

Reykir regarded himself and his companions, who looked as though they had just stepped out of a brawl in a seedy tavern. *Aie, yes, we do look a mess,* he thought.

"Perhaps you should go talk to them first," Craig said, making himself comfortable by leaning up against a felled log. "While we wait here."

"For once I agree with you, brother," Alaire said. "Of the three of us I've managed to retain some semblance of civilized garb."

Reykir wanted to disagree, but remembered that, despite his disheveled appearance, Alaire was his master. Alaire strode up to the cottage and knocked on the door. Moments later, it opened, with an audible creak. Another moment later, Alaire waved for them to proceed.

Craig groaned and slowly followed Reykir to the cottage; apparently he was ready for another nap.

A rugged farmer and his timid, pregnant wife invited

them inside with hand gestures. The farmer was tall and wiry with the thick, calloused hands of a hard worker. Despite his rough appearance he looked friendly and eager to help them. Reykir wanted to suggest that Craig remain outside to have his nap, but the couple seemed determined to be hospitable, and invited them all in. Reykir seated himself on a bench at a simple table, painted in blue with streaks of marbling. The farmer was younger than himself, Reykir noticed, perhaps only seventeen. *Already with a pregnant wife,* he thought, grateful that he was not in the same situation. *I'm not ready to give up my freedom just yet!*

As soon as the young father-to-be spoke, he knew they were in Suinomen. He spoke the language of the Suinomen folk, none of which Reykir understood, except the garbled utterances of "Althea" and "Suinomen" and other place names. Alaire spoke some of the language, but it was evident from his halting speech that it wasn't very much. On the dirt floor Alaire drew a jagged line, which Reykir didn't recognize at first. Only when his master drew the border between the two countries did he recognize it as a map. More haggling over place names. Silver City, down here. Rozinki, up here. Alaire pointed to the farmer and the cottage with a questioning look. *Where are we?* his look seemed to ask.

Understanding passed over the farmer's features like a lit fire, then he pointed to a spot just south of the Suinomen capital.

Alaire whistled. "That storm blew us a lot further than I thought," the Bard said. "Not only are we in Suinomen, we're maybe two days from Rozinki!"

Reykir didn't know if he should take that as good or bad news. "I don't much like traveling in unfamiliar territory in our condition," he pointed out. "But I guess we don't have much choice."

"That's right, we don't," Alaire replied. "At least it's not winter. That will help. Though the nights do get cold here."

The wife approached Reykir cautiously, holding her skirt just above her feet, waddling just a little with her ample, pregnant belly. The boy didn't know what she wanted until she touched the flute hanging around his neck. Then she smiled, and said something to her husband.

"I think," Alaire said, getting up off the ground, "that she wants to hear some music. Why don't you play them a few tunes while I see what kind of shape my harp is in. It might persuade them to feed us."

Playing for his dinner was nothing new to Reykir, but his fingers were sore and his heart wasn't really into it. Still, even though his dance tune came out sounding like a funeral dirge, the couple seemed delighted with the performance. The wife pulled a loaf of bread out of the oven and broke it on a wooden slab, offering Reykir a large, steaming chunk for his trouble.

As he bit into the bread, a movement by the window caught his attention.

:*Feed yourself first,*: a voice seethed in his head. :*Worry about me not!*:

"Rak!" Reykir said around the mouthful of bread. He hurried over to the owl, who stood fluffed up on the windowsill. "You've lost some feathers," Reykir whispered, holding his hand out. The owl stepped up on his hand, limping slightly. "Look who's here!" he said to Alaire. "This little pest made it after all."

Alaire looked pleased. "Ask her why she took so long to find us. I think I already have an idea."

The owl seemed to be a step ahead. :*Large thing. Gone?*:

Reykir was uncertain what she was talking about, then he remembered their new companion. *Of course. The wingrat. No wonder she stayed away!*

"She was afraid of Low Moon," Reykir said. "Probably thought she would eat her."

Alaire looked amused. "We don't know yet if she wouldn't. We'll have to tell Low Moon about Rak."

"True," Reykir admitted, then turned to Rak. *:Large thing. Wingrat. Comrade. Friendly.:* The boy sent as many hospitable feelings and images to the owl as he could come up with, but in spite of his efforts Rak didn't look convinced.

"This may take some time," Reykir said, sounding only a little discouraged. Training the owl had required patience, which thankfully he had plenty of. "Rak has never seen a wingrat before." He brought Rak over to the table to introduce her to their hosts, and finish his bountiful meal of fresh bread.

The farmer kindly allowed Alaire, Reykir and Craig to sleep in the barn, and when the three awakened the next morning their host and his wife served them a fine breakfast of sausage and fried eggs. Alaire noted that their thin leather boots, designed for city life, were far from appropriate for long hikes, but there was nothing to be done for it. He was not about to ask these kind folk for more, since they were, when it came down to it, peasants and could ill afford what they had already provided. Alaire thanked them as best he could with hand gestures and made a promise to himself to somehow repay these kind people as soon as he returned home.

"If we stay close to the shore, we should find the road I remember," Alaire said, trying to lift his brother's spirits. As usual Craig was sullen this morning, and Alaire wasn't looking forward to his company on the long trip to the Suinomen capital.

For most of the morning they followed the farmer's directions to what they hoped was the road to Rozinki, encountering a creek along the way where they all drank their fill. Apparently hungry after the few candlemarks of travel, Reykir examined a bush covered with berries, pronounced them edible, and started picking them for lunch.

"I'm not hungry," Craig said when offered berries. He hadn't eaten much for breakfast, which was the norm, but Alaire knew that if he was going to keep up with them he would have to at least eat something to keep his energy levels up. *Even if it means shoving food down the damn fool's throat!*

"Craig, let me explain it to you this way," Alaire said carefully. "We're looking at two, perhaps three days of travel. As I have been in this territory before, I know that food will become even more scarce the further north we go. We have no weapons to hunt with, though it may be necessary to stop and construct a snare if hunger gets to be too much of a problem." He hesitated before mentioning Rak, uncertain if she could find enough meat for the three of them. "If you eat now, that problem will not be on us as soon. Which means we will arrive at Rozinki sooner. And once we are there I can guarantee excellent food."

"Then perhaps I am hungry after all," Craig said, seeing the wisdom in his brother's words. He reached for the bush. "These berries, they look like little grapes."

"Stay away from the green ones," Reykir warned. "Not ripe yet."

The Bard had seen no sign of Low Moon that morning. The creature still puzzled him, as did the revelations about the other race of Arachnia. *I have other things to worry about,* Alaire reminded himself. *I have a murder to solve. After all, the death of our ambassador is why we're on this ill-fated journey.* As best he could, Alaire put all of these worries out of his mind. Their immediate needs for surviving the passage to Rozinki would require all their concentration.

After gathering and gorging on as many berries as they could, the party of three proceeded inland. Here the terrain started to look a little more familiar to Alaire, and when they came across the coastal road he'd taken on his first visit, he knew they were heading in the right direction. Mountains rose on the horizon in the west, and beyond the ridge they had just negotiated lay the ocean which had so rudely spit them onto land. The road was considerably more rutted than he remembered, probably because of the increase in overland trade since Alaire and Naitachal had established diplomatic ties with the northern country. With any luck, they might find transportation to where they were going.

At least we're not walking around in circles, Alaire thought, feeling his own spirits lift at the familiar sights around him.

Chapter Six

A small caravan, a wagon drawn by dieren and a single mounted horse, appeared on the road behind them. Alaire signaled for Craig and Reykir to stop, evidently hoping to persuade the newcomers to give them transportation.

The dieren were large domesticated beasts with cloven hoofs and enormous branching horns; they were the work beasts of choice in the north. Reykir had only heard descriptions, as they were rare in Althea, but as soon as saw the beasts he knew what they were.

Reykir was grateful for free trade between the two countries, particularly after he learned the identity of the other travelers. The caravan turned out to be a group of friendly Althean traders, and they were all too happy to help the Bard Alaire and his party once they were convinced of Alaire's identity. The boy noted that Alaire had failed to mention Craig's title, perhaps out of embarrassment for himself and his brother.

"Ah, you are indeed the Bard Alaire, brother to the king," the swarthy, older trader and apparent leader said. "I recall some work you did earlier this year. It's a shame Bardic magic did so little to help the drought."

Reykir felt his master's mild humiliation at the remark, to which he didn't immediately respond. After all, it was true.

"Aye," Alaire finally said. "It's one of the reasons we've made this journey. There is powerful magic in Suinomen I may be able to use."

The trader's eyes raised at that last comment. "So there is," he said, sounding surprised. "Please, ride with us. There is room in the back of the wagon."

Indeed, there was. The wagon was much larger on the inside than it looked and was not fully loaded. As Reykir crawled aboard Rak objected to being moved from her comfortable perch on his shoulder, then settled down to doze on the edge of a barrel. Once Alaire and Craig situated themselves they were underway, and the boy, lulled by the rhythm of the rattling wagon, fell fast asleep.

Later, when Alaire woke him, Reykir thought that night had just fallen. He was starting to get annoyed, wishing his master would have let him sleep the night through, when he realized he *had* slept the night through. The dim light at the end of the wagon was a rising, not a setting, sun.

"I wanted you to see this," Alaire said, pointing to a rise in the road in front of them.

Reykir didn't know what he was talking about until they reached the top of a hill which sloped sharply down to a bay. A great city spread out along the shores on the opposite side.

Rozinki.

The city's size struck him speechless. Until then, he had believed Silver City to be not only a big city, but the *only* big city in the world. In this bay were hundreds, perhaps thousands of small boats moored to an intricate network of docks. The city was built on several hills, with what had to be the royal palace built on an enormous outcropping of rock. Somewhere down there a church bell rang, and above them sea gulls glided lazily in the still morning air.

The caravan rolled down the hill and stopped at the

edge of the bay, where a long ferry was moored and taking passengers. As Alaire conferred with the trader, Reykir caught a glint of gold changing hands. Presently, his master returned to the wagon.

"This is where we get off," Alaire said. "The trader has business elsewhere, and because his wagon won't fit on the ferry he'll have to go all the way around the bay. Another day's travel, easily." Alaire smiled. "He's lent us some coin to pay the ferryman."

Craig groaned as he got up, and slowly climbed off the wagon. Reykir marveled at how he managed to look hungover each morning without having so much as a drink the night before. Rak stirred as her master returned her to his shoulder, then fluffed up in contentment once she was back to her familiar perch.

As they made their way to the ferry, Reykir noticed Rak's crop was full.

:Hunt? At night?: he asked.

:Mouse. Mouse, rat,: Rak replied. She did not understand the concept of numbers, and communicated amount by repetition.

:Good. You're eating better than we are,: Reykir said, then said verbally to the bird, "You pig."

The passage on the ferry was uneventful, but Reykir noticed the other passengers keeping their distance from them. As the ferryman poled the craft across a shallow portion of the bay, the boy caught a mixture of Althean and Suinomen language among the passengers. Their nationality did not seem to be the reason for the others' aloof attitude.

When he mentioned this to Alaire, the Bard shrugged and said, "I suspect it's because we haven't had a bath in some time. I'd be keeping my distance as well."

"How are we going to convince the palace guards of who we are then? We have no papers, no baggage, not even decent clothing."

Alaire frowned and looked thoughtful. "That will be difficult. We don't exactly look, well, royal."

"That's for certain," Reykir said. *I looked more royal when I lived on the streets of Silver City!*

Alaire continued, "First, since we are here at the docks, we should find an Arachnian vessel. We need to tell someone what happened to our ship, and an Arachnia is more likely to know of her."

The docks were bustling with activity when they landed, and the other passengers quickly disembarked and went their separate ways. Some of the sailors and dockhands he saw there were dressed no better than they were, so the Bard's party of three blended in nicely with the crowd.

On one pier alone, Reykir counted twenty-two vessels, in various states of preparation for sailing.

"Ah, there's one now," Alaire said. The ship looked much like their own, and was probably built in the same yard. Arachnia scrambled in her masts, checking lines and making sure the sails were secure. The sight sent a pang of grief through the boy as he remembered the lost crew which had been most kind and gracious to them.

Alaire spoke with one of the crew, who quickly referred him to a human sailor. Evidently, these Arachnia weren't as fluent in human languages. As the sailor listened to Alaire's account his face gradually darkened. He asked Alaire a question or two, to which the Bard sadly shook his head.

"He knew our ship, and he knew Su'Beltor, the captain. He will pass the word along." He glanced back at the grief-stricken sailor, who slowly turned back and approached an Arachnian sailor, this one dressed a little more elegantly than the others. "I don't envy his task," Alaire said. "Apparently, Su'Beltor was thought highly of in the Arachnian clan. He was known as the Father of Arachnian sailing, according to the bloke I just spoke with."

Reykir's remembering the disaster triggered several dark thoughts. *How in the world did we manage to survive? Craig was drunk. And I can't even swim!*

But on a day as bright and comfortable as today, his spirits lifted. The air was cool, like early spring in Althea. *It must have been downright cold last night,* he thought. *And I was too sleepy to even notice.*

Alaire had no trouble finding the proper route to the palace, since he had been here once before; this was fortunate because here, in the city's interior, nobody spoke Althean. At least, he heard no familiar words, just the harsh, guttural tongue of Suinomen. Reykir imagined that asking directions would have been, at best, a frustrating exercise in pantomime.

The palace at Rozinki was even more dark and ominous than it had appeared from across the bay. A wall surrounded the palace, with two red and green Suinomen flags flanking the gate. Before reaching the gate, however, two guards approached them with drawn swords. Since Reykir had no weapon, and neither did his traveling companions, the group of three stood where they were and raised their hands in unison.

The young guards wore gray uniforms of a design that was at once alien and striking. Reykir guessed the guards were near his own age, and despite their ominous sword waving he found himself admiring them. One said something sharply in his native tongue, to which Alaire shook his head.

"We are Althean," the Bard said loudly in his full Bardic voice. "Sent by my brother Derek, *King* of Althea."

The guard, a hulking blond with blazing blue eyes, stepped back. "Althean, then," the guard replied, in halting monotones. "But not royalty. Look at you," he added. The other started to laugh.

As if we should have expected anything else, Reykir thought. *At least they haven't run us through yet.*

"Aye, that is true, we do look like bandits," Alaire added hastily; he evidently thought it safe to lower his arms. Reykir and Craig followed suit. "As I think anyone of royal blood would if they had endured what we have."

The mention of royal blood seemed to make the blond one a little nervous. His mouth twitched as he said, "It's true, we are expecting visitors from Althea. But not so quickly."

Alaire crossed his arms mockingly. "And yet here we are."

The guard now looked seriously doubtful, perhaps regretting his hasty judgment of the trio.

Reykir caught a glimpse of Alaire's expression, and bit back a laugh. The Bard's eyes rolled as he continued, "Really, now. Perhaps you will recall that thrice-damned storm a few nights ago."

The guards exchanged worried looks but nodded. "Your ship was lost?"

Alaire snorted and Reykir winced at the rudeness. "Now we are getting somewhere. Yes, in order to get here by speediest route possible we elected to travel by ship—and encountered that storm. All perished, except us. We've managed to secure a ride from some of our countrymen who happened along the way. But we have had little to eat, and the overland journey we have just completed, without benefit of coin or wardrobe, has tried my patience to the very end." Anger dripped off the Bard's tongue, and Reykir thought his master was about to strike the blond guard. "As you two are doing now. Summon someone at once to verify who we are."

The guards didn't answer right away. They seemed to be gauging whether or not Alaire was bluffing. Which, Reykir realized with some uneasiness, he was *not*. Alaire was about to explode, no acting involved.

"Did you have a particular diplomat in mind?"

"Well," Alaire said, offhandedly. "Since our ambassador has been murdered, don't you think it would be appropriate that I see King Kainemonen himself? We are, after all, good friends."

A white pallor fell over the blond guard; a hazy shade of green overcame the other. "No—no one in Rozinki knows about the ambassador. Good gods, I think you might just be who you say you are."

"Might?"

"I'll return shortly," the guard said, and started off at a brisk trot towards the palace's main entrance.

While they waited, Alaire said to the other guard, "You seem to be more reasonable than your partner. I suppose I would be as cautious if I were in your position, what with all the riffraff that I've seen in this country. And it was only a few short years ago that a coup in this palace nearly succeeded in seizing the crown from Archenomen, Kainemonen's father." He looked the guard over briefly. "But I think you would be too young to remember *that*. It was, after all, six years ago."

The guard shrugged. Whether or not he understood what Alaire said, Reykir didn't know. At any rate, Alaire seemed to be enjoying himself. If he was venting his frustrations on the guard so as to better present himself to Kai, he was doing a good job of it. There would be purpose in the mockery, if only to make a lasting impression on the guards. Alaire seldom did anything without purpose.

The huge twin doors, several paces away, slowly swung open. The guard and a striking young man appeared at the gate, hesitating.

Even at this distance, Reykir saw that he was dressed as a king should be. A black-and-purple velvet doublet hung over his slight frame, giving it more bulk than he'd guessed the king probably had. The dark jerkin was laced up the front with silvery cord, and around his waist was a black belt with a huge golden buckle, with a stylized "K" in the center. Black breeches which looked to be of silk clung tightly to his lower frame, but despite the thinness of his legs, he saw wiry muscle. The king stared at the ragged looking trio, then started towards them.

"Alaire, is that *you*?" the king said in perfect Althean.

Alaire shouted back, "At least I think so. There's not much left after what we've been through!"

The king came to a stop in front of them. "Good gods, it *is* you." He smiled, but not as broadly as Reykir would have expected. *I thought they were good friends? And they haven't seen each other in six years. I would have expected a warmer welcome, even if he is the king. Gods, Alaire helped save their kingdom from being overthrown from within!*

Alaire also seemed subdued, but this looked as though it was in response to his cool reception. "Good to see you, Your Majesty," Alaire said, bowing slightly. Reykir didn't know what the protocol was between a king and a friend, and apparently neither did Alaire.

Kainemonen gave him a strange, nearly *warning* look. "That is the last time you will address me as 'your Majesty,'" he said, a twinkle of mirth coming into his eyes. "It's Kai, to you, as it always has been." Kainemonen extended his hand, and they shook warmly.

"Tell me, old friend," Kai said. "What happened to your ship? We've had no news."

Alaire told him, and an angry storm cloud, harsh as the one that had sunk their ship, darkened his face.

"That is a horrible tragedy. Are you the only survivors?"

"As far as I know," Alaire said. "The others never washed ashore, but with Arachnians, you can never tell. They sometimes have more lives than a cat."

"And tell me," Kai said, apparently noticing Reykir and Craig for the first time. "Who are your friends?"

"My brother, Prince Craig Reynard," Alaire said as Craig stepped forward. He seemed surprisingly polite, given the circumstances, and afforded Kainemonen the respect due a king.

"I am honored," Craig said, with a slight bow. "This is my first visit to Suinomen." He glanced around, taking in the road they'd just traveled, the houses and shops. "This is a very beautiful city."

Kai seemed genuinely pleased. "Why, thank you," he replied. "And I hope the rest of your visit to our country is more sedate than what you've already experienced." The King glanced at the sky. "I remember that storm, a fierce one, that blew through here three nights ago." He regarded them with sympathy. "I had no idea it nearly killed all of you."

Kainemonen stepped closer to Reykir, who bowed deeply. Of those present, he was probably the least royal of them all, including the guards, and he let his gesture of respect reflect that.

"This is my apprentice, Reykir of Reynard. And Rakvel, who is, well, a companion," Alaire said. They had discussed his parentage early in his training, and while it was impossible to know who Reykir's family was, it was proper and fitting, particularly when living in the palace, for him to have *some* kind of lineage. Adoptions into the royal family were uncommon but acceptable, and they had treated this one more as a formality than an actual fact. Rakvel, as was her custom during daylight hours, slept soundly through the royal introduction.

"And a very great pleasure to meet you," the king said. "I hope that you become every bit the Bard your master is." He winked at Alaire as he added, "He did, after all, save our kingdom with his magic."

"Myself and *my* master, Naitachal," Alaire hastily said.

"And what of the Dark Elf?" Kainemonen asked.

"Alive and well. After I became a Bard, he took to wandering the countryside, working his magic."

"Well, enough of introductions," Kainemomen replied. "We can become properly acquainted tomorrow. For now, I believe you have a well deserved rest on your agenda." He dismissed the guards with a wave of his hand, a gesture which seemed to gratify Alaire no end, and led his guests to the palace.

The king showed them their quarters, a main bedroom with two antechambers, one of which led to a courtyard outside. The rooms were lavishly furnished, but smelled as if they'd not been occupied in a while. The main room had a tall, four-posted state bed with heavy linen hangings.

Kainemonen stood in the center of the room and addressed all three.

"I hope these rooms are acceptable," he said. "When we asked that you come to . . . investigate your ambassador's murder, we had these prepared for you." He shrugged apologetically. "The room you had on your last visit was not very well appointed."

"But then, you weren't expecting us," Alaire said politely. "Dear friend Kainemonen, after what we've been through, a spot on the floor next to the servant's fireplace would be heaven!"

Reykir felt a little chill run down his spine at the mention of *murder*. He'd managed to forget their purpose for coming here during the ordeal.

"Let's wait until tomorrow to discuss my investigation," Alaire said. "I am patient, but I'm in no mood to deal with assassinations this afternoon."

"Of course," Kainemonen said, looking relieved. He looked at Alaire and his features softened, as if he were beholding a long lost brother. "Alaire, it is so good to finally see you." The king approached the Bard and they clasped arms. Evidently, Reykir mused, male affection was more appropriately expressed in private. Alaire towered over the younger man, and in that moment they indeed looked like siblings who had been separated for years.

"From what I've seen, young friend," Alaire said, "you have done well as a king."

"I thank you, Alaire. The events surrounding your last visit forced me to grow up rather rapidly."

From the hallway came a loud metallic clank; when Reykir turned, he saw an army of servants bringing in three copper baths, towels, soap, and a dozen steaming kettles of what promised to be glorious hot water.

"Ah," Alaire said as his eyes swept over the offering. "This is too good to be true."

Kainemonen started for the door. On his way out, he said, "While you are having your baths, I will see what I can do about appropriate clothing. What you have on has seen, shall we say, better days?"

"I'll say. I was looking forward to a soft, comfortable ride aboard a ship and we packed accordingly," Alaire replied, but his eye was on the nearest copper bath, into which servants were pouring steaming water.

As they sat luxuriating in their baths, saying little except for the occasional groan of pleasure, other servants came in with an assortment of upper-class clothing. There were garments and accoutrements Reykir couldn't begin to identify; Alaire picked out some items for him, whispering under his breath that it wouldn't hurt to dress on the same level as everyone else in the palace, at least while they were conducting their business there. After the bath and a thorough toweling by yet another servant, Reykir slipped on a comfortable robe. Apparently they were supposed to rest up here, which Reykir had no objection to. The ordeal had left even his young constitution drained, and he was still aching from the wagon ride.

Alaire had picked out a short, high-neck houppelande

with baggy sleeves for Reykir to wear. The shoes, which came to an annoying point, were sewn with thousands of little stitches and such skill that they seemed to be made from a single piece of suede. The clothing was far more stately than Reykir was accustomed to, but he did not object, given the circumstances. *Do as the natives do, and you are more likely to survive.*

"Quite the royal treatment, isn't it?" Alaire asked. "Even if we are here under such ominous circumstances."

Of course, Reykir didn't mind one bit. A year ago, he had been sleeping on the street and wherever else he could be secure for an evening; now he was being dressed in royal finery that would make a prince envious.

As he was contemplating his finery, a cart on wheels appeared in their room. On it was spread a banquet of beef, bread, cheeses and vegetables of northern origin he wasn't familiar with. The sight, and the magnificent odor coming from the cart set his stomach rumbling.

No, I don't mind at all!

Chapter Seven

After a good night's rest, Alaire was up at the crack of dawn and looking over the garments the servants had left in their room. While debating over a well worn doublet that might have belonged to Archenomen, and a long tunic of more modern design, a hard, firm knock sounded at his door.

He reached for a weapon in reflex; in the same moment, he realized he *had* no weapon.

"Yes?" he asked the visitor. "Who is it?"

"Who do you think, you arrogant southerner? Are you going to spar with me today, or is some other commitment going to conveniently get in the way?"

The Althean was broken, but understandable. And it could only be from one person.

"Captain Lyam!" Alaire exclaimed as he opened the door. "I thought they would have put you out to pasture by now!"

The sight of the Suinomen captain of the guard brought back a flood of memories, some pleasant, most not. It was reassuring to see yet another familiar face. Though a little grayer at the temples, Lyam still looked as rough and solid as Alaire had remembered. The captain was an enormous man, filling the doorway, with a face that had seen many a knife fight, and suffered for it.

"No such luck for you, my boy," Lyam said, entering the room. As usual, he towered over Alaire, but the

Bard found nothing intimidating about him. "I'm here to escort you to our morgue," he said, his voice turning somber. His eyes met with Alaire's directly, as if to show he had nothing to hide.

Alaire found the gesture comforting. *Lyam, as usual, is on our side. But what is the other side this time?*

"Who is—" Alaire heard from behind him. Reykir stood in the doorway joining their two rooms.

"Captain, I would like you to meet my apprentice, Reykir," Alaire said. "My brother is here with us, but I don't believe he will be joining us today." *At least, I hope not.*

"My pleasure, Captain," Reykir said. "Rak is sleeping on a chair in the other room. I wrapped a towel around the back of it so she wouldn't scratch it."

"We have a . . . moment, before I take you to the morgue," Captain Lyam whispered. Alaire stepped closer, while Reykir pretended to be disinterested. "There are some issues I'd like to discuss with you in private, while I have the chance." Alaire glanced at his apprentice, and the captain hastily added, "No, I think this should be for all those loyal to our two respective crowns."

"I would trust Reykir with my own life," Alaire said, again grateful that his brother was nowhere around. *But Craig might be listening.*

Alaire checked the other room and found his brother snoring loudly. Satisfied of their privacy, he returned to Lyam.

"Kai has been a most capable ruler," Lyam began, "far exceeding *my* expectations."

"I've been impressed," Alaire said, stopping short before saying, *and surprised, too.* "Is there something going on here that might not be obvious to the casual observer?"

"I think so," Lyam said. "As I did shortly before Sir Jehan showed his true colors."

Alaire sighed, and took a chair. Lyam seemed content to remain standing. "I thought that mess was cleaned up years ago," Alaire said, quietly making a promise to himself to visit Suinomen some day when there wasn't trouble brewing.

"For the most part it was, thanks to you and your master, the Dark Elf. If not for you we quite literally would not have a kingdom to rule."

Alaire felt himself blushing. "Thank you, but I took my bows for that one years ago. What do you think is going on now?"

"I'm not certain. Until the ambassador was murdered, I didn't think anything was amiss."

"What about your spy network?" Alaire asked, remembering the excellent information Lyam had provided before.

"Still in place, but after we exposed Sir Jehan's plot our secrecy was compromised. We also had a few moles from Sir Jehan's camp in our organization, which did not help."

"But after six years . . . ?"

Captain Lyam was thoughtful for a moment. "Perhaps it was my fault that I didn't aggressively maintain my secret eyes and ears. Please remember, our spy network was originally fueled by a distrust of Althea. Once we established trade with your country, many other walls fell, including travel restrictions. We focused on developing our new markets in the south."

Reykir appeared to be trying to take this all in, but his face didn't register much. *Later, I will explain,* Alaire thought, returning his attention to Lyam.

"It would seem to be the thing to do," Alaire agreed. "I hope you're not here to tell me that another group is trying to overthrow Kai."

Lyam shrugged, a gesture which turned Alaire's blood to ice.

"Surely not," Alaire said.

"I don't know," Lyam said. "I do know that your ambassador is dead, killed within the walls of this palace, the very place where he should have been the most protected."

"Have you traced the murderer with magic?"

"We have, and it appears magic was used to cover the murderer's tracks."

This was all beginning to sound a little too familiar. "It must be easier to secure good wizards now that magic is legal."

"One would think so. But remember, we are behind Althea in that area. What might seem simple to you might prove to be very difficult to one of our mages. Our strength was in being able to control magic, and for the last six years magic has been deregulated."

"I see," Alaire said, but he wasn't really certain if he did.

"The trail is still fresh, and we are searching diligently for any clue that would lead us to a traitor. But we could use some help."

Alaire nodded, wishing he found this more assuring.

"Well, they'll be expecting us downstairs," Lyam said. "Shall we join them?"

The further they descended the steep, narrow stairwell, the cooler the rock floors and walls became, until Alaire's breath fogged before him. He caught the stench of something rotting. If Reykir smelled it too, he said nothing about it. The boy had become quiet, perhaps intimidated by the anticipated presence of the king. Alaire made a note to find out later how his apprentice felt about the situation. The boy's street smarts had often shed a different light on a problem and, with murder involved, Alaire wondered if Reykir might see something everyone else had missed.

Torches every several paces cast a dingy yellow light for them to see by, and the Bard had a flash of déjà vu, remembering the passages beneath the Association Hall which led to the Prison of Souls. *It was the same kind of rock as this,* he recalled with a shiver.

The morgue was a chamber not much larger than the guest room. The cloying smell of death was much stronger here, and there was no doubt as to its source. The ambassador's body lay on a table of stone slabs, with a single white cloth covering him to his waist.

Kai was waiting for them as a servant, who seemed surprisingly aloof to the body, lit more torches and strong cedar incense.

"Alaire," Kai said, turning to greet him. "I hope you slept well. I have to admit, I didn't."

Alaire was impressed to see the king with them at this early hour. He remembered how much *Prince* Kai liked to sleep in after a night of heavy drinking, which he used to do every night—at least while Alaire was present. *He is reformed,* the Bard reminded himself. *That's still going to take some getting accustomed to.*

Not wanting to spend any more time down here than was necessary, Alaire stepped closer to the body. "Well, let's have a look."

Yes, Alaire remembered this man. Erikson, of house Turonen, had been a faithful subject of King Reynard, and had gladly accepted the position here as his ambassador. Erikson was also King Reynard's close friend, and had accompanied the royal family on numerous outings. Alaire remembered the little gifts Erikson had brought to him when he was a child, some of them musical instruments. Erikson was one of his early influences, and had probably been the one to plant the seed of Bardly ambitions in the young Alaire.

"What killed him?" Alaire asked tonelessly.

Pasty and white, the elderly ambassador gaped lifelessly at the ceiling with a horrified expression.

"We have already done an examination," Kai said. "He was found in his chambers by the housekeepers. The gash, there in his neck, seems to be what killed him."

A jagged incision reached from Erikson's left ear down across the windpipe. Whatever made the cut had left a crooked tear in the skin. *Either the knife was dull, or the perpetrator hesitated before making the kill,* Alaire thought. Then, *Suicide?*

The ambassador's taking his own life was the last thing Alaire expected, but if he had learned anything from his master, Naitachal, it was to be thorough.

"Kai, when was the last time someone spoke to him?" the Bard asked. "If anyone knows."

Kai's look wavered momentarily, and he looked embarrassed. "The servants saw him walking to his room. He said nothing to them. And they didn't notice anything remarkable about him."

Kai was leaving something out. "Does anyone know what frame of mind he was in?"

"The last person to speak with him was myself," Kai said, after a pause. "We were discussing the drought in Althea, and how King Derek might seek some sort of trade agreement to make up for the famine he was expecting."

Alaire raised his eyebrows at this revelation. *Was he, now. True, Erikson was the ambassador, but that was information we were wanting to keep to ourselves for a while. Or so I thought.*

"Aside from the problems in Althea, the ambassador was in good spirits. For a man his age, he had more energy than I did, and he certainly enjoyed his work. Only last week he mentioned that he was looking forward to serving another year."

That much was common knowledge. Erikson had been ambassador for years, and Derek had said on numerous occasions that he was very satisfied with his performance. The ambassador commanded a great deal of respect without raising the ire of the younger generation around him, a rare talent not found in many senior diplomats. Alaire knew that Erikson was not easily replaceable, if he was replaceable at all; and nothing had darkened the ambassador's record to suggest his dismissal. Overall, Erikson was the perfect man for the job, with no suggestion from anyone, in Althea or Suinomen, to the contrary.

"This makes no sense," Alaire said.

"You're not suggesting the ambassador took his own life, are you?" Kai asked.

Alaire sighed. This was not the impression he wanted to give, but then anyone could see where his questions were leading.

"Excuse me," Reykir said, joining Alaire at the table. "Was the ambassador right- or left-handed?"

Alaire had to think about this one for a moment, but not for long; one didn't usually notice right-handedness, as it was so common. Left-handedness was something else altogether. The Bard remembered when Erikson had brought a lute for Alaire. Erikson had mentioned that, to make it a left-handed instrument, he would have to rearrange the strings.

"He was left-handed," Alaire said. "Why?"

Reykir leaned closer to the body. "Well, look where the cut is. If he were left-handed and had cut his own throat, wouldn't the cut be on the other side?"

Alaire looked at the cut again. "Indeed," he said. "I suppose that rules out suicide."

A thin, wispy voice spoke behind them. "Your Majesty, perhaps you should show them the other wounds."

An Arachnia stood in the doorway for a moment before entering the room, moving with the grace and silence Alaire had come to associate with the insectoid race.

"Prince Alaire, may I present my secretary, Su'Villtor," Kai said.

The Arachnia nodded ever so subtly, but did not offer a claw; the Bard had noticed a trend in etiquette lately between the two races that made the "handshake" optional. The Arachnians were never comfortable with the gesture, and neither were most humans, particularly when the pincers could snap fingers off in a moment.

"Your reputation precedes you," the Arachnia chittered. "The kingdom of Suinomen is in your debt, to be sure."

"Thank you, Su'Villtor," Alaire replied. He was starting to find the praise for something he had done six years before a little tiring, but being the patient prince he was, he held his tongue. "I would have preferred that we met under better circumstances."

Su'Villtor's head tilted to one side, an expression Alaire knew was the equivalent of a sigh.

Reykir helped the other young servant turn Erikson's body over. The apprentice gasped in surprise and stepped back, and the servant rearranged the cloth over the body.

"What in heaven's name are *those*?" Alaire asked, after a moment of silence.

On Erikson's upper back were two more wounds, but not gashes like the neck wound. They appeared to be punctures, made at the same time as the fatal wound.

"What do you make of these?" Alaire asked Kai.

The king shook his head. "No one has been able to determine what did that. Captain Lyam did an inventory of all the weapons in the training arena, and nothing even came close to matching those wounds."

"What about the kitchen?" Alaire asked, suspecting this angle would also be a dead end.

Captain Lyam cleared his throat before addressing Alaire. "We're not entirely certain the weapon was metal. The punctures, too, are jagged, like the neck wound. A stone weapon, perhaps, or a wooden one."

Strange, Alaire thought. "Those are the only marks?"

"We believe so," Kai said. "If you wish, you may examine further."

Alaire held a hand up. "That won't be necessary," the Bard replied, realizing his intense desire to be out of there. The odor, which had worsened when the body was turned over, was becoming quite unbearable.

"Very well, then," Kai said, turning with Alaire for the doorway. "I wish there was more I could tell you."

They all ascended the stairs and gathered in the palace's main hallway.

"After the assassination," Alaire asked Kai, "who did you question?"

"Why, Su'Villtor questioned all the guards on duty," Kai hastened to answer. "All servants were accounted for in their quarters by midnight. The assassination, we believe, happened well after that."

Alaire puzzled over this. While he didn't want to miss anything that might provide an important lead, he also didn't want to offend the king by suggesting impropriety or laxness on his staff's part.

Su'Villtor spoke up, looking as if he were ready to depart. "If you will excuse me," the Arachnia said, "I have a meeting with the Merchant's Guild to attend. Will you be needing my assistance?"

"No, Su'Villtor, go ahead," Kai said absently. "I think we can take it from here."

Alaire watched the secretary walk gracefully away on his stiltlike legs, noting how he turned his front claws towards his body when he walked. Something about what he saw in the Arachnia's movements nagged at him, but he wasn't certain what it was.

"Your Majesty, didn't Galdur use truth spells to extract information from the guards on duty that night?" Captain Lyam asked.

"Well, yes he did," Kai replied. "He turned nothing up. I didn't feel it was worth mentioning."

In response to Alaire's raised eyebrow, Captain Lyam continued, "Galdur is our head wizard. He assumed his post shortly after the coup attempt." The captain looked momentarily puzzled. "Your Majesty, wasn't he supposed to accompany us this morning in the morgue?"

"He told me last night he would," Kai said. "But he never did show up, did he? He probably overslept. Those wizardfolk keep strange hours." And with a wink to Alaire, added, "Like *I* used to. Remember?"

Alaire could not help but grin. "Yes, Kainemonen, I do. Things have changed, now that you are ruler."

"For the better, I hope," the king replied. "Yes, well Galdur should have been with us. But I doubt he would have provided any new information."

No, perhaps not, Alaire thought. *But his absence raises suspicions.*

King Kainemonen and Captain Lyam excused themselves to take care of some urgent Suinomen business, but before they left, the king invited Alaire, his apprentice and his brother to the noon meal. The Bard was glad the king had not included breakfast on their agenda; after dealing with Erikson, he doubted he would have had the stomach for it.

Before the king and captain left, Alaire asked, "Would you mind if I asked your head wizard a few questions?"

To which Kai replied, "Certainly not. In fact, I think that's an excellent idea. Where would he be now, captain?"

"Mostly likely in the Association Hall," Lyam said, and gave Alaire a somber look. "Yes, I know, Alaire.

There are a lot of bad memories there. But believe me, we've cleaned up the riffraff in this kingdom. The wizards you will find there will be legitimate, and on *our* side this time."

"Aie, yes," Alaire said. "I am certain of that." But privately, he *wasn't* so certain.

Someone killed the ambassador, and Suinomen's magic users had yet to determine who it was. I must look into every possibility.

Alaire remembered all too well where the Association Hall was. The short, squat building itself had changed little, the exception being a coat of white paint on the stucco. But the vegetation growing around it had come to life; where it was barren and desolate with dead trees before, there was a deep green forest, overrun with oak and wildflowers. True, it was now summer, not winter, but the Bard sensed more at work here than just a simple change of seasons. It seemed that with the demise of Carlotta, which had happened in the basement of this very building, nature had sighed in relief.

Alaire rapped on the door and waited. The door had been refinished since his last visit, but still gave a low, resonating tone to the knock that comes only with well-aged wood. Reykir looked nervous as well, perhaps because of the reputation the building already had; Alaire had told his apprentice about the Prison of Souls more than once during his lessons.

A nervous, mousy little man opened the door and peered up at them. He wore the familiar gaudy robe Alaire recalled seeing on Suinomen magicians the last time he'd been here; for an uncomfortable moment, Alaire thought this was Soren, the magician who had played a key role in the coup. But this magician was younger, and smaller. Still, the resemblance rattled him.

"Yes?" the mouse said. "What do *you* want?"

"I am Prince Alaire, of Althea," the Bard said. "And this is my apprentice, Reykir. I came to speak with Galdur, the magician. Is he in?"

The magician stepped back and gestured for them to enter. Inside, torches burned on the walls, giving some light to a mostly dark interior. Alaire noted that the installation of windows would have provided more light than the torches, but evidently this hadn't occurred to the magicians here.

"I am Galdur," the small man said at last, sounding as though Alaire's visit was the last thing he wanted this afternoon. "I assume you've come to question me about the assassination."

"I have," Alaire said, as Reykir closed the door behind them. "This was, after all, our ambassador. As well as a close family friend. His loss grieves me personally."

Galdur's expression softened, and in that moment he looked more like Soren. *Is this Soren in disguise?* Alaire wondered, but refrained from probing the wizard for glamories.

"Of course," Galdur said. "How may I help you?"

"I was hoping to see you in the morgue this morning," Alaire said, relaxing his shoulders and letting his arms fall limply to his side, a stance that he hoped would help put the magician at ease. He was going to be asking some direct questions, and the less defensive Galdur was in advance, the better. "But we studied the body anyway. It was a most distressing sight, seeing the ambassador dead like that. After all Althea has done to help preserve the Suinomen crown."

Although he delivered the statement in a calm, soothing tone, Galdur flinched visibly.

"I am well aware of the attempt by Sir Jehan to seize the throne," Galdur began, looking as though he was checking his anger. "And I am equally aware of the role played by the magicians then in power. My uncle, in particular." Galdur also relaxed, but the motion only made him look more nervous. "But that was long ago. This is not the same Association you would remember."

"Indeed," Alaire said quietly, but his mind was racing. "Who was your uncle?"

Galdur looked doubtful, then resentful. *Did he reveal something he didn't want to?* Alaire thought, but it was obviously too late for the wizard to backtrack.

"Soren is my uncle," Galdur admitted. "He was the head magician at the time of the coup. And yes, before you ask, he was involved in the revolt."

Alaire cleared his throat politely. "Yes, I am aware of that. I was present during those troubling times." *Need I tell him that Soren also incarcerated me in the Prison of Souls? That he was probably the second most significant figure in the coup? Why in the seven hells didn't Kai have the traitor executed?* For whatever reason, Galdur seemed to be oblivious to Alaire's near brush with the Prison, and the Bard saw no real reason to bring it up now. *Perhaps feigning some ignorance of this place might put him off guard.*

"That is interesting," Alaire said. "I remember Soren. What finally happened to him, after all was resolved?"

"In spite of my uncle's role in Sir Jehan's plan, King Archenomen pardoned him. Although Sir Jehan was defeated, there were still the many magicians who had conspired against the crown as well. Soren helped turn this element in to the proper authorities." Galdur stepped forward, his arms open in a gesture of frankness. "Without his help, there would have always been the possibility of some other element rising from Sir Jehan's organization."

But that still doesn't explain what happened to Soren, Alaire thought. *Answers come to those who wait.*

"The king was not without his gratitude," Galdur

continued. "He gave my uncle a post in one of the outer provinces. That is where he is now."

"I see," Alaire said. *This is starting to sound more like an exile than an assignment.* "Where is this province, I wonder?"

"It's to the north," Galdur said reluctantly. "On the coast. At least, one might call it a coast during the summer."

Soren's fate was gradually taking shape, and Alaire was doing his best not to burst out laughing. *I know of this province. It is covered with snow year-round, and is only accessible during a few weeks out of the summer! How fitting to exile Soren to that ice ball!*

"I am certain Soren's skills are not going to waste," Alaire said, trying, and failing, to keep the sarcasm out of his voice. *Now, back to business.* "I understand you questioned the guards on duty the night of the assassination. Might I ask where *you* were that night?"

"In bed, asleep," Galdur said immediately.

Too easy, Alaire thought suspiciously.

"I had spent the entire day inventorying our herb supply," Galdur continued. "To see what we needed to plant now to carry us through the winter. I was very tired and knew nothing of the assassination until the next day."

"And you heard nothing?" This would make it obvious if Galdur was telling the truth. The Association Hall was far enough away from the palace that a riot would not be audible at this distance.

"Nothing," Galdur replied. "Bard Alaire, I must ask you. Am I under suspicion of something?"

The question caught Alaire off guard, but for only a moment. "Oh, of course not," the Bard replied. "I am only trying to piece together what took place that night. Any information would be helpful."

The Bard declined to mention that he didn't think someone as small and apparently weak-minded as he would be capable of such a gruesome crime. *His dander is already up. Time to smooth the feathers.*

"I might also mention," Galdur said, "that during the coup I remained loyal to the king. True, I was only a stableboy at the time, but at no time did I take up arms against the crown."

"I am certain you were loyal," Alaire replied. "Your dedication to Suinomen is not in question either. And it is certainly not my place, as a prince of Althea, to question the decisions of another ruler."

Again, Galdur flinched visibly at the mention of his title, even though there was little chance Alaire would ever be king of Althea.

"When you questioned the guards, what did you turn up?"

Galdur seemed pleased for the subject to change from his loyalty to the assassination. "Absolutely nothing. The guards in question were stationed outside the palace. Two at the gate, two near the stable, and four walking patrol on the grounds. No one heard or saw anything. My truth spell made certain of that. There have been no incidents on the palace grounds since the Sir Jehan incident, so security is not a priority. You might do better to question Captain Lyam about that."

Alaire considered this. "There are no guards on duty within the palace at all?"

"Not to my knowledge, no."

"And no one came, or left, during the evening?"

"No one."

Which implied only one thing: the murder was committed by a member of the Palace staff. Perhaps, even, a high-ranking official of Kai's cabinet.

"I see," Alaire said, making a note to ask Captain Lyam more about this. "Thank you for your time, and your help."

Galdur took his hand and bowed graciously. "If I can be of any further help, please let me know."

Alaire and Reykir left the Association Hall and started towards the palace. A bell tolled nearby, twelve chimes, indicating noon.

"Is it time for lunch yet?" Reykir asked. "I am a little hungry."

At the mention of food, Alaire's stomach roared. "Yes, I believe it is. To the dining hall."

"Lead the way," Reykir said good-naturedly. "I'm still new to this place."

En route to the dining room, Alaire caught a glimpse of Craig at the far end of the main hallway, talking to the Arachnian secretary, Su'Villtor. As his hunger was more overpowering than his curiosity, he did not pause to think about this right away. *Probably just making some inquiries,* the Bard thought as the glorious aroma of potatoes and cooked pig wafted past his nostrils. *I'll have to ask him about that later.*

Servants escorted them to the king's table, where Kainemonen and Captain Lyam, who seemed to stick close to his side, greeted them warmly.

"I hope you have had a productive morning," Kai said after they had situated themselves.

Alaire hesitated about bringing up the issue of Galdur and his questionable family ties. *Best to save the matter for after dinner,* Alaire decided, and proceeded to devour the feast before him.

When lunch was over, Kainemonen invited them to his private chambers. On their way there, Alaire remembered that his brother, Craig, had not turned up at the dining hall. *Probably not even hungry,* he thought. *Come to think of it, neither did Su'Villtor.*

Alaire mentioned this to Kai, who replied, offhandedly, "Oh, Su'Villtor usually doesn't eat with humans. He finds it, shall I say, offensive?"

Still, something seemed odd about his brother's encounter with the Arachnia. *Craig doesn't like strangers, even less the nonhuman ones. Where have they gone off to?*

Before the Bard could puzzle over his brother's whereabouts too long, King Kai led them into his chambers.

"I would offer you wine," Kai said apologetically, "but I don't keep it in the chambers, even for visitors."

"Is it still a temptation?" Alaire said, hoping this was not an insult. He seated himself in a heavy oak chair. A tall window opened onto the garden, and a warm afternoon breeze wafted past the king. Reykir took a smaller, less ornate seat, and promptly blended into his surroundings. *The boy must work some magic to make himself invisible,* Alaire thought.

"Yes, I do still go for it," Kai replied. "But as soon as I do I remember the last time I was drunk. The night those two 'bandits' jumped us. And I almost didn't survive."

He hasn't had a drink since then? Alaire thought, a bit ashamed that the revelation astonished him so. True, Kai had matured into a man, but his stiff attitude made him seem so unlike the Kai Alaire knew that the Bard thought he was someone else.

"I remember," Alaire replied. "But that was so long ago. We should discuss the problem at hand. My brother Derek wishes to know what happened. And so do I."

Kai looked grim. "Of course," he said. "We are doing what we can to find the perpetrator. But we have turned up nothing." The king met the Bard's eyes directly, and he added, in a softer voice, "Do not worry about offending me. I am terribly saddened and embarrassed by this whole affair."

"Althea is not blaming you," Alaire said hastily. *At least, not yet.* "There must have been a reason for this."

Kai sat down behind a huge wooden table, looking

far older than his twenty-three years. "I've had doubts for a year now. Since we purged Suinomen of Sir Jehan's followers, I had assumed we had done so thoroughly."

Alaire waited for him to continue, his interest piqued.

"Then one of our secretaries, an assistant of Captain Lyam, was murdered in much the same way as your ambassador."

"When was this?"

"About this same time last year. The secretary was a young man, about the age of Reykir here. He had been studying old Arachnian texts, which Su'Villtor had in his study."

Now this was most interesting.

"I know you're probably thinking, Su'Villtor might be the likely suspect. But he was with me, personally, when this murder apparently happened."

Aie, yes, but is there any way to prove that? Alaire thought frantically, still not wanting to voice his doubts to his friend.

The Bard walked a fine line between friendship and pursuing his role as investigator, and he didn't want the two to clash, at least not this early in the game.

"I don't think Su'Villtor killed either the secretary or your ambassador," Kai said.

"Are there . . . other Arachnias in the palace?" *Careful, now.*

"Su'Villtor has an apprentice, Su'Quon, sent by his family to train under him. Su'Quon is a relative of some kind. I don't even pretend to try to figure out relations among Arachnians."

"And what of this apprentice?"

"Accounted for," Kai replied, but Alaire thought he detected a bit of doubt in the ruler's voice. "Su'Villtor vouches for him, or her. I'm not certain of the apprentice's sex."

So. Now we're back to the beginning. "A moment

ago you mentioned Sir Jehan's followers. Do you think perhaps some were not discovered?"

Kai expelled a loud breath. "Gods, I hope not. That's the last thing I need. But it would help to explain the ambassador's death."

"Did you not find the secretary's murderer?"

"No," Kai said. "I'm afraid not."

An uncomfortable silence filled the room. Alaire broke it by saying, "I spoke with Galdur, your head wizard. What do you know of him?"

"I had questioned his loyalties as well," Kai admitted. "Even though he assisted in cleaning up the grand mess Soren left behind."

Alaire chose this moment to bring up the suspicious relationship between Galdur and Soren. "Are you aware that Soren is Galdur's uncle?"

"Of course I am," Kai replied. "Soren has been assigned to another province. Far to the north. I thought it a just punishment, given that he helped us break up the conspiracy."

Did he, now? Probably in order to save his own skin. I cannot imagine Soren doing anything unless he had something to gain from it.

"Galdur is beyond suspicion?" Alaire asked.

Kai shook his head. "Nobody is. But I don't suspect him myself. Captain Lyam has brought up the question of Galdur's loyalty several times. But then, Lyam is suspicious of all magicians."

Not all, Alaire thought. *He does seem to trust me.*

The meeting broke up when Kai announced he had another meeting to attend. The Bard had decided that Kainemonen might be a capable ruler, but if there was a conspiracy to dethrone him, the boy would probably not see it until it was too late.

Reykir went to tend to Rakvel, and Alaire went to the gardens to contemplate the fine mess they had been sent to clean up, arriving at no real conclusions.

"All things come to those who wait," Alaire whispered, remembering the lyrics to an old ballad. He pulled out his harp and played through the song a few times, finding the patience he sought.

Give it time, he thought. *Sooner or later, the guilty parties will make a mistake, just like they did last time around.*

Chapter Eight

For what seemed an eternity, Reykir stared up at the enormous canopy over his head, trying to figure out why he could not sleep. It wasn't as if his bed were uncomfortable. On the contrary, the silk pajamas, sheets and goose down pillows were the ultimate in comfort. He had to admit, he was not yet accustomed to upper-class living, having lived at the very lowest rung most of his life. He was still exhausted from the trip, so sleeping should have not been a problem, particularly in such opulent accommodations. But it was.

The bedroom window opened onto the courtyard, and an occasional cool breeze brushed past the curtain. From outside he heard guards making their rounds, which became less and less frequent as the evening progressed. He had turned Rak loose to go hunting, and she had been gone a good part of the night. It wasn't concern for his owl that kept him awake. When she was done feeding and wanted to return, Rakvel would find the correct window easily enough by tuning into Reykir's thoughts.

In the other room Craig snored loudly; he'd managed to get completely drunk at dinner, along with several merchants who had arrived that afternoon to discuss new accounting laws with the king. Though they shared no common language, except for the language of drink, they seemed to have had a good time together. And, fortunately, Craig did nothing obviously embarrassing.

If Alaire had been bothered by his brother's behavior, he didn't show it. As they prepared to retire, the Bard seemed to be quite worn out by the day's activities, due in no small part, Reykir guessed, to the frustration of not coming up with a single lead to the ambassador's murder.

It bothered him that he couldn't sleep; he knew what condition he would be in the next day if he didn't sleep, and this would not be a good thing. Since Craig would most likely be fairly worthless tomorrow, Reykir felt responsible for being alert for both of them.

And this is not to be if I lie here awake all night! he seethed. *The last time I had trouble sleeping . . .*

Ah, yes. The last time. It was some years ago, but he remembered it well. He was sleeping in a barn somewhere in the northern part of Silver City, tossing and turning much as he was doing now, for no apparent reason. Then a thief had entered the barn, knife drawn, and Reykir pretended to be asleep. That is, until the thief tried to cut his throat. Reykir had drawn his own knife, hiding it under his cloak, which he was using as a blanket. The blade entered just above the thief's stomach, below the rib cage, and an amazing amount of blood had poured from the wound. Reykir had carefully cleaned his blade, relieved the thief of the coin he had on him, and crept off into the night.

Only later had he realized what had happened. *If I had slept, I would have died. My magical sense saved my life by keeping me awake.*

Lying in the state bed, surrounded by luxury, the boy began to wonder if the same thing was happening all over again.

If it is, then it is a surprise for us all. I doubt a palace can sound more asleep than this one. . . .

Suddenly, Rak swooped in through the window, circled the room once, and landed on the edge of the bed.

:Wake! Up! Up!: the owl mindscreamed. *:Attack!:*

Reykir sat bolt upright. *:What are you talking about?:*

Before he could ask more, he heard a shout, a scream, and the unmistakable clatter of arrows against the palace walls.

"Attack?" Reykir asked. *:Who?:*

Shifting frantically from foot to foot, the owl replied with a garbled image of wingrats and Arachnians. *That makes no sense,* Reykir thought. But whatever Rak had seen, it had scared her senseless. She was so puffed up she was practically a ball of feathers, a sight that would have been comical if not for the imminent danger that had provoked it.

Alaire stirred in the adjoining room. "Reykir? Are you up?" he called.

"Aye," the boy said, rushing to his feet. Already he was hopping out of the silk pajamas and throwing on some thick breeches.

"What's going on outside?" Alaire came in, partially dressed, clutching a shirt and a sheathed knife, and looked at Reykir. *"What is it?"*

From outside came another shout, followed by the sound of something *big* swooping past the window.

Alaire's eyes told him he'd heard it too. *"What in the seven hells . . ."* he began, rushing to the window. Reykir joined him, casting a nervous glance back at Rak, afraid for her sanity, afraid for all their safety.

"Look, over there," Reykir said, pointing to a darkened area of the grounds. Two guards had rushed into a shadow, swords drawn. Two more guards, perhaps the ones who had been on patrol, ran under their window towards the commotion.

"We're going outside," the Bard said, tying the large

knife and sheath to his forearm, then throwing the shirt on. "Did Rak see anything out there?"

"Wingrats and Arachnia," Reykir said, then studied his pet again. :*Arachnia* riding *Wingrats? That's what Low Moon told us . . . :*

No time to think on that. Reykir instructed Rak to stay in the room and followed Alaire to the courtyard. On his way out he grabbed a sheathed knife and stuck it under his belt.

Before they had reached the courtyard, Reykir knew something major was going on. At least ten guards, some of whom looked as if they'd just wakened, filed down the hallway before them.

"Follow them," Alaire said. "They've got bigger weapons than we do."

Reykir and his master took a position behind a large, opened door, giving them a view outside. The apparent source of the ruckus was out in the corner of the courtyard. Two large shapes thrashed in the darkness, several paces away. More guards swarmed towards the disturbance, swords drawn.

"Probably a thief found his way over the wall," Alaire said, but he sounded more hopeful than convinced.

Reykir sensed a presence immediately behind them, and whirled around. His right hand was around the hilt of his knife before he saw that it was Su'Villtor.

"What isss thiss?" The Arachnia said, some of his words slipping into a heavy Arachnian accent. "Invaderss?"

"We don't know yet. Maybe we'd better . . . " Alaire began, but Su'Villtor brushed right past them.

They turned their attention to the situation outside. Two of the guards had produced lit torches, which illuminated a wide oval in the courtyard.

"Lyam's out there," Alaire said, as the torchlight fell on the captain. Reykir focused on the largest of the assembled guards, and indeed it was their friend. With him was a younger guard with a crossbow, which was aimed at the thorax of an Arachnia. The insect was darker and larger than Su'Villtor, who had approached the scene but kept a respectable distance, and wore an elaborate system of leather armor. *Something that crossbow would penetrate in a flash,* Reykir thought, transfixed by the scene. Two other guards were examining what at first looked like a fallen horse behind the captain's group. As the torchlight flickered over the still form, he saw it was no horse, but a wingrat.

"Low Moon," Reykir whispered, and started for the door. Alaire clutched his shoulder before he got too far.

"It's not Low Moon," Alaire said. "Different color. Still has the collar on." He squinted at the fallen animal. Its belly faced them with a pair of arrows extending from it. "And it's male. Nevertheless, we should investigate. That Arachnian soldier resembles the one we encountered on the ship."

Of course, Reykir thought, now knowing why the bug looked so familiar. Even with the armor he saw that it was darker than Su'Villtor.

No other officials from Kai's office were present besides Lyam and Su'Villtor. Once they were closer to the invader, Reykir saw an arrow projecting from the Arachnia's claw, apparently rendering it useless. As they approached the scene they heard a guard explaining to Lyam what had happened.

Reykir didn't understand the Suinomen language, but he was able to follow the gist of what had happened. The guard had spotted three or more wingrats and their Arachnian riders landing just inside the palace walls. As he had never seen such creatures before, and the visitors had made no hostile moves, the guard thought this might have been an ill-timed and ill-aimed rest stop, and tried to hail them. In return, the visitors had started shooting with bows and arrows. Other guards, who had been observing the intruders, began shooting at them from the wall. One arrow caught one of the wingrats, and as it plummeted to the ground another arrow struck it.

The wingrat lay on its side, its chest heaving, face pinched with pain. The Arachnia who had ridden it didn't seem concerned for it, indeed, it only seemed concerned for its own hide. Surrounded by crossbows, it didn't look as though it could do much of anything besides stay where it was.

"Alaire, what do you make of all this?" Lyam asked as he gestured towards the wingrat, sounding completely baffled. "I've never seen a beast like this. That it can be used for assaults from the air . . . that is very disturbing indeed."

"They are wingrats," Alaire replied. "Slaves of these Arachnian masters."

The captain eyed him suspiciously. "You know of these creatures? Why didn't you mention them earlier?"

Alaire shrugged, and approached Lyam, speaking only a short distance from his ear. Even with his voice lowered, Reykir heard what he was saying. "We encountered one of these creatures after our ship sank. They are quite intelligent, but evidently have been enslaved by this other race of Arachnia."

Lyam shook his head. "Other race? You mean there are two races of these . . . " Lyam said, but looked up as Su'Villtor drew closer.

"I was waiting for a better opportunity to discuss this with you," Alaire said. "I would prefer to speak in private, if you understand," he added, nodding toward Su'Villtor.

"Indeed I do," Lyam replied, but his eyes were on Su'Villtor, who without hesitating approached the captured Arachnian. Standing side by side, Reykir saw their differences clearly. The captive was larger, though this might have been an illusion caused by the armor. The two insects began speaking in Arachnian.

"You, Su'Villtor, stay away from that prisoner!" Captain Lyam bellowed, but the secretary ignored him.

Without warning, the captured Arachnia lunged for Su'Villtor. Reykir stepped reflexively backwards; they moved with incredible swiftness, and in an eyeblink the two were locked in a death struggle. The guards nocked and aimed their arrows.

"Hold!" Lyam shouted. The other guards stirred anxiously, but with the two insects moving as quickly as they did, with their bodies intertwined, it was difficult to tell the two apart.

As they watched helplessly, the prisoner suddenly froze, then fell backwards. Its thorax, though shielded with leather, was pierced. In moments, two arrows pierced the Arachnia through the head, followed by a third. The insect continued to quiver, but for all intents appeared to be dead. Nevertheless, Reykir kept his distance.

"Stay back," Alaire said needlessly. "It's likely to strike out at anything now."

Su'Villtor approached the captain, and bowed just the slightest bit. As they were probably equals in rank, the gesture suggested an apology of some sort.

"What in the seven hells happened?" Captain Lyam demanded. "What did you *say*?"

Su'Villtor cast a brief glance back at the fallen Arachnia. "It is something I have feared for some time now, Captain Lyam," Su'Villtor replied. As the secretary spoke, more guards surrounded the slain Arachnia, which continued to twitch.

"What, then?" Lyam said, his voice lowering. "Who is this creature and why do they dare attack the palace?"

Su'Villtor paused, as if catching his breath. In spite of his recent struggle, the secretary appeared to again have full possession of the human language. "This Arachnia is from a distant hive called the Roksamur. We know very little of them, except that they dwell on a distant island, far at sea. They have never been in contact with our hive."

Interesting, Reykir thought. *If they've never been in contact, then how do you know of them, Su'Villtor?*

Alaire looked as though he wanted to question the secretary, but held his tongue. As visiting diplomats from Althea, Reykir knew this was not their place. Also, he suspected he would learn more by eavesdropping. Su'Villtor acted as though he didn't see Alaire or Reykir. *Perhaps he* wants *us to hear this.*

"We have been enemies for an eternity," Su'Villtor continued. "This is why the prisoner attacked me."

Too neat, Reykir thought. *Su'Villtor, what are you hiding?*

"They do not trust our hive, particularly those who work for humans, as I do. They find this . . . disturbing."

Captain Lyam rubbed his temples. "Are you saying these invaders came to kill you, and not attack the palace?"

Su'Villtor nodded, "Indeed, Captain. I doubt the palace has anything to worry about." He paused, glancing into the dark night sky. "They would have been the only ones sent. Their hive wouldn't risk more."

Lyam gazed fiercely at the Arachnia, his disbelief evident. "Su'Villtor, how do you know so much about them if they live on a distant island?"

"I am Arachnian," Su'Villtor said simply, as if that should explain everything. "I think I should prepare my report for the king." The Arachnia bowed. "If you will please excuse me."

Su'Villtor turned and walked back to the palace. Lyam shook his head.

"I don't like it," the captain said. "Su'Villtor seems to know an awful lot about these creatures."

"I agree," Alaire said, glancing to the sky. "And I am not ready to believe there are only three, as Su'Villtor claims."

"Nor I," the captain said firmly. "I think I will put the entire guard on alert. I don't like the smell of this one bit."

Alaire ventured closer to the dead Arachnia, who had now ceased moving completely. The creature lay in a curled position, with portions of its leather armor flayed and missing. The Bard studied the body for some time, then suddenly looked up.

"Captain," Alaire said. "Come look at this."

Lyam approached the body. "Its a dead bug," he said, after a moment of study.

"But look how he died," Alaire pointed out. "Two ragged tears. One behind the neck, and the fatal wound across the thorax. Or, on a human, that would be the throat. When did we last see a wound similar to this?"

At first the burly captain looked puzzled. Then his expression turned to anger. "The ambassador," he said. "Su'Villtor killed him?"

Alaire shrugged. "Perhaps." He looked again to the night sky; a quarter moon hung just above the palace, providing some light to see by, but not much. "It would be a good night for an invasion," Alaire said finally. "Killing the ambassador must have been a diversion," he added.

"The king," Lyam said. "We must—"

"I'll go to Kai. We need *you* to organize the army." He glanced again at the sky. "A perfect setup. If I hadn't noticed those wounds—"

"Aye," Lyam said. "I'll call my officers. Go to Kai, now! He must be told what's happening."

❖   ❖   ❖

"I should have known, dammit, I should have known!" Alaire fumed aloud, only vaguely aware of Reykir following him. While they had discussed matters outside with Lyam, servants had begun lighting lanterns and candles in the palace. Apparently, this was going to be an early morning for everyone.

Guards looked nervous, all pretense of sleep now forgotten. Word that the palace was under attack must have traveled quickly; that, or the guards thought it a drill. *With all the ruckus outside, it would have to be a pretty realistic drill to get me stirred up!*

"There you are!" Galdur called, approaching them frantically.

Does he know something we don't? Alaire wondered.

"You must go to the king now," Galdur sputtered. He looked as if he'd been running through the palace, and was quite out of breath. "He requests your attendance immediately."

"That's precisely where I'm going now," Alaire said. "If I recall, the king's chambers . . ."

Galdur shook his head. "He's in a secret place," Galdur said. "Down below. It's a special fortress we keep for emergencies."

Alaire stared at him. "Galdur, what's going on? What aren't you telling us?"

The wizard took Alaire's arm and began leading him to a set of stone stairs. "It would be much easier to show you," he said, but Alaire pulled away from him.

"I would like to know *now*," Alaire said. "The guards intercepted an invader on the grounds. An Arachnian invader. Where is Su'Villtor, by the way?"

"He's with the king," Galdur said quickly. "Please, if you'll follow me. It's very important."

Alaire sighed. "So be it. Reykir, go to our rooms and rouse Craig. *If* you can. Stay there until I get there."

"Yes, master," Reykir said, and scurried off.

"Okay, Galdur," Alaire said patiently. "Let's go."

"Thank you," Galdur replied, sounding relieved. *Relieved over what?* the Bard thought. *At any rate, the answers, whatever they may be, are waiting for me below.*

"Rak. Rak?" Reykir called out as he entered their rooms. "Where are you?"

He was too panicked to use mindspeech, knowing that if he did, his question would come across to Rakvel as a deafening scream. Standing in the middle of his quarters, he saw nothing.

Reykir jumped at a sudden movement from under the bed. A beak, followed by a round face of feathers, peered at him from under the edge of a blanket.

:Safe?: Rakvel queried.

"Don't know," Reykir said, holding his hand down. The owl took this as an affirmative and hopped on, then the boy transferred her to his shoulder.

"Craig," Reykir muttered to himself. "Gotta see if Craig . . ."

One look in Craig's bed told him everything. *He's nowhere around.* Reykir sat on the edge of the bed. *Think, think, now where could he have gone . . .*

On his shoulder, Rak hissed. Reykir looked out the window, and blinked.

Oh dear gods, no, he thought. *This must be a nightmare.*

Knees shaking, Reykir went to the window to get a better look. He wished he hadn't.

A swarm of wingrats, hundreds of wingrats, with mounted Arachnia, flew towards the palace. Down in the courtyard a bell rang loudly, and throughout the palace grounds Reykir heard an army rising to fight. The first wave of invaders swooped towards the guards manning the wall, spearing them and knocking them over. The soldiers down below seemed just as stunned as Reykir was; the sight of so many flying creatures with armored Arachnian mounts froze a good many of the guards where they stood.

We're doomed, Reykir thought morosely as he stared out the window, unable to move.

The stairwell to the underground chamber was at the other end of the palace. Alaire didn't remember this particular passage, though he had discovered a fair number of secret tunnels throughout the palace grounds the last time he was here. It left him wondering how many hidden passages there *were* in this place.

"Down here," Galdur said, but Alaire had paused beside a tall, narrow window. It was obviously a much older part of the palace, as the stone looked much more streaked with soot and grime. The style suggested a design at least a century old.

"Look, out here," Alaire said. The window looked over a narrow section of the grounds between the palace and the main wall. Dark shadows passed through the sky. First one, then a few. Flapping, flying creatures swarmed the sky.

Wingrats. The palace is under attack!

Galdur was waiting for him by the stairs. "Down here," the wizard whispered urgently. Alaire tore himself away from the window and followed the wizard down the stairs.

"Galdur, why did you move the king down *here*?" Alaire asked, picking his way carefully over the stone. Parts of the steps had crumbled, leaving a hazardous path of loose rocks for him to negotiate. "Did you know something was going to happen tonight?" As they descended into the darkness Alaire began to suspect he might be walking into a trap.

Not again, he resolved, remembering his last experience with Rozinki wizards.

"Just a precaution," Galdur replied, but the answer

left more questions than it answered. "The king can answer your questions better than I can."

The wizard paused at a large wooden door, pounded on it three times, then pulled the huge wooden handle. Torches lit the room brightly, blindingly, so that Alaire had to shield his eyes. The Bard followed Galdur inside, and the door slammed shut behind him.

Alaire blinked as his eyes adjusted to the brightness.

What is my brother doing down here?

Craig appeared to be in deep conversation with Su'Villtor, but as soon as Alaire entered, both looked up. Alaire did not like the expression he saw on his brother's face, a mixture of surprise and glee; at his feet was an uncorked bottle of spirits.

"Ah, brother," Craig said, approaching Alaire. The smell of alcohol carried clearly across the room as his brother spoke. "Good of you to join us."

Alaire was in no mood for polite conversation. "Craig, what the hell is going on?"

Craig replied with a stupid grin.

Alaire ignored him. "Su'Villtor, what do you know of this? We're under attack!"

Su'Villtor shrugged with an expression of incomprehension.

Exasperated, Alaire continued, "Galdur said the king was down here? *Where is he?*"

"Why," Craig replied innocently, "he's sitting over there. Say hello to your friend Alaire, would you?"

Alaire looked deeper into the shadows beyond the torches, afraid of what he would see. As soon as his eyes adjusted and he saw the dark shape lying there, an urge to run came over him. Kai lay shackled and unconscious, wearing only a pair of breeches and a heavy fur mantle.

He whirled around on his brother, who had stepped

back. Alaire wanted to strangle him. *Time to get out of here,* he thought. *I'm outnumbered.*

As he turned to leave the chamber, something sharp jabbed his rear end. It wasn't a knife or an arrow, or even a sword; but it was, he knew immediately, something equally familiar.

It was the same now as it was then, when the Swords of the Magicians paralyzed him with a poison dart. Only this time Galdur had evidently shot him with it. Alaire collapsed, turning towards the door as he did so, catching a glimpse of Galdur and the little reed used to launch the dart.

It's the same poison, he thought, his mind darkening. In moments the paralysis took over, and his vision faded to black.

Reykir stared out the window at the invading forces for only a moment, suddenly aware of Rak digging her claws into his shoulder.

We're not getting out of this, he thought. *At least not now.*

Holding his fist up to Rak, he said, "Up." The owl stepped onto his fist, panting with a wild look, nearly turning her head completely around. *She's our only hope,* Reykir thought.

He looked into the owl's eyes directly, willing the creature to relax, sending her calming, tranquilizing thoughts. Soon the panting slowed, and Reykir had her full attention. :*Fly. Home now:* he sent.

For a moment Rak's expression was strangely sad and human, as the realization seemed to sink into her that Reykir might not survive.

Reykir fought back tears. :*Go. Now!:* he ordered in a mindshout, taking Rak over to the window. The harshness of the words seemed to prod the bird into action. :*Fly home now. Tell King Derek what happened!:*

Rak hesitated, and Reykir leaned out the window. :*Home! Now!*: the boy commanded, pushing the owl into the sky.

The gesture left a painful scratch as the owl tore off his fist and launched herself into the night, but it accomplished the goal. He felt a thin line of blood drip down his wrist as he watched his friend swoop away into the night, amid the wingrats and Arachnian soldiers who continued to pour in from the sky by the hundreds.

:*Fly, my friend,*: Reykir sent, but Rak did not reply.

He watched for several long moments as Rak vanished around the corner of the palace, having no way of knowing if she made it beyond the palace grounds or not. *She can't help me now. I must deal with my present situation by myself,* he thought. *What did Alaire tell me to do? Stay here until he returns?* With the enemy swarming over the area, that seemed to be the wisest move.

In the room was a large wardrobe with two large doors adorned with intricate wooden scrollwork. Inside hung some of the clothing given them by the king, but that wasn't what he was looking for.

"Not a weapon anywhere, except for this damned knife," he muttered aloud, touching the hilt of his dagger. He was torn between joining the battle and saving his own skin. Being Alaire's apprentice had taught him some bravery and a sense of responsibility; they were under attack by a well armed and well trained army, who were making mincemeat of anyone who defied them. At that moment, he saw nothing brave about walking into a battle with only a dagger to inflict damage. Stupid, perhaps. But not brave.

Reykir opened the doors and pushed past the clothes, finding a place to stash himself. Then he pulled the doors shut behind him, and began the long process of making his body and spirit completely still.

❖   ❖   ❖

Alaire opened his eyes, the only motion he was capable of. He had been dreaming about the Prison of Souls, the crystal jail cell his soul had been stored in; as he woke, he felt the walls of a coffin at his side, but this was only a part of the fading dream. He lay on his stomach, his face turned to the right, his cheek pressed against a cold, damp stone floor. Kai lay next to him, his eyes open, his wrists bound in shackles. He might have been unconscious, or not. The drug the wizards here seemed to favor had subtle, yet overwhelming effects.

Somewhere above and behind him, he heard movement, and voices.

"We have captured the palace," an unfamiliar voice said. "Except for the west wing. There is some . . . resistance there."

West wing? Is that where Reykir was? he thought, hoping the boy had listened to him and stayed in the room. Perhaps he would find a place to hide, and perhaps he would escape. *I pray to the gods that he has. Derek must know what's going on! Once these Arachnia capture Suinomen, if they do, then Althea is certainly next!*

"Very well," someone replied. Alaire flinched inwardly when he recognized the voice. *Craig.* "Su'Villtor, what do you suggest now?"

A rustle, followed by an unintelligible Arachnian chitter, then, "I think we should move the prisoners as soon as possible. We may have the palace, but we do not yet have the city."

At the sound of his brother's voice, Alaire withered inside. If there was any doubt about his loyalties before, his last statement laid it to rest. *Why is Craig betraying us? And where the hell are they taking us?*

Alaire felt some feeling return to his fingers, and he moved them tentatively. As the feeling spread, he sensed that his arms were bound behind him in shackles like Kai's.

"He's waking," Galdur hissed.

"We must keep him down," Su'Villtor said. "Dose him again."

A pause, followed by a sharp pain in his right leg. In moments, the darkness returned.

The wardrobe made a stuffy hiding place at first, but as the boy willed his breathing to slow, his muscles to relax, he became aware of a draft coming in from beneath him. Soon he was comfortable, and discovered he would be able to sit there indefinitely.

As calm as he made himself on the surface, he felt as though he was on the very edge of hysteria. Though muffled, the sounds he heard coming from around him in the palace were not encouraging. At first it was a frantic scraping, as though someone was dragging a sword down the hall, followed by a flurry of pecking noises. The floor vibrated with the motion, and he had to concentrate further to still himself. When he heard Arachnian shouts, he realized the odd sounds were Arachnians, searching.

He resisted an urge to bolt out of the wardrobe and run like a frightened rabbit. This would not make sense, he knew, even though the enemy was so close.

I must remain here. If for no other reason then because Alaire told me to stay here! When logic fails, submit to a higher authority. He'd heard that somewhere, but could not quite remember where. It had made no sense when he heard it, but now, as he sat on the bottom of the wardrobe, trying to become one with the wood, he realized the quote was the only thing keeping him sane.

Someone entered the room, and then came the thud of something big and heavy falling over and breaking.

For a moment, Reykir stopped breathing, until the wardrobe doors flew open.

Two armored and well armed Arachnians stood regarding him for a moment, then chittered away at each other, sounding *amused*. Their suddenly relaxed stance indicated he was not the threat they had anticipated, and he didn't know whether he should be relieved or insulted.

A claw reached out and plucked the dagger from his belt, then tossed it aside. "Human. Come with us," the Arachnia said. If they recognized him as a prince's assistant, they didn't show it. *And why would they? I'm just another human so far as they're concerned!*

They stepped around the large thing that had fallen over—the state bed. The canopy lay in splinters and the mattress lay in a corner. Arachnians, Reykir concluded, could toss heavy furniture as easily as they could a saucer. He cast a wary eye towards his dagger, which had fallen beneath the window, but saw no way to retrieve it. *Not that it would do me much good,* he thought. *If anything will help me now it will be my head, not my blade.*

As the Arachnia marched him down the stairs, he saw more of the invaders, but no humans. They seemed to have seized the palace, apparently without much resistance.

Craig was nowhere to be seen, and neither was Alaire; but then, he had said he was going to the king. Whether he had made it there or not remained a mystery, unrevealed by what he saw in the great hall. Servants, children, women and a few wounded soldiers had been herded there. They looked up hopefully when Reykir entered, and just as quickly, their eyes fell.

This annoyed the boy more than anything. *Hmmmph. I haven't even tried to help yet, and they think I'm useless! Well, I'm not!* He glanced at their captors, clusters of three or four Arachnians standing at all the exits, each wielding a crossbow. *As if,* Reykir thought wryly, *we would try to get past those claws.*

As he looked over the captives, he saw how scantily most of them were dressed, due in no small part to being wakened in the middle of the night. However, he wore rather expensive looking breeches and shirt, and even though these items looked as though they had been thrown on, he still felt as though he looked conspicuously *noble*.

And noble is probably not a good thing to be at this point, he thought, and looked about for ways to rectify the situation.

He moved past a gaggle of maidservants, tittering away in their Suinomen tongue, and started looking behind the dining tables for what he needed. The room had been swept and cleaned after dinner, but the invasion had changed the neat appearance of the hall. On the floor, near a pile of spilled dinner plates, he saw what he needed.

The apron was soiled and dirty, with what looked like hog's blood on it. *The messier the better,* he thought, hoping some of the blood would stain what he was already wearing. The apron was for a large man, and it reached nearly to his ankles, wrapping him completely around the back. The shirt still looked a tad gaudy for a servant, but it would have to do until he found something grungier. In the meantime, he moved among the other prisoners, who cast nervous looks at the Arachnian guards.

The speed with which the Arachnians had taken the palace surprised Reykir, and on the surface it seemed as if history were repeating itself; from what Alaire had told him, Sir Jehan, the traitor who had nearly succeeded in taking the throne six years before, had worked as quickly.

But Sir Jehan was on the inside, he thought.
Is there . . .

The thought stopped him cold. *Su'Villtor?*

Chapter Nine

Low Moon stirred from the nest of weeds and branches she had made for herself in the thickest part of the forest she could find. As night fell, lights came on in the vast human city down in the valley. At first she had thought it was on fire but no local animals were upset; then she remembered the lanterns used by the Arachnia at home, and guessed this was just a more expanded use of the same.

Before nesting, she had found more game, and had enough left over to eat the next day. Low Moon hung the game from a tree, but even this was not enough to discourage scavengers; she had warned three wolves off before she curled up to sleep.

Now she woke because of something else, a distant sound chasing away the fragments of a dream, a memory of her home. She dreamed of brothers and sisters, of collars and Arachnia. Home again, she felt the prison circling her neck, changing her thoughts, guiding her actions. For a time it was a comforting feeling, as it was meant to be. She did not have to take care of herself, the masters did that for her; they fed her, and when she was in season they provided a mate to sire her litters—if she obeyed.

As she woke in her nest, she remembered the flight from Roksamur, the storm, the freedom, the humans

130

who helped her, the human city below. And rose from her nest with a start.

She sniffed the air. *Sisters?*

The scent of her clan was undeniable, overwhelming and everywhere.

Low Moon peered into the sky, uncertain for a moment what she was seeing. A storm cloud seemed to have a life of its own, and moved with great speed. But there was no wind; in fact it was a still night, the sounds of insects loud and resonating. She smelled no rain, just the strong odor of other wingrats, male and female, young and old, with the underlying scent of Arachnia in the background. The scent of the latter stirred fear in her, reminding her that she had not been free for long.

Can they reclaim me? she wondered, terrified at the prospect. The hair on her back rose, and her wings rose reflexively, ready for flight. *Are they . . .*

Then she saw that this was no storm cloud. It was a swarm of wingrats, so many that they filled the sky, blotting out the moon and stars. The only sound was the beating of their wings, a low thrumming that sounded like distant rain. Low Moon ducked beneath a tree, hoping it would conceal her, and watched the swarm pass overhead.

This is what they planned, she thought. *This is why they sent me.* Low Moon knew this shouldn't surprise her, but the sheer numbers of her kind stunned her. She'd never seen that many wingrats in one place; in fact, she hadn't even known that many existed. *There must have been colonies elsewhere on Roksamur, away from the rest. Whole clans in training. How can the Arachnia control so many?*

Her speculation startled her. Contemplating the power of her masters was not something she would have done while imprisoned by them. She knew their spells prevented independent thought, turned her kind into mindless followers. While bound, they were focused only on their duties to their masters and the slim rewards dispensed when they obeyed. With startling clarity she saw what an injustice had been done to her race. The humans had liberated more than her body. Her spirit was now reborn as she took in the entire picture.

The others must be freed, she thought, but the sheer numbers of wingrats staggered her. *How?*

Afraid of detection, but more afraid of doing nothing to help the others, she reached out with her thoughts. She found a familiar shield surrounding each wingrat she probed, a black curtain supported by the collars each wore. Also, there were curious inquiries from some of the more adept Arachnia who knew their defenses were being probed. Fortunately, they were more concerned with the invasion at hand, which, from what Low Moon could read, seemed to be on the threshold of certain victory.

Out of the sea of beating wings, she picked up a pair of wingrats without riders, carrying bundles underneath them. They were flying in the opposite direction, away from the city. She concentrated on these, probing for clues to their identities and destination, and found only the dark, concealing curtain.

But the bundles underneath were not shielded, and they were, Low Moon discovered quickly, humans.

Not only were they humans; one was the human who had freed her. He seemed to be confused and not as sharp as when they first communicated.

What are they doing with them? she thought, her wings once again flexing. *Are they taking them . . .*

Then she saw where they were going, the only other place they could go.

They're returning to Roksamur, she thought. *I owe that human my freedom, and now that human is imprisoned by my former masters!*

She took to the air, and flew after them, grateful that much of her strength had returned and that she now had a task to perform again.

I must go after them, even if it means losing my freedom again. . . .

The moment Alaire woke from the darkness, he knew that someone was carrying him somewhere; but his awareness stopped there. He drifted in and out of sleep, wavering between the comfortable darkness of drugged slumber, and a less agreeable windy chill which cut through it. In time the drug wore off, leaving a numbing cold which sliced through his body.

He recalled a lucid dream concerning the Prison of Souls, the cold having summoned those distant memories. The experience was imprinted on his soul, for his soul was what had been imprisoned and separated from his body. Those soul memories surfaced during the dreams, clear images of the crystal that had become his new home. Cold, numbing cold crystal . . .

No! he thought, coming wide awake now. He tried to sit up, but found himself wrapped in something, a blanket, or, from the scent of it, leather. It felt like a hammock, suspended between two trees, only he knew he was moving, the icy wind whipping through the leather like it was tissue. His hands remained bound in front of him, but now with leather bindings, which turned out to be as effective as the iron shackles without as much discomfort. Rough and chafing, at least they were not carving away at his wrists as the shackles had, and in this frigid cold he was at least grateful for that.

I'm awake now, he thought, though not entirely convinced that he really was. *I still feel the drug. Distant, fading, but I still feel it.* He yawned, as if to emphasize the fact. *If they think I'm awake, they'll just dose me again. Better to feign sleep, and keep my ears open, than to not be able to hear anything.*

But he heard no people, no Arachnia, no horses or dieren, not even the sounds of a palace being taken over. Only a loud wind. Occasionally, he was jostled left, then right, as if his captors were carrying him up mountains. He heard what sounded like flapping, along with the wind that blew deafeningly against him. Most likely he was nowhere near the palace. But where? Out to sea?

He sniffed the air, but smelled no salt or ocean; the air was actually quite thin, and only smelled strongly of the leather which bound him. It was not cowhide or even dieren, but it must have been from a large beast, as it seemed to be mostly of one piece. That, or it had been so skillfully assembled that he couldn't tell. But the smell, he'd smelled it before.

The leather. Smells like rodents.

The hammock he hung suspended in was more like a cocoon, and as he ran his bound wrists along the inside he felt wool and leather reinforcements lining it. The cocoon sagged in the middle, as evidenced by his stiff back. Above him was a cluster of five holes, probably installed to allow air in what might have been an airtight leather bag; it was also the source of the biting cold.

Well, better to be cold than to suffocate, he reasoned, working his way towards the holes and, hopefully, a glimpse outside.

As he wriggled towards the holes, he felt the cocoon shift, and the wind came from another direction. If his captors objected, or even noticed that he'd moved around, they said nothing. Or they were not . . . concerned.

Where in hell am I?

His face drew closer to the light, the chill biting into it as he moved. Tears ran down his cheeks as the wind invaded his eyes, drying them so fast that blinking once or twice didn't help; but he kept moving. He had to get a look at the outside.

As his right eye moved over a hole, which was just big enough to put his index finger though, he found himself looking out.

At first he saw only a wide area of greenish gray, and for a moment he thought there might be a second layer of fabric surrounding the cocoon. But as he kept watching the dingy green, he saw, here and there, the whitecaps of waves. They were enormous waves, he realized, but seemed small because of the great height the bard had found himself at.

"*Egads!*" Alaire shrieked. *I'm flying above the thrice-damned ocean!*

Then the scent of rodent began to make sense. As did the wind and the flapping he'd been hearing.

I'm being carried by a wingrat!

Cautiously, he turned his eye away from the ocean far below, and looked up through the other holes. Indeed, he saw what had to be the fittings for a leather harness to which his cocoon had been attached, secure fittings, he noted with some relief, with a wide patch of brown fur beyond that could only belong to a wingrat. To either side he saw the great wings which carried him to his unknown destination; long, graceful wings, their motion resembling that of a soaring seagull. But then, it would make sense to glide as much as possible, saving energy, making use of the wind.

Alaire evaluated his arrangement with cold calculation, trying not to panic or scream. Evidently they wanted him alive, or they would have killed him already. He looked for, but didn't see, another wingrat with a similar cocoon. That would have been Kai, he thought, but even though he didn't see one that didn't mean much with his range of vision limited to five little holes. Somewhat regretful that he had bothered to look, he slithered back down in his former position; he had a few other things to worry about now.

Like . . . where are they taking us?

For a horrible moment he thought they had intended to dump him in the ocean. The cocoon he was in would be perfect for getting rid of their bodies, particularly if weights were attached to either end. But the fear came and went. Whatever they had in mind, it did not involve killing them.

At least not yet.

Then he saw what should have been the obvious reason for taking them.

Ransom.

The memory of Craig and Su'Villtor, making a deal, left him feeling cold and empty.

He needed something to hit, hard, but nothing suitable came to mind as he hung suspended only the gods knew how far above the ocean.

He remembered the cryptic conversation Craig was having with the Arachnia Su'Villtor when Alaire had arrived in the chambers. Though Alaire's recent past was fuzzy, blunted by the wizard's knockout drug, the scene burned vividly in his memory.

After a time, he felt the angle of the wingrat's flight change drastically. He got up and worked his way to the airholes. Halfway into a banked turn, he saw, far below, what had to be their destination. It was only an island, but a large one, which jutted upwards from the sea like the bow of a sinking ship. An entire range of mountains, topped with snow, made up most of the island, and instead of a gradual descent to the shore, the terrain made a sudden drop to the water. Enormous cliffs faced the entire side of the island. Now he saw why they had to fly.

There's nowhere to dock a ship.

Then Alaire noticed something odd about the mountains; one of them was billowing a thin stream of smoke. This made no sense to the Bard, who began to wonder if it was a forest fire, or if his eyes were playing tricks.

Not that it much mattered anymore; they were going down faster now, close enough to the ocean to hear the waves. He looked up, and flinched. The cliff wall was coming straight at them, and it looked as though they weren't going to clear it. At the last second he felt the wind rush beneath them, urging them up and over the cliff. The wingrat glided into a valley, deep and green with few trees and a blanket of grass and wildflowers. Wind rose here as well, and the ground dropped away; they were up again, but this time over solid land. Alaire didn't know if he should be relieved or not.

The valley wove through mountain passes, which became steeper, taller, and narrower. He looked down at a distant river, twisting through what had become a canyon, with only the brown and white of rock and sand. The air also became thinner, and Alaire suspected they were climbing again to some higher point, perhaps atop the mountains themselves.

Then suddenly, the wingrat began backflapping rapidly, and Alaire's stomach lurched as he watched them drop down to a rocky mesa, a smooth field of granite that seemed to go on forever. The cocoon scraped the rock slightly before they came to a complete halt; the wingrat walked, or rather waddled, a short distance. Then the leather bindings came loose, and the cocoon dropped free of its carrier. Now a prisoner of gravity, Alaire dropped, smacking his head on the hard rock beneath.

As suddenly as the wingrat had landed, the Bard watched it take a brief run, then launch itself once more into the air.

Alaire lay on the hard stone surface, uncertain if he should move or try to get out of his leather prison.

When he decided to move, he found he could not; his limbs and joints were numb with cold.

The only portion of his anatomy that seemed to be working was his ears. Even they told him little, only that the wind blew up here as well, and that there didn't seem to be any bird life. A few moments passed, and as he lay prone on the rock, he felt heat issue through the leather, warming his stomach, chest and legs. In another moment he was able to move, and rolled over, warming his backside.

Though the wind blew hard, it not as cold as what they had flown through, and carried a wide range of organic scents he wasn't accustomed to. He reached up with his bound hands and started working at the top of the cocoon. While the bindings were on the outside, he was able to loosen the noose that tied the cocoon shut, and blessed air and sunshine poured into his prison.

Only to be interrupted by the largest, darkest Arachnia Alaire had ever seen.

The insect's head filled the opening; then the Bard saw that it was not a head, but only *one* of its eyes. As he gaped at the creature, something pulled at the cocoon near his feet, and in seconds it dumped him inelegantly onto the warm stone. Alaire scraped his palms as he rolled, banging forearms and elbows, and rapping the back of his head, again, on the stone. Even so, solid ground felt good, and it was a relief to be out of that cocoon.

Alaire peered up at the Arachnia, who was considerably larger and taller than Su'Villtor, or the captain of their ill-fated ship, who had been a large critter himself. Another Arachnia, evidently the one who had dumped him out of the leather sack, stood at his feet. The two giant insects regarded him for a moment before one of them spoke, in broken Althean.

"You will come with us, prisoner," he said. "If you try to escape, we will cut you in half."

To demonstrate, the Arachnia reached down with a claw, and clamped around Alaire at the waist. The creature exerted just enough pressure to let him know he meant business; Alaire's knowledge of those claws convinced him that they could snip him in two with very little effort.

Bad news in any language, Alaire thought, holding his breath.

"You will obey," the Arachnia said.

Alaire nodded slightly, but apparently the Arachnian wanted a more substantial reply.

"You will obey!" the Arachnia said, and with a wave of the massive claw knocked Alaire aside; he tumbled onto the warm stone, and lay there a moment, waiting to see what else the creature had in mind.

"You will . . . obey," it repeated.

Now Alaire understood this to be a question, which he had not properly answered the first time.

"Yes, I will obey," he said, and slowly climbed to his feet. *As if I had a choice . . .*

Standing between the two Arachnia, Alaire noticed, off in the distance, another leather cocoon. A similar pair of Arachnia stood near it, and dumped its contents out much as they had Alaire's.

Alaire recognized the fallen, crumpled form. *Kai!*

The king didn't move. *Frozen to death, or just under the dart?*

The Arachnia closest to Alaire tied a rope about his wrists with the other bindings, and gave the other end to his companion.

"Come with us," the Arachnia said, tugging at the rope as if it were a leash, and he was no more than a pet.

The two giant insects led him across the featureless mesa towards a cluster of boulders, jerking his rope for no apparent reason, except maybe for sheer annoyance.

They're toying with me, he thought. *It will take some work to get to me.*

Alaire glanced back to see that the others were carrying Kai, rather clumsily, between two of them. Either the king was truly drugged, or was acting the part very well; the Bard remembered that he'd had a low tolerance to the drug before.

Amid the boulders at the edge of the mesa was the mouth of a tunnel, leading down at a sharp angle. Inside he saw a hint of light, but for the most part they were entering darkness.

If he was going to escape, now would be the best time. *If I summon Bardic power now, I might be able to free us. But Kai is unconscious and unable to run. We are outnumbered. And if I got away now, where would we go?*

His urge to flee lessened. With difficulty he walked down the steep slope, stumbling twice on rocks, feeling warm, moist air waft past him. When his eyes adjusted he found glowing green and yellow lichens clinging to the rock above them, which became more dense and numerous as they descended.

At least there's something to see by, Alaire thought, hazarding another glance backwards. He saw no others following them, and wondered if they planned on keeping him and Kai together, or separated. The lichens' light was soft and dull, but much better than nothing. His captors didn't seem to have any trouble navigating by it.

Well, these Arachnia would have little to fear on this island, the Bard thought dismally. *It's not like the Suinomen army will be knocking at their doors anytime soon. I don't even think Kai's kingdom knows of this island, and if they did, they don't know this is where we are.*

The passageway made a sharp right turn, and on their right was a series of hollowed out rooms or, the Bard thought more likely, cells. They came upon a large chamber with an opening secured with stout wooden bars, made from the trunks of trees, with crossbars to match. It was lit by a concentration of the luminescent lichens and he could see. Inside were a table, chairs, and a pile of straw in one corner. It was the first furniture Alaire had seen since entering the Arachnian lair, so he thought it likely that this cell had been provided specifically for humans. But Alaire could see no way into the chamber. Then the leading Arachnia moved a huge, flat boulder aside, revealing a doorway leading into the cell.

"We will send for food presently," the apparent leader said. "Tend to the other human. It doesn't look very healthy."

Alaire watched the two Arachnians carry Kai in and lay him on the hard stone floor. Without another word, they left the cell, and the leader replaced the enormous boulder over the opening.

Wonderful, Alaire thought, leaning over Kai. *Just bloody wonderful.*

"Kai," Alaire ventured, lightly slapping his cheek. "Time to get up."

The king groaned slightly, raised his arms over his face. "Is it morning yet?"

Alaire looked around the dimly lit cell. "That's kind of hard to say."

"Huh?" He moved some more, but not very enthusiastically. "Oh, drat. Let me sleep. I don't want to be king today."

Alaire sat on one of the crude chairs and crossed his leg. "I would say that is pretty much in the cards, given our circumstances."

Kai rolled over, threw his arms over his head again, and appeared to be attempting to go back to sleep.

"Shoo the servants away," Kai said dreamily. "I'll have breakfast in my chambers. Tell Paavo to have my shoes polished. . . . "

Alaire sighed. *Out of it. Totally bloody out of it. How much did they drug the kid, anyway?*

"Yes, Your Majesty," Alaire replied somberly. "Oh, and will you be receiving this afternoon?"

"Hmmm." Kai seemed to be considering it. "Let me sleep on that. . . . "

In moments, Kai was snoring.

Which is just as well, Alaire thought. *He should go ahead and sleep it off, then I can break the unpleasant news that we are in the enemy's dungeon, not curled up all comfy cozy in the palace.*

Alaire dragged him over to the straw and made him as comfortable as possible. Seeing Kai lying there reminded him of their first night out on the town, when *Prince* Kai got roaring drunk, and Alaire had to help him out of the carriage.

Alaire scratched his chin thoughtfully; now Kai was every bit the dignified king he was supposed to be. *A bit overboard with the formalities,* he had to admit, *but still, much reformed. Perhaps he has stopped drinking.* Alaire cringed, remembering how difficult Kai was to handle when drunk.

No, not difficult, he amended. *Impossible. The boy didn't have a responsible bone in his body when he was drinking, and once he started, he didn't stop until every drop in sight had been consumed.*

Kai stirred, moaned, said something unintelligible. Alaire went over to the bars to see how well they were being guarded. Just outside the cell stood not one but two Arachnian guards, complete with thick leather armor.

I suppose that means we're not going anywhere for a while, Alaire decided.

"Paavo! Bring me my tea!" Kainemonen shouted from the hay. Alaire heard rustling and returned to his friend's side.

"Kai, are you up yet?" Alaire inquired, pulling a chair

up beside the pile of straw. "I have something important to tell you."

Kai's eyes flickered open. Slowly, he looked over at Alaire, and brought both hands up to massage his temples.

"Alaire," he said, sounding confused. "What are . . ."

Then he sat up suddenly, wincing at the sudden headache that must have resulted, and looked around.

"We're not in my chambers," Kai said. "Where are we? The dungeon?"

Alaire shrugged. *This is going to come as quite a shock. Here goes.* "Well, yes and no."

To Kai's confused look, he continued, "Yes, we are in a dungeon. No, it is not yours."

"What do you . . ." Kai began, then looked down, at the floor.

"Kai, what can you remember of the evening?"

The boy crossed his legs, evidently to make himself more comfortable, but it didn't look like he succeeded. "First the servants came with word that an intruder had been arrested on the palace grounds. I didn't think it was anything important, so I went back to sleep."

"The intruder was an enemy Arachnia," Alaire said. "Anything after that?"

"The servants came a second time. Galdur—" He stopped there, his eyes widening.

I think he's starting to remember, Alaire thought.

"Damn them all to the *seven hells*! Su'Villtor had me *kidnapped!*"

Alaire nodded. *At least I don't have to convince him who our enemies are.*

Kai was on his feet now, fuming, pacing in the small cell. A brief inspection of the bars that held them in, and the two guards outside, seemed to convince him that they were, indeed, prisoners.

"Su'Villtor has been a faithful servant for years. How

can he do this to us?" He pounded at the bars with his fists. "Alaire, where are we?" he asked, looking up at the glowing lichens that illuminated their cell. "What manner of growth is this?" he asked, peeling a bit of the lichen off.

"Roksamur," Alaire said woodenly. "We're on the island of Roksamur."

Kai flicked the piece of lichen across the cell. "No, I mean, *really*. Where are we?"

"I told you," Alaire replied, and met his eyes.

"How did . . . what ship . . . " Kai looked confused, but apparently was willing to believe what Alaire told him.

"We didn't take a ship. We flew. Wingrats . . . " Alaire began, then listened to his own words. *He won't believe this.* "Wingrats flew us here. We landed on the island, and Arachnian soldiers took us down here."

"When you say 'wingrat' what precisely are you talking about?"

"Well," Alaire began, "wingrat is really just our description of them. They are large creatures, the size of a horse, only they resemble rats. Rodents."

"You are serious about this?" Kai said, his voice mocking, but his eyes betrayed another emotion: fear.

"Quite," Alaire replied. "They have large wings with which they fly, and are used as beasts of burden by these Arachnians. They are a different race, these Arachnians, from the race we are already familiar with."

"So the legend is true," he muttered. "I thought it was a myth."

"I am not manufacturing any of this," Alaire said.

"Oh, I don't assume for a second that you are," Kai said, and took a seat in one of the chairs. "Roksamur. Years ago my great-grandfather returned from a long sea voyage. I never knew him, but my father told me he had encountered a large island, surrounded by several tiers of reef. He saw the remains of several ships on the shore, and did not attempt to land himself."

"There must have been survivors," Alaire said. *That would explain their apparent familiarity with humans and their needs. Chairs, tables. That's a human thing. These chairs are too small for them anyway.*

"If there were, they never left the island," Kai said. "There have been legends of a giant race of Arachnia," he said, casting a wary look towards the front of the cell. "And of dragons, flying above the island."

"The dragons have brought us here," Alaire said. "And they are not a myth. Back at the palace they drugged me, too. But when I awakened, I was in flight, over the damned ocean."

A hint of humor passed over the king's face. "That must have been disturbing."

"Other words come to mind to describe my feelings at that moment," he said.

"Su'Villtor must have been behind it," Kai said. "And Galdur, he's the one who led me down to that room."

"That's where I was led as well," Alaire said, and hesitating for a moment before going on. "I think my brother Craig is involved, too."

"Nothing surprises me anymore," Kai said, stretching. "You don't think this is something he had planned earlier, before you arrived in Rozinki, is it?"

"Who's to say?" replied Alaire. "But I doubt seriously he knew anything of the invasion before we arrived. In case you haven't already noticed, my brother likes to drink. Including him might have been a second thought."

"In what? A coup?"

Oh, damn. He doesn't know. "Yes, a coup. Arachnians, mounted on wingrats invaded Rozinki. Took the palace. As near as I could tell, the takeover was complete by the time we were subdued. I caught a glimpse of some of them. Too numerous to fight."

"In one night," Kai said, "my kingdom is taken. By *rodents*," he spat. "Alaire, has it occurred to you that when we're together, we spend more time in trouble than out of it?"

Alaire wanted to say that all was not lost, but after thinking about that, he realized all *was* lost. For Kai, anyway. *And what is this army's next move? Althea? Most likely.*

"There is the chance," Alaire ventured, "that Reykir has gotten word to Althea. They might have time to set up a defense."

Kai did not respond.

Then again, Alaire thought morosely to himself, *there is the chance that the both of us will sprout wings and fly home ourselves.*

Midway through Low Moon's flight to Roksamur, the wingrat realized, too late, that she had made a serious mistake.

The wind currents which, despite the storm, had aided her voyage to the other land were now blowing against her. While in superb shape when beginning the journey, well rested and well fed, she had depleted most of her energy far sooner than expected. Her masters had taught her that if she faltered while over the sea, she would not survive; her kind were designed for flying, not swimming.

In pain and terror now that she saw her fate, she studied the two wingrats she pursued; they were mere smudges in the moonlight, their wings now dim flickers, pausing to glide more often than not.

She didn't understand why, while she bordered on exhaustion and certain death, these others flew without apparent difficulty. They had flown the same distance as she, and had no time to rest or feed, while she had. Also, she flew unencumbered, while the others were burdened with passengers. While not large beings, the humans were no light package to carry.

Gradually, as the others drew further away from her, her hope also slipped away.

Why are they succeeding, while I . . . her dazed thoughts began. Then she noted where they were in relation to herself. *They are higher. They . . . fly with little wing strokes, while I struggle to stay aloft.*

Low Moon squinted to see the others, barely dots in the night.

The wind currents, she thought. *They change. . . .*

With everything she had left, Low Moon pounded the air with her wings, reaching for *up* instead of *ahead.* The sudden flurry of activity numbed her back muscles, and stretched her wing membranes painfully. But she knew she had no choice, it was this or dying at sea.

When she thought her life had burned itself out, she felt a subtle change in the wind. The headwind weakened, then shifted; renewed with hope, she reached further for *up.*

Wind changes, she thought, excited and renewed with the prospect of surviving. *Wind is . . .*

Soon she saw why the others flew with such speed. While still giddy with exhaustion, she sensed uncertainly that the wind had shifted completely, giving her a slight push. That, or it was an illusion, caused by the sudden absence of resistance. While the wind was thinner and dryer up here, she flew with ease. In time she gained on the others, and had to adjust her speed to stay behind them.

I may survive after all!

Finding the winds more navigable, she fell into the rhythm of long flight. Instead of focusing on the pain in her wings, she allowed her consciousness to drift just beyond her body, so that her physical awareness was secondary.

Once in the rhythm, time passed quickly. The dawn of a new day broke as Roksamur appeared on the horizon.

The sight both comforted and intimidated her. While saved from drowning, her fate from her former masters was more uncertain. Would they become her masters again, and punish her for defying their laws, by allowing others to remove her collar?

I must replace the collar with something else, something that appears to be the original, she thought. *In time. First I must see where these brethren take the humans.*

The wingrat followed her brethren over the cliffs, taking advantage of the stiff updraft that rose from the sea along the cliff wall.

Only one valley from this direction provided passage to the interior; a wide area of grass gave way to a bare canyon, carved deep into the mountain range. The winds picked up here as well, and low clouds obscured the way. But by now, she knew where they were going.

This place was far from the training grounds, where the middle class Arachnians lived. This was the palace itself, the home of Saurboar, queen of Roksamur. A place where no servants, wingrat or Arachnian, were allowed.

I must go, I must follow, Low Moon thought, surrendering again to her fate, that of reenslavement, punishment, or death. It didn't matter, she owed her life to these humans. Freedom equaled life, and for the first time, Low Moon knew she would rather die than be imprisoned again.

The fear sharpened her senses; around the next curve in the canyon, she saw a mesa, above a larger plateau. She flew towards it, landed, and folded her wings in.

Where are they? Ah, there they are, she thought,

looking down on the expansive plain. Two wingrats landed, deposited their leather baggage, and flew off. *As well they would have to. Wingrats are not permitted anywhere near Saurboar. They must have adjusted the boundaries to allow them even this far.*

She watched the two leather bags, looking much like seed pods left to germinate. For a fleeting moment, she considered swooping down there and collecting the bags, and secreting the humans elsewhere on the island. One of the methods used to train them for long-distance flight was to fill long leather bags with rocks, and transport them from mountain peak to mountain peak. These bags looked like the very ones they had used, and even if she didn't have a harness, she might be able to carry . . .

Her musings stopped short when four Arachnians appeared. They were of the warrior class, and one, she saw from the amulet around his thin neck, was a wizard. Even if she reached the humans before they did, they would see her, and if the wizard didn't strike her from the sky with his powers, he could summon an army of wingrats who would. She watched helplessly as the warriors carried the humans away, and disappeared in what had to be the entrance tunnel to Saurboar's lair.

For what seemed like forever Low Moon listened to the wind whistle against the rocks. Her head pounded, and her nervous exhaustion came back, with a vengeance. Without fully realizing what she was doing, Low Moon curled up beside the boulders and dropped into a deep sleep.

Low Moon woke at nightfall, having slept the entire day. Her wings were stiff and sore, as was the entire mass of muscle along her back. It was tempting to consider walking as opposed to flight, but she remembered that her present perch was reachable only by air.

Tentatively, she flexed her wings, shrieking as pain shot through them. She had never flown this far before in her life.

Where to go? she thought. *The humans are imprisoned in Saurboar's palace.*

Torn between her debt, and her desire to stay free, she considered hiding on Roksamur until she was well enough to fly. But there was no food up here, or anywhere else on the island. Arachnia guarded the fields carefully, using food as a way to control the wingrats. Her choice now was only to raid them at night. Which, she noted with some relief, was upon her.

First, food, she thought. *The fields are below. I may glide all the way there.*

She took to the air, just as the last of the sun dropped beneath the horizon. In the not-yet-night, there was some light to see by. Using the mesa as a reference point, she sought the landmarks that would guide her to food.

Moments into her flight, she sensed she was not alone in the sky and glanced behind her.

A mounted wingrat, with a small Arachnian rider, flew into the fading light of the day. Higher in the sky, the sun hadn't yet set on them. The other flyer shone brilliantly in the sky, and Low Moon realized that they were probably students, flying this late in the evening, and to be that size. It was traditional for beginning riders to be paired with young wingrats; this taught young Arachnia how to control their steeds by participating in their training. Low Moon hoped she was invisible in her position. A lone wingrat flying in this location would be suspicious indeed. If the Arachnia saw her, he would be likely to investigate.

She glided as long as possible, knowing that any wing movement would attract attention. Low Moon thought she might escape detection until she saw the other shift direction suddenly, and fly directly for her.

At the edge of her awareness, she felt the Arachnia trying to call her. But without her collar, the words came through weak and garbled.

They will want to know why I have no collar, she thought in panic. *If they learn the truth, they will execute me for certain.*

Pretending not to see them, Low Moon dove deep into the canyon. The updrafts were tricky here, she knew, but not so much that she couldn't handle them. The rider hesitated. *Uncertain if I am rogue, or if I simply didn't hear the call. His command of mindvoice might be questionable. Right now he must be deciding which course of action would get him into the least amount of trouble.*

To her surprise, the rider plunged into the canyon after her. For several moments she lost sight of them, but after a few turns she saw them, much closer now.

At the end of this canyon lie the training grounds, she remembered. *Now that they've seen me, I must pretend that I am returning from my mission! But will they believe me?*

A cover story for her long absence would have to come later. First, she had to find the training grounds, and as soon as possible, a fake collar. If she returned without her collar her master's suspicions would be great. A minor bit of magical probing into her recent past would be all that was necessary to betray her.

Past the canyon, in a valley thick with trees, she saw the outlines of her training grounds. Seeing her former prison made her wings freeze in position while she fought back an urge to fly in the other direction. She was still tired, and while the students following her were less skilled, they were probably far from tired. Outflying the pair would only delay her recapture.

I must have a collar, she thought, wondering if any Arachnians down there had seen her yet. As she made her approach to the southern field, she caught a glimpse of the pursuers, now much further behind. Taking a steep dive, to save energy as much as time, she swooped to the field. Backflapping renewed the agony in her wings, and she fought with her own pain to keep from making any sounds.

The field was desolate, but nearby, in round huts, were the workshops where they made the harnesses. The collars were made elsewhere, then sent to a wizard to be bespelled. But the harness shop might provide a good imitation of what was once around her neck.

Inside the first hut she found nothing usable, just raw hides in the process of being tanned. Now that she was no longer under the Arachnian's spell, she felt the horror of what the hides represented. The leather laid out before her was the skins of wingless rats used as pack animals. Though stupid, slow, and incapable of flight, they were relatives. Anger fueled her actions as she turned from the skins and found her way to the next hut. Here she found harnesses and several finished collars hanging on the wall.

The unspelled collars would not pass close inspection. Yet, she had no choice. One of these would have to work.

She selected the most ornate collar, and after letting out some of the slack, put it on. It fit comfortably in the notches in her fur, left by her previous collar. She left the hut, a place where she would never have been permitted to go in the first place.

The rider was close to landing now, but they appeared to have lost track of her. *I must find the overseer,* she thought. *I must make up a story. . . .*

In addition to the Arachnian masters, each training camp had a detail of overseers, whose job it was to maintain order and to watch for any predators which might feed on the young wingrats. Training was conducted by masters, who slept elsewhere. An overseer would not be as sensitive to magic, and would be easier to convince anyway.

Beyond the huts she heard other wingrats landing. Low Moon chose the opposite direction, down a path which she thought lead to the overseer's quarters.

That the training ground seemed more or less abandoned seemed odd; normally, at nightfall, the grounds would be bustling with wingrats and young Arachnian students.

Of course, they might have flown in the invasion, she reasoned. Still, some of the less skilled should have stayed behind.

A dark swarm passed overhead, answering her questions. Hundreds of wingrats and Arachnian riders flew as a unit to the landing fields, where the less experienced wingrats with riders could land with space to spare. Among the swarm was a master and two overseers; the rest of the riders were students.

I must join them at the field, she thought, with some regret. *Any other actions would be suspicious.*

The collar reassured her to some extent, but she was still worried about what the other rider had seen. *Was I out of the hut before they landed? Did they see me leave?* She had no choice but to find out.

As she approached the landing field, the students were still making their awkward landings. The master watched closely, no doubt making the fledgling wingrats, as well as their riders, more nervous. Low Moon remembered these training flights well, as she wasn't too far removed from them herself.

This master, an older Arachnia who had thought training students beneath him, was one she had hoped she would never encounter again. The Arachnia stood solemnly, with his highly trained mount standing without motion next to him, watching with obvious distaste as one wingrat after another made a less than tidy landing. Low Moon knew that the master was calculating who would be denied rations that night; she recalled that some of the more inept had starved to death under his tutelage.

The master turned slowly towards Low Moon, showing only one of his huge, multifaceted eyes. His claws, crossed before him, slowly unfolded as he seemed to recognize Low Moon.

The look turned her to ice. In that moment, she thought she was certain to die. *He knows the collar is false.*

For many long moments the master said nothing, looking as if he were deciding what form her punishment, or execution, should take. Then, the truth came to her.

He doesn't recognize me.

Never would a master admit that. To do so would show a weakness; all masters, and all Arachnia for that matter, were perfect, with perfect memories.

:*Master,*: Low Moon offered tentatively. :*I have returned from the voyage. To the other land, across the sea.*:

Then a slow bobbing of the Arachnia's head indicated recognition. Low Moon didn't know if she should be relieved, or if she should try to make a run for the mountains.

:*Long time it has taken you to return,*: mindspoke the master. :*Where have you been, this moon?*:

Low Moon quickly tallied the six days she had been gone, and constructed a lie to account for them. The story was mostly the truth, seen from a certain viewpoint.

:*A great storm cast me south,*: she sent, conjuring her actual memories of the lightning and hail, leaving out how the lightning muddled the spell. She had nearly perished in the storm, and sent the appropriate images to convey this, emphasizing what had actually happened, knowing it would be easier to convince the master of the truth. She was new at this lying game, and didn't trust her expertise in manipulating falsehoods just yet.

:*Did you see the great city?*: the master sent. :*Report!*:

She bowed her head sullenly. :*No city. Saw some humans in little huts, but the city, I saw not. I must have been blown off course.*:

The master did not look convinced. :*You reported back not promptly. Are you hiding something?*:

:*I hide nothing,*: she sent. *I returned as soon as I could. Please, allow me to redeem myself!*:

The master's claws snapped twice, making her flinch. She'd seen those claws clip through wings, an unusual but not forbidden form of punishment among the masters. Eventually, the wingrat died from shock; it was not a painless death.

:*You have shamed yourself. You have failed in your mission, and you dare insult me by spending twice the allowed time to return.*:

Low Moon took a tentative step back, ready to run. If the master knew her obedience spells were no longer in place, he kept this revelation to himself. Not that she stood a chance of escaping. The best she could hope for was an instant death by spear or arrow, rather than the prolonged agony of a clipped wing.

:*You will work among the human slaves as your punishment. You will not be allowed to fly. You will learn to obey when out of spell range. You will know your place, and you will never forget ours.*:

Low Moon hung her head low, but her mind was assessing what the master had said. *So the spell does weaken with distance!* she thought, careful to keep her mind shielded. *And he doesn't know I am unbound, even though I am standing before him.* If the master thought that sending her to go work with the human slaves was punishment, then so be it. She perceived it as an opportunity to help the humans who had helped her. *If that is where they send the two humans.*

Acting appropriately chastened, Low Moon bowed her head even lower, letting her wings droop accordingly.

:Yes, master,: Low Moon said, with as much sadness as she could summon.

Chapter Ten

Reykir realized too late, that despite finding an apron and ridding himself of some of his finer clothing, his plan to blend anonymously with the rest of the kitchen staff had a major flaw.

He didn't speak Suinomese.

Soon after the invaders had herded the palace staff into the great hall, they began interviewing them in the kitchen. They were looking for someone, and that someone might very well be himself. He still had no idea where Alaire and Kai were, but he suspected they had been lured into some sort of trap, and were now being held captive somewhere. At any rate, the Arachnians would discover him as soon as they began asking whatever questions they had; unless he played an idiot. Which probably wouldn't work either, and would in fact attract more unwanted attention. Remaining invisible was becoming more difficult with each passing second.

How many Altheans can there be in this group? he wondered. Once they determined his nationality, it would only be a matter of time before they figured out what role he played in the Althean court.

I'm the assistant and student of a Prince of Althea, he thought morosely. *In other words, an excellent hostage.*

He looked for ways out of the great hall, but each

exit was covered by Arachnians. His only other hope had been to find allies in his fellow prisoners. But once they had learned he was from Althea, and therefore a foreigner, they quickly withdrew.

Three of the staff and Reykir were the next to go in; an Arachnia pushed them roughly into the kitchen's interior. Torches cast harsh light on a table where two Arachnians and one human sat. Guards stood on either side of them.

"So here's the little rat Alaire brought with him," came a loud voice from the table. " 'S about time we found him!"

Craig.

The prince sat between the two Arachnia, one large and impressive, with military decorations of some kind. The other was Su'Villtor. A large, opened jug of wine sat before Craig.

Now there's a surprise, thought Reykir. *Is there ever a time when that sot isn't drinking?*

Reykir observed something peculiar: a leather collar around Craig's neck similar to the one they'd found on Low Moon, complete with jewels and glittering stones. A thick aura of magic surrounded the collar, which Craig seemed oblivious to.

"I'll have you know, you little cockroach, that your master, Alaire, is safe and sound. *On another continent.* You, on the other hand, are in a much more dangerous position." He turned to Su'Villtor, whispered something, and the Arachnia replied in kind.

"Come with me," Craig said, venom dripping from his voice. "We have a very great deal to talk about! In private, of course." The Althean prince pulled a long sword from its sheath, and gestured toward Reykir. "After you, my little rat."

With the aid of two Arachnia guards, Craig led Reykir into the great hall, under the watchful glares of the remaining prisoners. He tried hard not to sneer at them; finally, with a sword at his back, he was able to show them that he *was* on their side all along.

The room they took him to was not the king's chamber, but very close to it, in proximity and furnishings. With a jug in one hand and the sword in the other, Craig took a seat behind a large, ornate desk and promptly propped his feet on it.

"You may leave," Craig said. "We must speak in private."

Evidently the guards spoke Althean, or had enough of a grasp to know when they were being dismissed. Reykir sat in a sturdy oak chair facing the desk. Behind Craig was a large bay window looking over the palace grounds, visible now in the early dawn.

"I will ask the questions, and you will answer them," Craig said, taking a long pull from the jug and putting it on the desk. He continued to hold the sword, but unsteadily. Reykir wondered if he might be able to jump him. "First," Craig said, wiping his mouth with the back of his sleeve. "Where is that thrice-damned harp of yours?"

"The harp?" Reykir answered, confused. "Well, it was lost at sea. Don't you remember?"

Craig looked pained, then annoyed. "Of course I do. That was Alaire's instrument we destroyed, not yours."

So they found and destroyed Alaire's harp, Reykir thought. *Not that he was in any position to use it.*

The boy resisted an urge to reach up and feel the wooden flute he still wore around his neck. Under the shirt it was invisible, and he wanted it to stay that way. *I can still make magic with it*, he thought. *If I had time to play a sleep spell before Craig impaled me with that sword, I would.*

"This decision to turn coat," Reykir said cautiously. "Is this something you planned on by yourself, or is this merely the collar around your neck speaking for you?"

Craig's face glazed over, as if he were staring at something behind Reykir. He opened his mouth to say something, then he smiled sardonically.

That collar is controlling him, Reykir guessed, seeing the faintest trace of a struggle in the prince's face. *He doesn't even know he has it on!*

"You know, you seem like a fairly intelligent boy," Craig said. Reykir winced inwardly at the word *boy,* but kept his irritation to himself. "If I remember correctly, you were once a street urchin, were you not?"

Reykir shrugged noncommittally. Clearly, Craig was intent on discussing anything but the new item of ornamentation the Arachnia had given him

Craig continued, "Why would a member of the royal family decide to take you under his wing, hmmm? Had it occurred to you that Alaire had his own private agenda when he took you on? That maybe he would want to use you, in some fashion, once you were a Bard?"

The boy considered the words carefully, then looked beyond them, to what he thought Craig was really trying to tell him. *Is he making me the same offer the traitors offered him?*

"I never really gave it much thought," Reykir said, doing his best to look uncertain. "Granted, I was a nothing when Alaire took me in. I had perhaps a little talent." He fixed Craig with what he hoped was a convincing look of suspicion. "I always wondered about that. Were there not other, more qualified youngsters of noble birth who also wished to study under him?"

"That is correct," Craig said, his face alight with success. "And he would have taken them on as students, had they been more, well, malleable? The sons of noblemen have strong families behind them, each with their own ambitions. You, on the other hand, had none. All you wanted was to be a Bard; you had no one of importance to fall back on."

Discussing his past in such demeaning terms angered Reykir more than he would ever admit, even if he weren't held captive by a traitor, in the middle of what was, so far, a completely successful coup.

If I look the stupid street child, he'll think he can use me, he thought. *Can he be that simple?* He glanced at the jug which, judging by the angle Craig held it to his face, was nearly dry. *Yes, I think he can be that simple. With the help of what used to be in that jug. What if the wine is making the collar's job that much easier?*

Craig shifted upright, setting the jug down loudly. "These warriors, who have not sailed but *flown* from a distant island, have overwhelmed the entire Suino-men army in less than a candlemark. The city of Rozinki doesn't even know what is going on, and when they learn of the invasion, what will they do against a race of giant Arachnians?"

Reykir pretended to consider this. "Probably not much. These Arachnians, given their size, could probably take on the entire armed population of Rozinki."

"Precisely," Craig said. "The army of Roksamur doesn't intend to stop here. Their goal is the entirety of the Lored Lands."

Feigning shock, the boy said, in a trembling voice, "You mean they're going to attack Althea?" He slumped back in the chair. "They're doomed," he said, in a weak voice.

"Yes, Althea is doomed. *But we are not.*"

Craig let that last bit hang in the air, apparently for dramatic effect. Reykir took his cue, "So what are you saying?"

"When they take Althea, they will put me in charge of the kingdom. I will have the *throne*, you silly boy. Do you know what that means?"

The boy summoned the most stupid look of confusion he was capable of.

Craig slapped his hand on the desktop, hard. The jug did a little jig before it came to a rest. "I will be the king. Perhaps I'm already the king. Galdur, the wizard, had been promised a position, but when Su'Villtor became aware of me, they eliminated him in favor of me. He's dead, like half the soldiers in the palace!"

He must be a fool if he trusts someone who turns so easily, he thought. He also found himself unable to grieve over the wizard; Reykir had distrusted him from the beginning.

"You have an opportunity to secure for yourself an important position in the new regime, if you play your cards just so."

Reykir folded his arms and studied Craig, whose glance wavered, from drink or exhaustion, or both.

"What guarantees do I have?"

"Guarantees?" Craig sounded amused. "Who said anything about guarantees? What I am offering, my little friend, is a place by my side if we succeed in taking Althea. To do that, we will need your help."

The spell must be clouding his thinking. If it isn't thinking for him, Reykir decided. "What do you want from me? I mean, what can I possibly provide for you?"

"You forget so soon," Craig said oilily. "What you are. Althea knows nothing about this little venture. Nothing!"

"Not yet. But soon. So tell me," Reykir said. "What did you have in mind for me to do?"

"You mean, we flew in on one of *those*?" Kai exclaimed, pointing at one of two wingrats perched at the end of a long tunnel.

"No, we each had one of our own," Alaire corrected.

"I don't think one could carry two humans. Not the distance these did."

Two Arachnian guards escorted them to the long, tall tunnel, saying nothing as they led them through a complicated network of tunnels and passages. The tunnels apparently made perfect sense to the natives, but left Alaire completely confused. Not that he would want to, but he doubted he could find the cell they had been in, much less the entrance where they had come in.

Their passage widened after a sharp turn and they suddenly found themselves facing the Queen of Roksamur in her throne chamber. From atop an elevated mound of polished stone she glared in the direction of the two humans with the usual unreadable Arachnian expression. She had to be the largest Arachnia Alaire had ever seen, even at this distance. She wore a long robe of purple, with a silver amulet hanging just over her thorax, but gave no indication that she'd noticed them yet. Yet, with her multifaceted eyes, he doubted she was missing anything.

Long icicles of rock hung from the ceiling and jutted up from the floor. On these was a thick coat of luminescent lichens, these being a deep, blood red. An unsettling color, Alaire had to admit, given the circumstances.

Standing on either side of the queen were two wingrats. Compared to the queen's massive size, they looked more like pets than guards. Each wingrat wore a gaudier version of the collar they had removed from Low Moon; remembering their friend back in Rozinki made him feel a little sad.

But when their escorts prodded them sharply, urging them towards the queen, Alaire began to feel a lot afraid.

I don't really want to have this conversation with the queen right now, Alaire thought. For a fleeting moment, he wondered if they were being offered as some exotic snack for her royal highness.

Alaire saw no purpose in having the wingrats there, unless it was to give a sense of perspective to the queen's size. They drew nearer the queen, who rotated her head slowly towards them. Another Arachnian appeared from behind a cluster of polished boulders, this one wearing a black robe covered with odd symbols which could only be magical runes.

Ah, Alaire thought. *An Arachnian wizard. The one who put the obedience spells on Low Moon? And all the others, for that matter.* Considering the number of wingrats he had seen pouring into the palace grounds before, his admiration for the wizard's abilities moved up a notch. *The power must be coming from somewhere.* He resisted an urge to probe for the powers then. Doing so would only alert the wizard.

"You will stop there," said the Arachnian wizard. Alaire didn't know if he should kneel or bow. He felt assured they would correct him if he did something wrong. "I will translate for the queen. She does not speak your filthy human tongue, and she never will." The words came out smooth and languid, more polished than Su'Villtor's had been.

Where in the worlds did he learn to speak Althean? This queen is starting to sound hostile already, and she hasn't even said anything, Alaire observed. He did his best to keep his face a solemn, emotionless mask.

The translator chittered something to the queen, who chittered something back.

"You are a prisoner of Queen Saurboar of Roksamur," the translator said. "You will refer to her as 'My Queen.' Is that understood?"

"Yes, your . . . " Alaire said. "Who did you say you were?"

"My name is not important," the translator replied. He sounded, despite his awkward accent, a bit annoyed.

Kai stepped forward a step and spoke directly at the queen, whom he had to look up to. "My *Queen*," Kai said, his words soaked in sarcasm. "I demand to know why you have invaded our land without a formal declaration of war! And why, my *Queen*, we have been taken hostage in this godsforsaken place!"

"Silence!" the translator said, stepping forward. He slapped Kai back with the flat of his claw.

Alaire caught him as Kai stumbled back and whispered frantically, "Kai, this is not the time to assert your authority!"

"Speak for yourself," Kai said softly, standing upright.

The translator said, "You will speak only when spoken to. And *when* you speak it is to be with the utmost respect."

"As much as I've been afforded, I'm sure," Kai said under his breath, but the translator apparently didn't hear him.

"Kai, I think you should reconsider your attitude," Alaire whispered, but the words didn't seem to be having any effect. Kai seemed determined to get them in deeper than they already were, if that was possible.

The two Arachnias chittered briefly.

"Which of you is the king of the humans?" the translator finally said.

The two humans looked at each other.

"What?" Kai asked.

"Which of you is king?" the translator repeated.

Kai stepped forward, cautiously. "I am Kainemonen, King of Suinomen, the country which you have so rudely invaded. The humans don't have a king . . ."

"Yes, we do," Alaire interrupted. "Kai, trust me," he whispered, out of the corner of his mouth. "Our king is rather modest," he continued. "He rules us all with such wisdom, he hesitates before taking full credit for his accomplishments."

"So," the Arachnia said. "*You* are the king. I might have known, given your lack of respect."

Kai shrugged, "If you had arranged a diplomatic visit instead of this absurd invasion and kidnapping, my behavior might have been a little different."

Alaire observed the queen, uncertain what kind of reactions, if any, he was looking for. Her large, bulbous head tilted, but with distinction and grace.

"The queen admires your bravery. May I remind you that you are here on our terms, not yours," the translator said, after a series of sharp clicks from the queen.

"What terms would those be?" Kai shot back.

"Ransom, of course," the translator said.

"What are you asking?" Alaire asked. "What is the ransom?"

If the Arachnia was pausing for effect, he could not have timed it better. "Your kingdom, of course."

Kai and Alaire looked at each other.

"Our queen is the hive mother. From her all life comes. We require a great deal of vegetation which, on our rocky land, is becoming scarce. We have multiplied fourfold in the times I remember and are in need of more land."

"Is *that* all?" Kai said incredulously, sounding a little relieved. At what, Alaire didn't know. "Well, in that case, we can work something out, I'm sure."

"Most excellent," the translator said. "Will you instruct your subjects to hand over your kingdom?"

Kai replied evenly, "No, I will not, but certainly . . ."

"It would seem," Alaire said conversationally. "That this race has not yet mastered the concept of *sharing.*"

"To the contrary," the translator replied. "We understand the concept of cooperation, but only with beings of equal stature. You *humans*," he said, in an acid tone, "are mere animals."

Alaire saw Kai's face turn red, but was grateful he didn't act on his anger. Thankfully, the king said nothing in reply.

"We have two more females of bearing age," the translator continued. "We intend to establish more hives. We will swarm throughout this world."

Two more egg layers? Good gods, Alaire thought. *We'd better stop this now, before they get really populated. Unless it's too late for that.*

"We will send you to the human colony on Roksamur," the translator said, and started moving them back away from the queen, towards the entrance. "There you will find food to your liking. Here, in the royal section of the island, we stock only for the hive."

"More humans?" Kai said. "Who do you . . ."

"The ships," Alaire reminded him. "The ones that have wrecked over the years. I knew they must be somewhere." Kai didn't reply.

"Some of the humans have become good slaves," the translator said. "The rest, we have eaten."

"That's good to know," Alaire said. Kai had turned white. *Perhaps he's finally seeing the depth of the trouble we are in.*

"The only path off Roksamur is by wingrat, and they will obey only us. If you attempt to escape, we will kill you. But I don't think you will have that opportunity."

I get the idea, Alaire thought. The other two guards appeared and directed them to yet another set of tunnels. These, Alaire noted hopefully, tended to angle up.

Fresh air was the first sign of liberation, at least so far as being kept underground was concerned. They left the royal "palace" from a completely different exit, this one opening on a small valley, with no sign of the vast plain of granite in sight. The sky was overcast with storm clouds, which was just as well, as his eyes were sensitive to the light. If it rained, it might even give them an informal shower. The Bard had noticed a ripe smell coming from them both, and a bath of any kind would be likely to help their morale.

Waiting for them was a crude cage on wheels, made of bars of the same stout timbers as their underground cell. The wheels were hewn from a solid piece of wood and mounted on an equally simple axle. Alaire groaned, anticipating an extremely bumpy ride. The two Arachnian drivers, each without armor but still formidable in appearance, instructed them to climb in through a door facing the front of the wagon. Before complying with this last command, Alaire studied the two beasts of burden who would be pulling this monstrosity. Giant rats, similar to a wingrat, but without wings. They were harnessed to the wagon with a crude yoke. Next to the driver's seat was a long pole with a sharp point on the end. *To get the rats moving*, Alaire figured.

The Arachnians said nothing more as they secured the door, and the driver prodded the beasts in front of them sharply, as anticipated. The wagon lurched forward, and both Alaire and Kai tumbled to the back of the cage. What might have been Arachnian laughter chittered from the translator, who stood in the road, watching them pull away.

"That knot doesn't look too hard to undo," Kai said. The Arachnians had tied the door shut with a length of rope.

Alaire considered. "They would see us the second we jumped out. I don't think we'd have a chance to get away."

Kai looked grim, and in that moment suddenly seemed ten years older.

"Besides, there's food and other people where we're going. It would be best to ask them about this island before we try to escape, don't you think?"

Kai didn't answer right away. He shifted around until he was cross-legged and looked relatively comfortable. "Why don't you use Bardic magic to get us out of here? Even without the harp, you can sing."

Alaire considered. "I suppose I could. Then what?" He looked outside at the dismal surroundings, devoid of any vegetation. "How long do you think we would last out there? And more important—how long would it take for a few of those Arachnians and their wingrats to see us? I see no cover anywhere."

Kai sighed. "I suppose you're right."

Alaire leaned against the back of the cage. "But that doesn't mean I won't use Bardic magic. If the right time happens along, I will use everything I have."

Chapter Eleven

"It will be quite simple," Craig informed him. "You shall be my lieutenant. You will carry to Silver City our ultimatum. The prince's ransom shall be his brother's kingdom."

"That's a clever plan," Reykir said, though he didn't see anything clever about it, at least for Craig. *But he's sending me to Silver City. I can warn them of what's going on.*

"You have a deal, Your Majesty," Reykir said. "Thank you for this opportunity to better myself. I am in your debt."

He got up and bowed, as deeply as he could, while stifling a peal of laughter that threatened to slip through his lips.

Craig looked ready to pass out. His eyes fluttered shut for a brief moment, then snapped open.

"Into that next room," he said, getting slowly to his feet. "I must meet with my colleagues."

"Aye," Reykir agreed. *It may take time to assure him of my "new loyalties." Better to cooperate than give my true intentions away.*

Reykir went willingly into what looked like a servant's room. It was a small room, with basic furniture. It must be some sort of study, he guessed, for the working class of the palace. Craig slammed the door shut behind him, and a sound which could

170

only have been his sword sliding through the door handle raked noisily. He had expected total darkness, but from a skylight three stories up morning light poured in.

The boy put his ear against the door, expecting to hear Craig's retreating footsteps. Instead, he heard his snores. Guessing by the direction his snoring was coming from, Craig had decided to take a nap on the floor just outside the door.

A quick survey of the room revealed no other doors or windows. A hole in the plaster towards the rear revealed that the walls were solid rock.

He tried the door, which didn't budge. However Craig had wedged that sword, the door was securely locked.

Craig's sleeping. I'm tired. Maybe I should do the same, he thought, and curled up on a wooden bench. For a while he listened to the Arachnians skitter through the palace, but after a while, the place was silent.

Calm now, Reykir let his mind wander, then urged it gently towards the sky.

He considered sending a message to Rak, but that would have required far more energy than he had at his disposal. A subtle contact would tell him much, and let him know where Rak was.

Reykir fell deeper into trance, drifting to the very edge of sleep. He thought his efforts would be for nothing, until, suddenly, he was free of his body and looking down on a forest from some great height.

The sensation was jarring, and when he had first tried it, the effect had been so disturbing it had shaken him from the trance. Practice had tempered his fear. Flight was a natural thing now, as he rode Rak's mind, seeing what the owl saw, feeling what she felt.

Coastline. She followed the line of sand south, the

only certain landmark she had, besides the winding dirt road that connected the two countries. Reykir realized her eyes were in pain, as she was flying in the daylight, an unnatural environment for a nocturnal beast. But she knew she had to carry her message home, to the human her master had directed her to. Exhaustion pulled deeply at her, and Reykir knew she would have to rest soon.

As long as she's alive, Reykir thought, relieved. He didn't know where exactly she was, but she was going in the right direction, at least. *There's still hope she'll make it.*

His let his thoughts drift, and his own exhaustion soon took over. Easing from Rak's mind, he fell deeper into his own darkness.

Despite the increasing sunlight, Alaire was getting colder. It was not as numbing as what he had felt in flight, but here, in the open cage, he was less protected from the force of the elements than he had been in the leather cocoon. The path their wheeled cage followed tended towards the high roads, and as they passed a half dozen valleys, it became clear that they were climbing higher into the Roksamur mountains.

Each jarring bump sent pain shooting from his tailbone through his spine. Kai had somehow managed to sleep during short intervals, but each major bump had roused him. Alaire hoped that the humans who lived at these altitudes would have appropriate clothing, and enough to share. The two Arachnian drivers, from what little they could see of them, didn't seem to be bothered by the cold, even though they didn't have the thick leather armor he'd seen on the invaders.

Kai stirred, then sat up. They were negotiating a particularly rough stretch of "road." *If anyone could sleep through this, they'd be dead,* Alaire thought. He moved around himself, to take some of the stress off his spine.

In front of them the rats plodded on like oxen, the Arachnia's sharp spear urging them up some of the steeper inclines.

"Any sign of where we're supposed to be going?" Kai asked groggily. He looked around him with the most extreme look of annoyance Alaire had ever seen on a person.

"Not yet," he replied. "But wherever we're going, it seems to be *up.* The air's getting thin again."

"The air's getting *cold,*" Kai corrected. He sniffed the air. "What is that smell?"

As they ascended the mountains, Alaire had noted thick fog—or clouds, more likely—and an unfamiliar acrid smell. They'd passed several hissing steam springs, which the Arachnians had carefully avoided. Alaire would rather have gone a little closer, to benefit from some of the warmth, but their captors had other ideas. He caught a few glimpses of the mountain peak ahead of them, and from its top spiraled thick gray smoke. He hadn't the first clue what caused the smoke, but he suspected that was the source of the smell.

"The mountain's on fire," Alaire replied without enthusiasm. "Hells, I don't know." He was getting grouchy, and he knew it. *Who wouldn't?*

Kai wasn't paying much attention to him; instead, he was glancing somewhat fearfully at the terrain outside. They were negotiating a particularly narrow stretch of road which ran along the edge of a steep slope. Down below, over the edge, was a small, rocky valley. The wheels of their wagon cleared the edge by a hand's length.

While taking in their precarious situation, Alaire felt a tugging on the edge of his mind, as if someone, or something, were trying to contact him.

Throwing caution to the wind, he dropped his mental shields and opened his mind to whatever was trying to reach him. As soon as their minds met, he knew who it was.

Low Moon.

The rear of their cage gave him a view of a ridge of hills they had just passed through. Above these, in a layer of cloud, Alaire saw the vague shape of a wingrat kiting in behind them.

Kai looked where Alaire had, squinting to see what was so interesting. His eyes widened suddenly.

"*Quiet,*" Alaire whispered. "It's Low Moon."

"Who?"

Alaire was watching her sail towards them. "A friend." Her presence here was welcome, if somewhat bewildering. The Bard reached through the thin cloud cover with his mind, probed tentatively. *:We're captured. Taken from our home. Help us?:*

Low Moon sent back an affirmative. *:Wait. Must distract Arachnians.:* Then, stronger, *:I carry weapons.:*

Which is what we both need right now, Alaire thought to himself. *The weapons had better be big ones, to deal with these two.*

Alaire watched in silence as the wingrat glided towards them. Beneath her she carried a long sack, like the ones used to kidnap them from Rozinki. The wagon continued to trundle on, and its driver, given the lack of Arachnian speech coming from up there, had evidently not seen Low Moon. Yet.

Low Moon released the sack moments before sailing over them. *No,* Alaire thought, as the bag struck the side of the valley, and began rolling downwards, out of sight. From the resounding *clank* that came from within, he could tell it held swords. And they had fallen where he could not reach them easily.

Alaire had only a moment to consider this before Low Moon "distracted" the drivers.

A piercing Arachnian scream shattered the relative silence. The wagon slammed to a sudden halt, and Kai and Alaire slid forward, to the front door. Amid Low Moon's powerful backflapping, and the raging scream of the Arachnians, Alaire caught sight of what had happened. Low Moon hovered above an Arachnian, writhing in agony, apparently blinded. Gray matter dribbled from one eye. The Bard saw how the shimmering surface of the Arachnian eye would make an excellent target for an aerial hunter.

The rats pulling the cart began to panic. A wingrat flapping wildly overhead was apparently not something they were accustomed to. The yokes harnessing them to the wagon didn't allow for much peripheral vision, so when they tried to look around, the entire wagon shuddered.

"Alaire, we're about to . . . " Kai began. Then he saw what they were about to do.

The wagon rocked back and forth as the rats reared up, emitting their own dull roar, which vibrated through the entire cage; Low Moon backed off from her attack and soared off. Hovering like that, Alaire suspected, took a lot of energy. But in that short span of time, she had apparently done precisely what was needed.

The injured Arachnia continued to scream, while the other tried in vain to get the beasts pulling the wagon to calm down. The rats seemed determined to panic, and their fear apparently overrode whatever training they had. The rocking motion increased, and Alaire felt a wheel slip off the edge of the road. Slowly, the entire wagon, rats and all, tumbled into the valley.

"*Hold on!*" Alaire screamed, but it was useless advice.

They tumbled over each other as the wagon bounced down the valley. In one moment, he was looking at sky. The next, he was face to face with an Arachnia as the cage rolled over it, the ruined, rounded eyes poking through the bars. Then he heard a loud *craaack*, as the wagon shattered. Amid the splintered debris, Alaire rolled, and came to a rest against a large boulder. Then everything was silent.

For some time Alaire lay stunned, the sharp edge of the boulder jabbing him sharply in the back. It was this immediate pain he reacted to; awkwardly, he rolled over onto wagon wreckage, which was worse.

He heard something moving nearby, but he didn't know if this was Kai or an Arachnia. Then, a muffled groan, which could only have come from a human.

Above, Low Moon flapped and then landed nearby. *Clank clank drag. Clank clank . . . draaaag.* Alaire looked up, and saw that Low Moon was dragging the swords over to him. *There's an Arachnia or two around here. Where—*

Then he saw where. Rising from under one of the big wagon wheels, an Arachnia checked itself for damage.

Alaire grabbed the sword, his first reflex. Then he wondered if it were even *possible* for a human to slay an Arachnia.

As he hefted the sword, he looked around for Kai, who was lying still, too still, some distance away.

:Battle. Now!: Low Moon shouted, and took to the air. No time to check on Kai. The Arachnia standing was not the one with the damaged eyes.

Too bad, he thought. *Where is the other one?*

Alaire and the standing Arachnia squared off. The Bard noticed that this Arachnia hadn't escaped injury either. Its right claw tilted at an angle, probably broken. *Good. Now maybe we'll be even.*

Alaire held the sword up and charged the Arachnia. Not as quickly as he would have liked, but it was apparently not the reaction the Arachnia was expecting.

The creature neatly deflected the blade with its remaining claw, but didn't press the attack. Alaire stepped back and reassessed the situation, just in time for Low Moon to strike again.

Again, she came in from behind, and Alaire guessed this was an Arachnian blind spot the wingrats knew of. He raised his sword again, mostly as a distraction, and backed away to his right. A moment later, Low Moon hit, this time without as much success; the large insect staggered but remained upright. One of its legs appeared to be injured or broken, as it favored the other. Alaire searched for an opening.

I wish I knew what was vulnerable in these thrice-damned things, Alaire thought as he dodged the creature's claws. He had never been on the opposing side of one in a fight. Nor, before this trip to Rozinki, had he expected to. He struck, then struck again, his blade glancing off the thick shell. *That's not going to work,* Alaire thought, and he began considering an all-out retreat.

I'm never going to get a better chance . . . he thought, quickly discounting the notion of withdrawal. *If we leave this bug behind, he will only notify the others as to what happened.*

Behind some wagon debris Alaire saw movement, followed by the glint of a blade.

Kai? Alaire thought, and watched as his friend tried to get to his feet, using the blade as a crutch.

The insect whirled around, apparently alerted by the sounds behind him. Low Moon circled, high above.

:*Attack. Again?*: Alaire sent, but the wingrat didn't reply. *Probably preoccupied at this point,* he thought, looking again at the unsteady insect, which continued to regard the two humans as if they were a very real threat. *It probably has no idea how banged up Kai is,* Alaire thought. *If I can turn that to our advantage . . .*

Low Moon dove, and in the instant her shadow passed over the Arachnia, it turned to face her.

The wingrat's two rear claws swiped at the Arachnia's face, one of them connecting with a multifaceted eye. The insect screamed, its claws waving wildly at the air. Low Moon hovered momentarily, struck again, missed, then flew off.

Before the bug could turn around, Alaire struck with his sword, hard. This time his blow had enough force to topple it over. It fell sideways, writhing in a cloud of dust.

"Kai, strike it!" Alaire called out. Kai made a few steps forward until it was within striking range.

The Arachnia rolled towards Kai, who released his raised blade. The blow missed the creature's head altogether, blade sinking into the ground.

Alaire ran around to the other side, failing to negotiate around the injured claw with enough clearance; it struck out with amazing swiftness, and closed around his ankle.

The Bard screamed as the pinchers closed around his leg; he had no choice, he had to kill this thing now, or he was going to die from a severed foot.

He hacked madly at the Arachnian's head, connecting with the large eyes with a gratifying *splootch*; his blade, as he withdrew it, dripped with more of the gray goo.

The creature shrieked again, and the Bard was certain his foot was about to be snapped off at the ankle. He struck at the beast's head. Blade and shell met; shell cracked, then blade penetrated. Leaning with all his weight, he pushed, and with a smooth, sliding motion, the blade sank completely into the Arachnia's head.

Alaire rolled off, now aware that the claw had released his foot. *Now, for some distance between us,* he thought, crawling away from it.

The Arachnia still lay squirming, its claws and body quivering, making no apparent effort to remove the blade from its head. Soon the motion ceased altogether, except for an occasional, random spasm.

Alaire's chest was heaving in the thin air. He felt light-headed, now that the immediate danger was past. Kai lay nearby, apparently suffering from the altitude as well.

"Thing looks dead," Kai managed to gasp. He lay on his back, but had looked over towards the creature, then got up on his side. "What about the other one?"

"There were two of them, weren't there?" He saw no motion as his eyes tracked across the wagon wreckage. Then his eyes fell on the other insect, unmoving, evidently dead, pinned beneath the debris.

Low Moon backflapped into a landing near the wreckage, and after studying the other Arachnia for a moment, loped over to Alaire.

:*We must leave, now. Others will come soon.*:

The Bard nodded, but not liking the prospect of negotiating this terrain with damaged bodies.

"Kai. Kai?" Alaire called.

The king had managed to get to his feet, and hobbled slowly in a wide circle around the Arachnia. He was bleeding, but not as badly as it had first seemed.

"*Now* we can make our escape," Alaire said. "And we'd better get moving before they start wondering what happened to these two."

The sound of the sword sliding from the door handle woke Reykir abruptly; the door swung open, and Craig stood, framed in the doorway, holding the sword to one side. He looked as though he'd just awakened.

"*There* you are," Craig said.

Reykir sat up on the wooden bench, uncertain of Craig's mental state. *Either drunk or sober. Most likely somewhere in between.*

"This way," Craig said, waving the sword.

"As you wish," Reykir said, yawning. In spite of having slept on a hard bench, he felt renewed. He doubted Craig felt the same way, given his bloodshot eyes.

Their destination was the palace grounds near the front gate. There Reykir found a large, healthy looking dieren loaded down with supplies. The rest of the place was aswarm with Arachnian soldiers, resting, eating the vegetation, poking about what had to be an alien environment to them: a human palace. The wingrats, hundreds if not thousands of them, were gathered sedately on a nearby hill.

"Go to Derek and inform him that we will kill Alaire if he doesn't surrender his lands," Craig said. "I hope I can trust you, little rat. However, if you do turn, I will simply kill you when we take Silver City by force."

"Your *Majesty*," Reykir said, looking hurt. "I have every intention of remaining loyal to you. I have little to gain by helping Derek and everything to gain by throwing in with you." Reykir shrugged, a gesture of acceptance. "But I suppose it will take time to convince you. Time, of course, will tell."

"Very well," Craig said, with a wry grin. "Perhaps you do see the truth, after all." He looked up at the dieren. "Ride hard, my little rat. I shall see you when we invade our former home."

Reykir bowed before Craig again, this time a little stunned that the man was actually going to let him ride out of here. *The bespelled collar must make him think he is so powerful he can turn loyalties with ease.*

From atop the tall riding beast he looked down on Craig, who looked every bit the part of a man who thought he was in complete control of the situation.

Evidently so . . .

The reality, Reykir knew, was that he was a drunk making a drastic mistake.

Chapter Twelve

Rak stirred briefly under the healing spell's power, stretched, and struggled to her feet. With obvious gratitude, the owl accepted the bit of meat offered by the court wizard, Nechtan, and gobbled it down hungrily.

King Derek sighed with relief. *Perhaps this creature's flight wasn't for naught, after all.*

There was little the wizard and king could do now, except nurse the owl back to health through mundane means; the remains of supper's turkey carcass sat on a silver plate near the owl's new bed, a small wine keg that had been sawed in two and lined with pelts of fox fur. Outside, a thunderstorm raged, as it had for the last day and a half, shaking the shutters with each peal of thunder. Althea's drought had broken with a vengeance.

No small miracle this owl managed to fly through this storm, the king thought. At first, the owl's return had astonished the King, as soon as he recognized who it belonged to. Then, as the implications of Rak's arrival hit him, the king began to worry. *My brothers were at sea during this storm,* he couldn't stop thinking. *And now, this owl, who was on the ship with them . . .*

As soon as she had arrived, Rak collapsed in the wizard's hands. Nechtan had immediately brought the shivering, soaked creature down here to his workshop and began the healing spells which had revived her.

"Can she tell us what happened, do you think?" the king asked impatiently.

"Perhaps," Nechtan said, scratching his long gray beard thoughtfully. "This youth, Reykir. He didn't bespell her in any way, did he?"

Derek considered this a moment, then shook his head. "I don't believe so. They communicated without words, or so Alaire told me. Reykir was an apprentice, but hadn't been granted full Bard status. Alaire would never let his students practice the art unless he knew for certain they knew what they were doing."

The old wizard gazed at the bird evenly, and for several long moments said nothing. Rak didn't appear to be paying any attention to this human's attempt at communication, but then the king knew this didn't always mean much.

Slowly, Nechtan's face fell from a mask of concentration to an expression of sorrow, or fear. *Dammit all, why doesn't he tell me what he sees?* Yet the king knew that to hurry the wizard might require that he start over from the beginning.

"Sire," Nechtan said, after a long, painful pause. "This is . . . disturbing."

"*What?*" the king demanded.

"The ship sank at sea. The only survivors were your brothers, and the apprentice Reykir. And, of course, this owl."

The king exhaled a sigh of relief. "The Arachnians are excellent seamen. But, alas, they cannot swim very well. What became of Alaire?"

The wizard had returned his attention to the owl, and carefully scratched under her chin. "They encountered traders, who gave them transportation to Rozinki. I saw images of King Kainemonen and his palace, the guest rooms they'd provided our emissaries."

The king noted he'd avoided the use of the word "ambassador." *He must know I still grieve over Ambassador Erikson.* "If they made it safely to Rozinki," the king said, "then why did they send Rak back to us?"

"After their arrival, the palace was invaded," Nechtan said solemnly.

"Bandits?" the king asked, but he knew there were no bands out there powerful enough to overthrow a *kingdom.*

"Not . . . exactly," the wizard replied. "This is going to be rather difficult to believe, but I assure you, this bird saw what she saw. The invasion was carried out by an army of Arachnians."

Derek looked down at the owl, who had begun to doze. "That *is* surprising," he replied, remembering how peaceful the Arachnians tended to be. Granted, they would protect their hive if called for, but he did not see how an invasion of Rozinki would help them. "Why in the world would they want human lands?"

"You are assuming, Sire, that the Arachnians in question are ones we are already familiar with. From the images this bird gave me, I don't believe this to be the case."

Derek frowned. "Go on."

"This is another race of Arachnians. They are larger than the ones we know of."

The king was getting impatient, and he no longer cared if it showed. "And?"

"Their mounts were flying creatures," the wizard said. The king stared at him. "The invading force was a swarm of these creatures. Furred animals, with wings."

"Flying?" The king couldn't believe it.

"The owl doesn't lie," the wizard insisted. "Within a night, they conquered Rozinki. They're not just under attack, Sire, the palace has *fallen.*"

"Gods," the king replied, hiding his face in his hands.

"There must be another reason," he said, to no one in particular.

"They sent the owl to warn us."

The words hung heavily in the air, and the king's eyes narrowed.

"The images, the wave of flying creatures, the armed Arachnians in armor," Nechtan continued. "They may not stop in Rozinki. We may be next."

"It doesn't matter if they attack us or not," the king said. "Suinomen is our ally. We must come to her defense, send forces to Rozinki. If nothing else we need to find out *what is going on*. Gods, what a mess!"

"A general alert throughout the kingdom might be in order," the wizard offered carefully. "Until we know more."

Derek nodded. "Yes, of course. And it sounds as if these *flying* invaders might be formidable opponents indeed."

Since Low Moon's successful raid to free them, Alaire and Kai had followed a barren, rocky valley. Kai's injuries were painful, but mostly bruises with no broken bones. Alaire wasn't so lucky. His ankle had swollen considerably, and he was unsure if the bone was broken, or if his ankle was just sprained. Either way, it was painful going, even with the piece of splintered timber he used as a walking stick. He might have tried a healing spell, but he was uncertain if the magicians on this island were sensitive enough to detect it; the relief wasn't worth the risk of giving away their location.

The wingrat had pointed them in the general direction of the human settlement, which was not very far away; she had waited until they were almost there before attacking, to make the distance they would have to cover shorter. Her plan had been to hide the wagon and release the rats. The former had been taken care of when the wagon crashed into a thousand pieces, which was *not* part of the plan. The beasts of burden who had been pulling the wagon had been turned loose from their yokes and were free; Low Moon communicated with them with a series of whistles and grunts. Whatever they were saying, it didn't sound as though it was very complicated. Though related, the wingrat was clearly the more intelligent of the two species.

Low Moon had returned to her masters, after explaining to Alaire that she thought she could trick the ruling Arachnians into thinking she was still bespelled with obedience magic, using a plain collar as cover. Her only choice, she had explained, was to blend in with her brethren, or else she would be discovered. Before leaving, she reassured them that she would see them soon, as she had been reassigned to Fastur, the human colony, as punishment for her poor performance during her reconnaissance of Suinomen.

The locals expected them and would meet them at the edge of the settlement. Low Moon had apparently set this up beforehand, but before Alaire could probe for details, she had bid them farewell and taken to the sky.

"That must be the human colony," Kai said once they had cleared the top of a ridge. "Low Moon was right."

Alaire gritted his teeth against the pain in his foot. Down below, in a shallow valley, he saw a small village.

Humans.

There were roughly thirty mud-and-stone homes, roofed with thatch. A handful of emaciated cattle, sheep and goats huddled together in a fenced-in area. Alaire and Kai stood near the edge of a large field of an unknown crop. Ten or so people were working the field, with little more than simple sticks.

Beyond the village, on a hill that overlooked it, was another group of buildings, which at first looked like large boulders. Then an Arachnia left one, and Alaire realized they were mud structures, like giant wasp nests.

"More of the damned bugs, over there," Kai pointed out. To the right of the cluster there was another wasp nest, taller and pointed, vaguely resembling a church. The Arachnians milling about wore black robes. A *religious temple?* Even though the Arachnians Alaire knew back home had always been a bit mysterious, it was difficult to imagine *this* particular tribe as having anything as introspective as a religion.

"Well, what now?" Kai asked. "Should we wait until the welcoming committee arrives, or do we march in and present ourselves?"

"Good question," Alaire said as he eased himself down on the ground. The Bard noted that Kai was very much in charge in his own kingdom, but once they were both beyond it, he deferred the decision making to Alaire. For the time being he was content just to take the weight off his ankle, and postpone any decision making for some future time.

A shadow crossed over them. Alaire turned to see what had stepped in front of the sun, and saw the outline of someone silhouetted brightly by an orange halo.

The two regarded the newcomer with bemused interest; though not sure who this was, Alaire felt no threat from this apparition. For one thing, it was human. For another, it was small.

As the boy came closer, Alaire made out features. Yes, a boy, perhaps fourteen, with long matted hair reaching down to his chest. He wore a crude tunic made of skins, and boots that had been sewn together from coarse leather strips. He looked wary, but for the most part seemed unafraid of them.

"This looks like our contact," Alaire said, getting to his feet. The boy said nothing, simply gestured for them to follow him.

The boy led them past the fields, paying little heed to their injuries. They struggled to keep up, and at times, the best they could do was to simply keep him in sight. Alaire saw the workers were dressed in the same coarse leather tunics, and as they hobbled and limped past, some of the workers looked up. Just as soon as they spied the two newcomers, they cast nervous glances back towards the Arachnians' camp, which was not quite visible here in the humans' village.

They must know what's going on, Alaire speculated, but there really wasn't enough to go on.

Soon, they came to a mud hut, larger than and set apart from the others. The boy pushed aside the hide covering the door, and led them in.

A small fire in the center of the hut pierced the darkness within. As his eyes adjusted, Alaire became aware of others sitting around the fire, some visible in the orange light, some lurking quietly in the shadows. One of the figures tossed a branch onto the fire, and a bright flame plumed, fully illuminating the hut's interior. The sudden heat felt good, reminding him how cold he had been outside.

The old men numbered eight, Alaire guessed, as his eyes passed from one to the other. They all stared at him and Kai with an intensity which at first felt like anger. Then, as the moments passed, and no one had spoken, the looks seemed to change to admiration. They wore the same leather tunics as the others they had seen, these trimmed with fur, with stones and bones woven into their hair and hanging around their necks on thongs. Each had a long beard, in varying shades of gray. Alaire shifted his weight on his leg momentarily, and moaned when his ankle throbbed.

:Please, sit. You are guests.:

The sudden message thundered in Alaire's mind; Kai had apparently heard it also, given his surprised expression.

"Give me a hand, would you?" Alaire said, dropping the stick. Kainemonen helped ease him down on a thick pallet of furs situated against one of the walls.

One of the men, who had been sitting in the center of the group, came over to Alaire and examined his ankle. He wore more ornamentation than the rest, with an intricate pattern of woven bones in his tunic. From the deferential stance of the rest, Alaire guessed this to be the leader of the group, perhaps of the entire village.

"Rest," the leader said. "I will heal this leg." Alaire was so stunned by his use of Althean that he forgot to reply. And there was something about the man's demeanor that put him immediately at ease.

The elder went to work, first by removing the boot, which came off with extreme difficulty. *I'd like to know what they think they can do to heal this!* he wanted to scream.

"An Arachnian claw," Kai supplied, as the elder briefly studied the marks on the boot.

"So we've been told," the elder said. "You will both be quiet now. Do not interrupt."

The elder placed his hands directly on the swollen ankle. Alaire flinched. With a warning look from the elder, he forced himself to relax. The old man closed his eyes, and, in moments, a warmth spread from the hands to the ankle. At first, the pressure felt like he was squeezing the sprain, but when Alaire looked down, he saw that the swelling was shrinking and that the direct pressure from the elder's hands was only slight. Filaments of light danced through his fingers.

This man is a healer, Alaire thought, pleasantly surprised. *His work shouldn't attract unwanted attention. They must be used to him by now.*

Though tender, Alaire's ankle quickly felt better. He was even tempted to put some weight on it to test it, but the elder gave him a severe look, as if he knew what Alaire was contemplating.

"Later," the elder said. "It still needs rest." The old man sat back and crossed his legs with a fluid, graceful motion. "My name is Konnongur and I am high priest of Fastur, the human colony you have found yourself in."

"Thank you, Konnongur," Alaire managed. "This is Kainemonen, King of Suinomen. And I am Alaire, Prince of Althea."

Konnongur nodded slightly; though a small gesture, it carried with it the full dignity of a deep bow. "So our friend has told us."

"Low Moon? The wingrat?" Alaire ventured.

"The same," Konnongur said. Then, with a distant, sort of whimsical look, added, "Althea. The kingdom of my ancestors."

Konnongur seemed to be waiting for a response. "Your people," Alaire started. "In this place, Fastur. Did you come from our lands?"

"Long, long ago," Konnongur said. "In ships which had the misfortune to stray near Roksamur. The island is surrounded by massive reefs, too numerous and expansive for any ship to navigate safely. The sea is always rough, as we are in the direct path of a major current. Most perished in the reefs, but a few, a very few, made it safely to shore."

Kai looked like he was having trouble getting comfortable in the furs. "My kingdom has been invaded by these Arachnia," Kai said. "Mounted on the wingrats. Is there any way to defeat them?"

Konnongur shrugged. "They are an impressive force,

the combination of weapon-bearing Arachnians and flying beasts. Once they mastered the wingrat mutations, they worked spells to control their mounts. If there is a weakness, it would be in those spells."

"Impressive, and fearsome," the elder continued. "Amber would have been impressed with their progress."

"You remember King Amber?" Alaire blurted, and immediately realized the foolishness in such a statement.

"No, no, young one. My *ancestor*, King Amber."

As the statement dangled in the air, the implications sunk in.

"You are related to Amber?"

Then, *we are related to each other.*

Through the thick beard and long hair, he saw the family resemblance. The eyes, in particular, reminded him of his father's.

"Amber's nephew, Duke Fionbharr, was exploring the northern coast of Suinomen. His ship encountered a storm, which swept the vessel off course and blew it to Roksamur." Konnongur's eyes gleamed, as if he were recalling personal history, instead of relating the story of an ancestor. "In the confusion of the storm he thought he was approaching Althea and set a course directly for its shores. When he struck the first of the reefs, it was too late for him to turn back. He lost half his crew, and those who survived did so by clinging to wreckage as it washed ashore."

The story sounded familiar; Alaire wondered how different his own fate might have been if he had landed on Roksamur instead of Suinomen when their ship wrecked.

"What of the other people here?" Alaire asked. "Are they subjects of Althea and Suinomen?"

"Alaire, that means—" Kainemonen began, then cut himself off.

"That is correct," Konnongur replied. "Of course, we're not all descended from royalty. Most who landed here were common folk, sailors who managed to swim ashore."

Kainemonen shook his head. "All those vessels, reportedly lost at sea. All perished, it was assumed. For centuries?"

"We've . . . lost track of time, here in Fastur. Four generations, at least, I can account for."

"Amber was a long time ago," Alaire said, remembering the long tales his own father would tell them of the royal line.

The others remained silent during the entire discussion, though one seemed to be getting restless. He looked as though he wanted to say something, but seemed unwilling to interrupt the high priest.

"Your father is now King of Althea?" Konnongur asked Alaire.

"My brother, Derek. My father passed away some years ago and passed the crown on to his eldest son." Alaire managed a laugh. "I never wanted to rule. I always wanted to be a Bard." Alaire mentioned this last reluctantly, unsure what connotations the word *Bard* had assumed here in the last few centuries.

"A *Bard*," Konnongur said, sounding awestruck.

"See!" the restless one finally blurted out. "There it is! The *prophecy*."

The others murmured excitedly, and Alaire had the uncomfortable feeling that somehow he and Kai were associated with this new revelation.

"The prophecy," Konnongur said, "has been told for generations." He said it as if this were some childish story, something which mature adults would not indulge in. "Humans and beasts alike, the winged beasts who brought you here, we are all slaves of the Arachs. Or, in the old tongue, Ar-*ach*-nee-ans."

"*Slaves*," Kai spat. "Why doesn't that surprise me?"

"So what does this prophecy have to do with our present circumstance?" Alaire asked. He flexed his ankle, and was amazed by the lack of pain.

"Everything. Or, perhaps, nothing. I am not as firm a believer in the prophecy as the others," Konnongur said, with an air of apology. "I've become complacent in my old age, having lived an entire lifetime under the Arachs. Their treatment of us has improved over the years, since they began making the flying beasts."

"Wingrats," Alaire supplied. "I call them wingrats. We've never seen them before. When did they start 'making' them?"

Konnongur stared off at something that wasn't in the hut. "When I was a young man," he supplied. "Many, many moons ago."

"And *prophecy*," Kai said, steering the conversation back.

"The prophecy tells of the day of our liberation," Konnongur continued. "We are to be freed one day, by a human from the old land, a human magician."

The group murmured their excitement, whispering to one another, casting hopeful, nearly worshiping looks towards Alaire.

"A human . . . *Bard*."

The murmuring grew, until a low chant began. Konnongur looked annoyed and waved them to silence.

I don't believe this, Alaire thought. *First I go to bed, then an invasion wakes me up, then a wizard trainee pops me in the behind with a drugged dart. I'm flown by a flying rat across the sea in a trail bag. And now I'm someone's idea of a hero.* He looked at the others, who had a look of conviction in their eyes, an expression which made him shiver.

"You are a magician, are you not?" Konnongur asked.

"Well, yes," Alaire began, looking down. "But I have no means to harness it."

"You do have your voice," Kai said, and Alaire gave him a look which apparently cut off everything else the king was about to say.

Konnongur continued, "The prophecy describes the breaking of the magic which keeps the beasts enslaved. We have, to a lesser degree, the same spell placed on all of us. If an Arach commands us to do something, the spell makes it difficult to *not* do it."

"How does this prophecy say to accomplish this?" Alaire asked. He tested his ankle again by slowly crossing his legs, first one, then the other, tucking them carefully. He felt a slight twinge of pain, but no more. "Or rather, how does this magic work? Certainly you understand some of it, as you have just healed my ankle, and remarkably well. Where does their power come from?"

"Their power," Konnongur said, with a touch of sadness, "is ground energy, earth energy. They track the ley lines from the flowing mountains, and it gathers in the valley. They protect it, under their temples. I am not strong enough to control much of it."

"What of the others?" Kai said, gesturing towards the others in the room. "Do they have the gift?"

"Some, to a lesser degree," the priest admitted. "But the Arachs have the temples guarded. Only a magician, a true magician, can break through the barriers."

The others grunted in agreement, nodding. Alaire was beginning to see where this was leading. He wanted a private conference with Kai, but he was afraid that requesting one might be an insult; after all, these people were risking all by hiding them.

"Uh, Alaire," Kai said. "Something just occurred to me. If this is where we were being taken anyway, what purpose did Low Moon's raid serve?"

Alaire had been wondering that himself, even though killing the Arachnians had been rather gratifying.

"That deserves an answer," Konnongur said. "The raid you speak of was my doing. The Arachs were going to imprison you in a separate building, a place reserved for humans who have not surrendered to their will."

"A prison," Alaire supplied. "Much like the one we just left, I suspect."

"Indeed," Konnongur replied. "They will tell you that they want to keep you from escaping. The truth is, the Arachs cannot tell one human from another. Keeping you separated like that is their only way of knowing your precise location."

Kai scratched his head thoughtfully. "Now *that's* useful information," he said. "In what way, I'm not entirely sure yet."

The boy who had led them to this hut came bursting into the room. The rest of the elders didn't pay attention to him but Konnongur slowly looked up.

"Arachs. Searching the village," their guide said, out of breath. "They're looking for . . . them." He pointed at Alaire and Kai.

The high priest slowly stood and gestured for Alaire and Kai to do the same.

"This was inevitable. We have made the appropriate plans," the elder said calmly.

The elders dressed their charges in native clothing and burned the civilized garb they had worn into town. Even the stick from the smashed wagon that Alaire had used as a cane went into the fire. It was no longer needed for his injury, and it would, according to Konnongur, betray them immediately.

"To the fields," Konnongur said brightly. "We have plowing to do, as it is. They'll never think to look for you out there."

Chapter Thirteen

Captain at arms Sir Romont responded to the call like the true professional he is, King Derek thought from atop his riding mare. *And that's a good thing, as we have made the Suinomen border in record time.*

The scout had arrived with the news that the border was a mere stone's throw away, and was unguarded as it had been for many years. Derek had hoped to find a Suinomese soldier to confirm the information Rakvel had provided, but it didn't matter. He trusted Nechtan's ability to draw the truth from animals' minds, and the wizard had made it quite clear that what he saw was a very real threat.

The day after Rakvel's arrival, an entire army had been assembled, and although Romont had done so in haste, the results were more than satisfactory. The king had decided to take the potential threat from the air seriously, and had requested over a thousand archers to complement their division of foot soldiers. Not knowing if they would have to breach the walls of Rozinki once they had arrived, Romont had recommended fifteen cannon to travel with the army. For the most part, the weather had held, another favorable omen for the venture. They used the road that wove above the seashore along a series of cliffs, the scent of the ocean blowing over them with a cool sea breeze. Now the army passed quietly into Suinomen without incident.

Rumors had passed throughout the army that they were en route to combat dragons, and the king had put an end to that by making an announcement the night before in a valley where they had set up camp. As he wasn't sure what they would be fighting, he didn't want to make light of the opponent. Captain Romont assured him that no matter what they found camped in Rozinki, they were prepared to fight with everything they had.

The captain rode alongside the king, with a division of cavalry, armed and armored, leading the way. Romont was commenting on the lack of wild game on their route, when the king heard a commotion some distance ahead of them. King Derek ordered the army to halt, and the captain rode ahead, to see what was going on.

Battle already, the king thought, drawing his sword. *If this is where they want to engage, then so be it!*

Yet the commotion didn't erupt into sounds of battle; instead, he heard what might have been celebration. Then Romont appeared with a dieren-mounted youth, a boy who looked familiar.

Reykir! the king thought, sheathing his sword.

The boy rode up to the king, dismounted, and bowed. "Sire," Reykir said. "I bear news of your brothers, Alaire and Craig." He said this last with a bit of trepidation, as if it might be bad news.

"Captain," the king said to Romont as he climbed off of his tall horse. "I propose a rest, here. It is midday, after all."

"Indeed," Romont said, "This is likely the best place we'll find for some time." The captain rode off to inform his army to make itself comfortable while the king and Reykir sought a private place to talk.

A short distance from the main road was a trickling spring. Beyond this was a grove of trees, within which the king took a seat on a felled oak.

"Your brothers live," Reykir said, evidently unable to hold the good news in. "Did Rakvel survive the voyage to your court?"

"Indeed she did," the king replied, loosening his boots. "She is safe and sound, recovering in Nechtan's workroom. For the distance she must have traveled, she was in remarkably good shape."

The boy looked relieved, but seemed unwilling to sit in the king's presence. Derek noticed this. "Please, rest. Tell me the whole story. Come, there's enough room on this trunk for the two of us."

The boy's hesitation reminded the king of the youth's background. It hadn't occurred to him that Reykir might not feel equal enough to sit with a king, having lived the life of a street urchin. Timidly, the boy took the king up on his offer.

"Then you understood Rakvel?" the boy said after a pause.

"Indeed," the king said. "Disturbing news of the fall of Rozinki. Brought on by the unlikely combination of flying rats and Arachnia."

The king let his eyes wander to the line of foot soldiers, who were taking advantage of the creek upstream from the horses. It had been a hot day, but nothing like the searing weather Althea had experienced earlier this month. The storm had broken the drought as well as the endless heat, but may have, the king mused, introduced another complication to their lives. *Did these invaders ride the storm in, like migrating geese?*

"It is true," Reykir said, meeting the king's eyes. "I saw them myself when they attacked the palace. Large beasts, larger than horses, with broad wings the length of a house. Arachnia rode them like we ride horses, and they were armed with arrows and spears. They took the palace before sunrise. Nobody was prepared."

The king nodded, knowing that had they chosen Silver City as their target, their fate would have probably been identical. *Who would have expected an attack from the air?* The situation might have been amusing, had the consequences of the attack been any less grim to their brothers in the north.

"So tell me, young friend," the king asked amiably. "Where do these mysterious foes come from? Certainly we would have known of them had they lived on our lands."

"True, we would have," the boy replied. "But they are not from our lands." He glanced back over the road, towards the ocean, where a thin sliver of blue was visible on the horizon. "They are from other lands, across the sea."

The king kept his face emotionless, while suppressing a little shiver of fear. Myths from his own youth, told by his father, Reynard, came flooding back to the present. *Perhaps they were not myths at all,* he thought, remembering the seafaring tales of delirious sailors, men who had seen dragons flying over the unapproachable island of Roksamur. *No, certainly not dragons.*

"Continue," the king said. "This is *most* interesting."

"Alaire told me to hide while he went to inform the king of Suinomen of what was going on. That was, I fear, the last I saw of him." Reykir's voice had softened, and the king had to strain his ears to hear his words. "The Arachnia, they were a different kind. They were larger, and darker, than the ones we know here."

"And considerably more warlike," the King added sardonically.

"I hid in a wardrobe. I thought they wouldn't find me, then they did and put me with the rest of the prisoners. They brought me before the leaders of the attack." The boy looked away. "Your brother, Prince Craig, was among them."

"As a prisoner?" the king asked.

"As a . . . as an accomplice."

The king stared at the boy, who had managed to meet his eyes despite the gravity of his news. "Certainly not," he said. "How do you know?"

Reykir proceeded to tell him of the brief conversation with Craig. Certain key phrases, words that Craig was fond of using, crept into the story, convincing the king that what Reykir spoke of was true. "The Arachnian wizards have placed bespelled collars on their mounts," Reykir added hastily. "They had such a collar on your brother, and I believe it was through this they were manipulating him. I don't believe he was a willing accomplice."

The king said nothing as he stood abruptly. He paced over to a tree, then back to the trunk, then to the tree again. He looked directly at Reykir. "You are telling me the truth?"

"Yes, Your Majesty," the boy said sincerely. "I am. Forgive me for being the bearer of such bad news."

The king looked past Reykir to the army strewn along the road, out of sight. *Am I going to slay my own brother this year?* Then he looked again at the dieren Reykir had ridden, a healthy stallion with a Suinomen-style saddle, with large leather bags. He became suspicious.

"How did you get away?" the king asked. "With such a fine mount, and supplies?"

"Craig convinced . . . or rather, I convinced Craig that I had pledged allegiance to him. He offered me a position in his new kingdom if I would do this one job for him."

"And this task was?"

"To tell you they are holding Alaire for ransom."

"Confound it all. . . . " The king fumed and resumed

his pacing. Sir Romont cast worried looks in their direction.

"They have taken Prince Alaire and King Kainemonen to the island. To Roks—"

"Roksamur," Derek finished. "Dammit to the seven hells!"

The boy shrugged and looked down. The King thought, *He's probably afraid I will punish him for being the bearer of bad news. Best to alleviate that fear now.* "Thank you, young Bard, for your truthfulness. I wouldn't have expected anything less from one of my own soldiers."

Reykir beamed proudly, then frowned. "Your Majesty, I am not a Bard yet. I am only an apprentice."

The king rolled his eyes. "If this situation is anything like the last problem we had in Suinomen, you probably *will* be a Bard by the time this is resolved."

Alaire and Kai carefully loaded the simple wooden cart with rocks, trying hard not to look obvious as they cast surreptitious glances at the party of Arachnians who were wreaking havoc in the village.

"They don't look pleased," Kai commented as he picked up a small boulder, dropped it, then tried again with Alaire's help. The field they had been sent to "plow" had turned out to be littered with rocks too large for their plain wooden tools to negotiate. Which was just as well, Alaire noted, as picking up the rocks allowed them more movement and a better view of the goings on in the village.

Shortly after Konnongur had sent them with the boy to the field, three Arachnians appeared. They had apparently ridden in on mule rats, which were tied to a lone tree some distance away. They reminded the Bard of the cart they had destroyed and the Arachnians they had killed; he wished at that moment he could render himself invisible.

Don't know any Bardic magic for that feat, he thought forlornly. *These fur tunics will just have to do.*

"They're not coming over here yet," the boy informed them, but Alaire saw that for himself. "But when they do, keep working. Do something, but don't look at them. They don't like that."

"I'll remember that," Alaire said, not caring much for his use of the word "when."

The party of Arachnians went from hut to hut, turning the inhabitants out while Konnongur followed. The high priest seemed to be trying to say something to the apparent leader of the group, but they all ignored him. One Arachnia pulled a woman from one of the huts, tossed her violently aside, then seized a man, likewise throwing him onto the ground. Even at this distance Alaire saw he bore a slight resemblance to himself; blond hair, with a somewhat broad build. But his face was bearded. The Bard felt his own face, which was thick with stubble, then turned to the boy.

"Do all the adult men have beards?"

"Most, but not all," he said. "Okay, look out. They're coming over here."

Alaire looked up, and indeed, they were coming right for them, with Konnongur immediately behind them.

"Just keep working," the boy said.

Finding more rocks to haul away became rather important, and Alaire, Kai and their young companion went about their task with renewed enthusiasm.

At the edge of the field were four other hands, who were doing the actual tilling. As the Arachnians approached, they stopped what they were doing and looked to Konnongur expectantly.

Without warning, one of the Arachnians struck one of the humans with a claw, sending him flying. The young man landed on his back, hard. When he sat up, blood was beginning to pour from a head wound.

A new anger came over Alaire, the deep, red-faced kind that brings forth all sorts of violent scenarios. His knuckles turned white as he clutched a large rock.

Kai noticed this and came closer to him. "I think you should reconsider, Alaire," he said softly. "That pebble you have there would probably just bounce off their shells."

"You're right," the Bard agreed. "But I don't like watching them just tossing people about like refuse."

Kai seemed ready to reply, then held his tongue as the Arachnians came over to them, kicking through the rows of tilled soil.

"They are more workers," Konnongur said. "Please, if you would just . . ."

"Silence, human," one of the Arachnia said in a rasping, grating accent. His armor, more decorated than the others, probably indicated a higher rank. "The escaped humans came this way, and there is no other place they could be."

Some of Alaire's anger turned to fear as they stopped a few paces away from him. Their presence reminded Alaire of their much larger size; these, in particular, were monsters. They regarded the humans with unreadable bug expressions.

"And who are these?" the leader said.

"Two of Treg's sons," Konnongur said evenly. "The boy is my grandson."

"*Animals*," the bug rasped. Alaire waited for its claw to come crashing down on him. Instead, it reached over and grabbed the edge of his tunic with a claw, then roughly pulled Alaire over to him. It chittered something to his colleagues as it examined the tunic, then Alaire's face. The Bard hoped he was appropriately dirty to pass inspection; it was, he suspected, why Konnongur had sent them here to work.

It released him suddenly, turned, and led the other two back to their mounts. The leader seemed to be speaking to Konnongur, who was gesticulating in a most placating way. Whatever the priest had said to them, it must have worked. The Arachnians mounted up and rode out of the camp.

"That was a bit close," Kai commented. "Looks to me like we just saved our necks by burning our clothes."

"I would agree," Alaire said, looking down at the full cart. "Why don't we take this to the pile? It looks like it won't be able to handle much more."

Even though the Arachnians were gone, they continued to work until the sun set. Alaire felt energetic, and he was grateful to these people of Fastur for hiding them in general and to Konnongur for healing his ankle in particular. Kai didn't seem to mind the work either, and by the time they were done, the field was clear of the large rocks.

Konnongur advised them to avoid the others, or at least to use caution, as some of them were more vulnerable to the obedience spell than others and might turn them in to the Arachs. All Alaire noticed in the other humans was a heightened interest in them, a natural enough phenomenon, but he decided to take the priest up on his advice. They were provided with their own small hut near the elder's shelter. At dusk Konnongur and the elders shared dinner with Alaire and Kai, a pig slaughtered in their honor. Newcomers and old-timers got caught up on history. They were fascinated as Alaire described his family and his Bardic path in life. Murmurs of the prophecy surfaced again.

"Come outside," Konnongur said when dinner was finished. "There's something I would like you to watch."

Alaire, Kai and the boy, whose name was Fion,

followed the priest outside. It was quiet; most of the other humans were inside their respective huts. The setting sun had left a red canvas behind, with clouds off in the distance beyond the mountains. The air had also cooled. Alaire shivered and pulled his tunic closer. He had seen leather cloaks and mantles in the hut they'd been designated to use, and now knew why they were there.

Konnongur squinted at the sunset, then pointed. "There. You can see them, coming in from the west."

"Those birds?" Kai said, looking like he was having trouble seeing whatever the priest had pointed to.

"They're not birds," the priest replied.

The tiny winged dots grew into wingrats, then wingrats with mounts. Konnongur didn't seem particularly alarmed at the sight. They cut a path across the sky, away from Fastur, towards one of the mountains.

"It is almost a full moon," Konnongur informed them. Alaire looked for, but didn't see the moon in question, which had not risen yet. "Each moon they begin the ritual, five days before fullness. Arachnian priests from all over the island come on mounts, and congregate on yon mountain."

"Is this some kind of religion?" Kai asked, but Alaire already had his own ideas.

"This is how they enforce the obedience spells," Alaire said, though he wasn't sure how he knew this. "What is on that mountain, anyway?"

Konnongur gave him a puzzled look. "It is not a true mountain," he said. "Liquid rock pours out of it every few years, burning everyone and everything in its path. This land of Roksamur came from these mountains, or so myth tells us. You see smoke billowing from it, which usually only happens around the full moon. We don't know why, but it has to do with the magic they make, the spells they cast."

Fion tugged on the elder's sleeve. Konnongur leaned down while the boy whispered something in his ear, then the priest shook his head. "No, no, young Fion. It is not because of what the prophecy tells us."

"What does the prophecy have to say about the liquid rock?" Alaire asked.

Konnongur looked apologetic. "The prophecy tells us many things, but it is a lie, I think, that certain of the Arachnia have put into our heads in order to placate us. When the magician from afar comes to liberate us, and we take to the air on the freed wingrats, the mountains explode and shower the land with burning rock. This destroys the Arachnia. The humans flee, and escape the final fire. It is all a myth." Then, a bit softer, "It is a child's story."

Alaire nodded. "Perhaps we should go see this magicmaking in the process," he said. "It may tell us something about these people."

Konnongur shook his head. "No, no, you must not go there," he said, sounding very sad, and at that moment, defeated. "You will die if they see you. They will discover who you are and then they will kill you."

"But the valley," Fion said. "The prophecy . . ."

"All lies," Konnongur said sternly. "Some day you will understand, young one."

Alaire counted around twenty wingrats, some coming from the west, others from the north and south. It did look like a serious gathering. On the mountain a tiny fire blazed, but to be seen at this distance it must have been a bonfire. *This really intrigues me,* Alaire thought. *Prophecy or not, this gathering might explain, or show, how we can escape this place.* He glanced over at Konnongur. *But will this old man let us go?*

Alaire silently debated the issue with himself, and decided, at least for the time being, to set it aside. So soon in their relationship did not seem a good time to push an issue which might cause friction, or worse, between then. Besides, he was tired after the day's exertion. *Perhaps tomorrow night,* he thought. *I might even work some Bardic magic to let him see things my way.*

Alaire spent many long minutes staring at the hut's crude ceiling, while Kai snored loudly next to him. He was bone weary, and normally wouldn't have had any trouble getting to sleep, but for some reason tonight was going to be an exception.

What is it about that mountainside that is so intriguing? He couldn't explain it, and in frustration had looked out the front door of the hut, which faced the mountain; the tiny fire was now fully visible in the darkness. As yet, the moon hadn't risen, leaving the night dark, the stars bright, and the gathering of Arachnia on the distant mountainside all the more interesting.

He must have dozed off at one point, because the sudden appearance of someone standing over him startled him into full wakefulness.

"I will show you how to get to the temple," Fion said in the semi-darkness. Moonlight poured into the tiny hut, framing the boy in silhouette. "They practice the magic til dawn. We have little time."

"Agreed," Alaire said, getting to his feet. Kai was still sound asleep, and for a moment the Bard felt a brief twinge of envy. *What I would give for rest right now,* he thought, feeling the beginnings of aching muscles as he stood up. He considered waking Kai, but realized he would not, in his exhausted state, be quiet company when they would be likely to need quiet the most. *And if I don't wake up myself, I'll be stumbling around making enough noise for the both of us.*

Silently, Fion led Alaire out of the small village

where there was not so much as a hint of life. Everyone, elders included, seemed to be very much asleep. A bright, nearly full moon cast a dull white light over everything. The boy led him down to a small ravine, which at first looked like a dry creek bed. But at the bottom of the tiny canyon Alaire sensed the stirrings of magic.

Ley lines, he thought, sensing the thin tendrils of power flowing down the middle. The stream of magic led towards the mountain, and became stronger as they progressed.

The source of this power is what they are using, Alaire thought as it became clear they had begun the ascent of the mountain. The ravine deepened as they climbed, and the Bard suspected the boy had chosen this path for precisely that reason. It was proving to be excellent cover.

They stayed in the ravine's shadows, following a twisting and turning path; in time their trail evened out, and Fion, who until now had scampered quickly ahead of him, came to a full crouch and held a single finger to his lips. Alaire heard a distant murmur, similar to the chirping of crickets, but considerably deeper and louder. It took him no time to determine that the sounds came from Arachnians, not little bugs.

The Bard caught a familiar whiff of manure. *Wingrats.*

A fire's crackle punctuated the murmuring. The ravine was deep, and to look over the edge required a bit of climbing. Alaire saw places where simple footholds had already been made.

Apparently Fion has been here before. He peered over the edge, slowly, following Fion's cues.

"The *prophecy,*" the boy whispered, and pointed toward the gathering.

Twenty or so Arachnia with robes had assembled around a large fire that had burned down to coals.

In the moonlight, Alaire had a clear view of the ritual. The robed creatures sat in the circle, chanting a low melodic hum, apparently oblivious to everything going on around them. Alaire dropped back down in the ravine, on his haunches, stunned by a sudden revelation.

They're using Bardic magic!

From his crouched position he listened to the chant, studied it, tore it apart. The melody was simple, even crude, but there was no doubt in his mind that they were employing the same kind of magic he had dedicated his life to. He glanced down at the ley line and saw a dull red glow pulsating with the chant. He closed his eyes and sank deep into a trance, carefully shielding his thoughts and being while reaching out, then down, to the source of the power.

Beneath them Alaire sensed a dense knot of power, along with intense heat, hot enough to melt rock. The two powers, magic and heat, seemed to be connected. He remembered what Konnongur had said about the rituals coinciding with the burning of the mountain.

As he touched the power with his mind he recoiled at its strength. The Bardic magic from the Arachnia was strong, but was not even grazing the surface of what was available. The chant guided very little of the energy to their purposes, which, he saw clearly now, was the imprisonment of wingrats and humans with the obedience spell. Carefully, he withdrew from his trance.

I've seen what I needed to see, he thought, standing.

"Fion, we must go now," he said urgently to the boy, whom he found sitting next to him. "Or I'm likely to try something right now I might not live to regret."

Chapter Fourteen

"Fifteen Arachnians dead within the palace walls in the past two nights," Su'Villtor hissed. "And you are the only human among us. Can you give us a good reason not to imprison you now?"

Craig didn't know how to respond to Su'Villtor's venom, which he didn't fully understand. The human had been sound asleep in the palace when the Arachnia had roused him, rather roughly, with his claw. *Something about Arachnians dying in the palace. Well, what do they expect? They're at war!*

There was something about Su'Villtor's urgency that suggested their arrangement might have undergone some changes while he was passed out. The Arachnia led him through the palace corridors, poking him occasionally with the tip of the claw, which made him feel more like a prisoner than a partner.

Whatever is about to happen, I had better start doing some fast talking.

Su'Villtor led him to what had become the staging area for the new command, the great hall. Tables had been moved aside, and various Arachnians sat on the tiered benches. He noted with some discomfort that he was the only human present.

Su'Villtor addressed the apparent leader in their chirping Arachnian language, then turned to Craig. "Su'Kanguer would like to know where the crossbow is."

Craig was dumbfounded. One of the first things the invaders had done was to search the palace thoroughly for weapons. Even the kitchen knives had been confiscated, along with some of the sharper smithing tools. The remaining soldiers had been imprisoned in the fighting arena. Once Craig had seen Reykir off to parley with Althea, his attention had turned to locating more wine. This didn't take long. The wine cellar was well stocked and easy to find.

"I'm sorry, Su'Villtor, but I don't know of any weapons. I hope you don't think I am responsible for these deaths?" He was still a little unclear about the situation; were these soldiers dying of old wounds acquired during the original raid, or was this something entirely new?

"We doubt your sincerity," Su'Villtor said. "But as you are spending your time drinking, we doubt you would have the ability to kill a dog, much less an Arachnia."

"That's true," Craig replied, even though he knew he was capable of a great many things, while drunk or sober. *Best to not let them know of this,* he thought to himself. "I assure you, I know nothing of this. I have an interest in your success, as you well know," he said, in the vague hopes it was still the case. *They had better give me the crown of Althea! It is my birthright!*

Su'Villtor and Su'Kanguer exchanged more Arachnian, then Su'Villtor continued, "The humans of this city are not putting up much of a fight. Their fighting forces, which we have put out of commission, seem to have been the only obstacle. Why, then, are our people dying within the very walls of this palace?"

Craig shrugged, and tried to come up with a way to answer the same question differently. "Perhaps a disease?"

Su'Villtor replied shortly, "They were killed by arrows,

which were ripped out of them when the assassin left. There are no other traces. If you have no other information, we should waste no more of Su'Kanguer's time."

"Forgive me, I know nothing," Craig continued. And for once, he was telling the truth. *Why won't they believe me?*

Captain Lyam stood in the cramped passageway, holding a small candle cupped in his large, calloused hands. The passageway had narrowed further, requiring him to remain here while his son, Erik, continued ahead. Though he was eighteen and every bit a man, his son was still slender of build and capable of negotiating the tighter spaces of the labyrinth of secret passageways located throughout the palace grounds.

Waiting for him to return from this particular expedition had allowed Lyam plenty of time to think. Which was fortunate; as captain of the guard, he had plenty to think about.

It happened so quickly. And with no warning. When the invading Arachnians swept over the palace walls, he and his men had put up a good fight, particularly against an invasion so unexpected, and an enemy so alien. The Arachnians wore leather armor over their already hard shells, a complication Lyam had solved, if a bit too late. *Damn them all, if we had known we might have beat them,* he fumed, even now, three days after the invasion. Bolts shot from longbows and crossbows bounced off the armor harmlessly, at a distance. For up close fighting, daggers, knives and swords had been the weapon of choice. But in this battle, these had proven to be useless. Only towards the end, when their forces had succumbed to the invasion, had Lyam and his men discovered an effective way of subduing the enemy.

A crossbow, when fired at *close* range, penetrated

the armor and shell with ease. A longbow had the same effect, but was an awkward weapon indoors. The large body of an Arachnia made the easiest target, while an arrow through the head caused instant death. There was a bit of wiggling and crawling after that, but those were only the death throes. The life had, they had learned through trial and error, already been extinguished.

Alas, they had made this discovery too late to be of any immediate benefit. The Arachnians had overwhelmed and occupied the palace in an eye blink, and Lyam, with as many men as he could gather in a moment's time, had hidden in the secret tunnels located throughout the palace and grounds.

King Maergach the First, who had ruled Suinomen a thousand years ago, had built his palace with certain features in mind. At the time, the kingdom was besieged by bands of barbarians which had overrun Rozinki more than once in its first few decades of existence. To provide a safe retreat for the royal family should this happen again, he had an extensive network of secret halls installed throughout the palace. Over the centuries peace became the norm, and the passages had slowly faded from memory. Until Sir Jehan's attempted coup six years earlier, the tunnels had been all but forgotten. Jehan and the Swords of the Magicians, the elite group of wizards who were allowed to conduct magic at that time were familiar with them. King Archenomen had heard myths of the passageways, but hadn't the first clue as to where they were or how to access them.

Then, six years ago, an assassin had tried to kill the Dark Elf, Naitachal, the Ambassador of Althea. He used the tunnels to attack, then to escape. It wasn't until Sir Jehan's coup had failed that the tunnels had become common knowledge, revealed by a horde of crooked wizards eager to get on Archenomen's good side. Captain Lyam had explored them extensively, but, other than a few skeletons, he found little of interest; the passages did, however, make eavesdropping on certain rooms quite easy. Now, with the Arachnians in control of the palace and Rozinki, the tunnels were Suinomen's only hope.

His first task had been to locate King Kainemonen and Prince Alaire, but this had proven futile. As near as he could figure, they were alive but being kept somewhere else. The drunken sot, Prince Craig, had spoken of them as if they had been moved to another land. This didn't make sense, and he didn't know what to make of it. The palace appeared to be the center of the invading forces. What better place to keep the king and prince?

At first the captain was puzzled that Craig was not imprisoned with the rest of them, but a few overheard conversations with Su'Villtor had explained everything. *The bastard turned against us, and against his own kingdom!*

The Arachnians had seized all the Guard's weapons, with the exception of a few crossbows they'd had hidden in various places. With the help of his son, he had searched the palace for three days, looking for the cache, with no results.

A foot scuffle deep in the darkness roused him from his thoughts. He stood to peer down the narrow space. Momentarily, Eric appeared with a large canvas bag full of something.

"Got another one," the young man said, at about the same time Lyam noticed his crossbow was empty.

"Did you find weapons?" Lyam asked, reaching for the bag.

"No, but something else we are in short supply of," replied Erik.

Lyam looked into the bag at about fifty candles and stubs. The captain tried not to let his disappointment show. "Aye, we need these, that's for sure," he said, transferring the flame from his dwindling stub to a longer candle. "What news have you, son?"

"The command is still in the great hall. They were questioning Craig as to the dead bugs." He paused, the candlelight catching a wry grin of satisfaction on his young features. "Have we really killed *fifteen* of the demons?"

Lyam considered this, then nodded. "At least. Do they have any clues as to what's going on?"

They started back down the hallway, towards the wider of their passages, which would take them towards the fighting arena via an underground tunnel. Erik shifted the bag on his broad shoulders. "They were accusing Craig. Nothing said of passages. I don't think they suspect these tunnels exist."

Lyam grunted. "That's the first good news we've heard." As they descended a flight of narrow wooden stairs, the captain noticed an arrow in Erik's belt, dripping with Arachnian blood. Arrows were also in short supply, and they had to retrieve each and every one they used, when possible.

A clatter of stone alerted them to someone, or something ahead. Silently, Erik set the canvas bag down, and nocked the crossbow.

A candle flickered into view; then, its bearer raised it three times. Waited, then lifted it again. Lyam returned the signal.

"Must be Geoff," muttered Lyam. "What is *he* doing down here?"

A large man loomed into view, carrying what looked like an empty canvas bag, followed by three more men. Lyam recognized them as part of the group imprisoned in the arena.

"*Geoff.* You had better have a good reason for coming down here," Lyam said evenly. "I left orders that no one was to follow us. What if they do a head count? What then?"

None of these objections seemed to bother Geoff. He was grinning broadly, like a wolf who has just eaten his fill of chickens.

"We know where they're keeping the crossbows," Geoff said. "And perhaps more. One of the servants, who is still in the palace serving the thrice-damned bugs, stumbled across them while fetching something."

Now, that's a good reason to disobey an order.

"Tell me where," Lyam said, "and if we can, we'll reach them through these tunnels."

"The larder," Geoff said. "The main palace larder."

Lyam frowned. "But we've already been there."

Geoff shook his head. "They just moved them today. They intend to burn them at dusk." He held up several empty canvas bags. "That's why I brought these."

"Aie, yes," Erik said. "Father, we'd better move now. Isn't there a tunnel that leads to the kitchen?"

"It's risky," Lyam said. "The great hall, that's where the most of them are." But even as he was finding reasons why such an expedition would be too dangerous, he thought of as many, or more, reasons why they should go.

Presently Lyam's party of five found itself at a narrow doorway and an even narrower door. Lyam listened carefully for what might be taking place on the other side; satisfied that the way was clear, he looked for and found the wooden pegs that kept the panel shut. Being the only one of the five small enough, Erik slipped through, once the panel was open. In a moment he returned with an armful of crossbows and arrows. The booty changed hands with amazing speed, until every last weapon had been retrieved. Erik slipped back in, and his father moved the panel back into place and secured it with the pegs.

In all, Lyam counted forty crossbows, with an ample supply of arrows. The bags filled quickly, and what wouldn't fit went over their shoulders.

"Now, we must get back," Lyam said. "And soon, we must decide *when* we are going to take back our kingdom."

Chapter Fifteen

Alaire and Kai rose to news that the Arachnia were searching the village again for them. Again, Konnongur didn't seem to be particularly worried for them, but his mood this day was decidedly grim.

"Since they haven't found you," Konnongur said, as he led them, with others, to the field to do more work, "they will be in a rather foul mood."

Somehow Alaire knew this was an understatement, but declined comment. The Bard was grateful for the diversion, as it would allow him the privacy he needed to tell Kai about the evening's adventures.

With their simple sticks, they went to work turning soil, watching five Arachnia go through the village. Konnongur slowly shook his head. As he walked away, he said, "Your only saving grace today is that nobody knows who you are."

Alaire didn't know what that meant, but whatever his meaning he doubted it was good news.

"Wonder what he meant by that," Kai said, just as Alaire spied two Arachnia pulling a human out of a hut.

"I don't like the look of this," Alaire said, and tried not to stare, turning his attention to the task before him.

Despite his best efforts to avoid being conspicuous, Alaire couldn't help watching the unpleasant scene unfold. The Arachnians dragged the man, by a foot, to the center of the village. Ten or so humans came out of their huts, evidently to see what the ruckus was about. Konnongur hurried over to the Arachnians, and while his words were inaudible, his gestures clearly showed some gallant attempt to placate the beasts.

"If I had a longbow, I'd kill them all," Alaire heard Kai seethe beside him. "These people must be free of this slavery!"

"Actually, I'm working on that. I may have a solution," Alaire said, jabbing at the soil. But Kai didn't seem to be paying any attention.

Alaire had a sickening feeling that the Arachs had come to the end of their patience. Konnongur continued to plead with his hands, others in the village came over, then promptly looked away; whatever was about to happen seemed to be anticipated by everyone.

Not the first time something like this has happened, is it? Alaire thought, wishing he could take his eyes away. But it was impossible.

"I can't watch this," Kai said.

An Arachnia held the human up by an ankle. The man struggled momentarily, then suddenly stopped moving. The other Arachnia looked over the humans briefly, and without warning pierced the dangling human's abdomen with a claw. Blood spilled, and the man fell to the ground, without motion or any sign of life.

"Dammit all to hell, Alaire, he *killed* that man," Kai said. "What did he do?"

"Probably nothing," Alaire replied, with an amazing lack of emotion. "Just setting an example." But despite his deadpan delivery, he felt the blood drain from his face. "We must act tonight," Alaire said, and Kai looked up. "Or we're all dead."

"What did you have in mind?" Kai asked, somewhat sarcastically. "Arm wrestling?"

"Not exactly," Alaire said. "Do you remember what

they said about a 'prophecy'? Well, last night Fion woke
me and led me to a magical scene that I can only
describe as Bardic in nature. . . ."

"They will kill one of us each day until they find
you," Konnongur explained to them when they returned
from the field. Alaire felt the beginnings of a sunburn
on his shoulders and arms, but he didn't care; the plan
had seized his imagination, stirred his adrenaline. Kai
was whistling an Althean folk ballad that had been
popular at the Rozinki taverns.

"They will, will they?" Alaire said. "Someone in
Fastur must have noticed us. Why haven't they turned
us in?"

"Everyone believes in the prophecy," Konnongur
said sadly. "They believe it to be true, and that you
are the instrument of the prophecy. The myths just
happen to fit the circumstances."

They walked a bit further, tossed their sticks on
the pile of similar tools, and paused, watching the
spectacular sunset. Konnongur looked up, and stopped
in his tracks when he saw Alaire's face.

"Konnongur, you don't seem to be a believer in this
prophecy, and to tell you the truth I have my doubts
as well. So for now, let's set myths and legends aside.
Let's stay with what we know is real, and what we
know is real is *magic.*"

"Aye," Konnongur said, squaring his shoulders. "You
called me on that one. I don't believe in the prophecy, as my father, and his father before him, passed
the story down as a way of giving us hope. False
hope, granted, but a glimmer of hope that no one
in this village would have had otherwise. But *magic,*
yes, I rely on it." His eyes narrowed, and a slight smile
creased his aging features. "I suppose you've had a bit
of time to think things over, out there in the field."

"We have," Alaire said, then proceeded to tell him

about his trip to the mountain with Fion the evening before. "They are working a form of Bardic magic, crude and primitive, but on a level I can use."

Konnongur looked away, to the horizon as Alaire outlined his plan. The first of the mounted wingrats was making its sedate way from the west. Beyond it, another.

"Can you do it?" Konnongur asked, not taking his eyes off the wingrats.

"I will not know until I try," Alaire replied. "I will need the help of the elders. I cannot do this alone."

Konnongur gradually turned his face towards Alaire. "When?"

"Tonight," Alaire replied. "Before any more of your people die."

"So be it," Konnongur whispered, and started walking slowly towards the elders' hut.

Alaire led the group of elders and, at Konnongur's urging, some of the younger men and women of the village who had shown magical aptitude, to the edge of the long, jagged ravine.

Kai stayed behind. This was no commentary on what Alaire was about to do. He just didn't feel he could contribute. Some of the other elders stayed behind, for the same reason.

The group situated itself at the end of what Alaire had at first perceived as a dry creek bed. This was, in actuality, the edge of a massive field of underground power, a spider-webbing of ley lines. Alaire had only explored a fraction of it the night before. Directly beneath them was a major stream of this power, a river of energy sweeping down from the mountain.

"We will begin here," Alaire said. He had instructed the group to not mention the prophecy, by name or by thought. He was afraid this would contaminate what he was trying to do here, which was to wrest the power

away from the Arachnians, who were congregating
upstream on the mountain. These people's belief in him
was all he needed to work Bardic magic in a group.
They would create a strong vessel; he would be the
oarsman.

Please, gods, don't let me muck up, he thought as
the villagers gathered around him. Some of the prom-
ising mages were barely in their early growth, and
some of the young men, he positioned close to the
center. They would be working with raw power, and
their raw youth, he believed, would aid in guiding it.

"Another," someone whispered, and all eyes turned
to the sky. The Arachnia above didn't seem to notice
the group of humans congregating beneath it, as its
mount's wings beat softly at the sky. Konnongur had
been keeping count of the wingrats as they flew overhead; meeting Alaire's eyes, he nodded, indicating this
was the last one who would be gathering on the
mountainside.

Alaire closed his eyes, feeling for the soul of the
island. The ground had a new feel to it, as if this island
had not existed for very long, and the newness felt
powerful. The ground in Althea had been in existence
for millennia; this ground was much younger.

Then he saw why: The land he stood on had leaked
from the ocean itself, from deep below in the heart
of the planet, like a bleeding wound. He stood on
the cooled scar tissue of that wound.

Alaire nodded to Konnongur, his signal for the
group to begin raising its power, then closed his eyes.
He didn't know precisely how his Bardic skills and
their earth magic would mix; provided the two were
directed toward the same goal, in a positive manner,
he doubted there would be a problem. Perhaps they
would even complement each other.

We must try, Alaire thought, as a chant rose around
him with its native sound.

Nam-mu, *Nam*-mu, *Nam*-mu, *NIN*-ma, *Nam*-mu,
began the chanting, and Alaire tuned into the direction
their power was going, down, down into the rough, gray
soil. The ley line glowed brightly now, and he followed
its path up, towards the Arachnian wizards he had seen
the evening before, to the cluster of similar lines their
circle had been established upon. He saw them now,
around their dimmed fire, their multifaceted eyes
focused on the glowing coals, a dim reproduction of the
true power flickering beneath. Their power was crude,
not just simple, but crude; that he could sense. They
knew nothing of the spy now looking over their work,
or what Alaire and his group were about to do.

The song was old, centuries old, as old as the prophecy itself. Konnongur had produced it once Alaire had
decided to make this attempt, knowing the magician
needed something with which to focus.

When the Arachnians' magic had reached its peak
power, Alaire began to sing . . .

> Bindings of the thousand born,
>> Onto this land of Roksamur.
> Tied and caged to masters lay
>> Allow the bound to fly away.

Alaire took in what the others were chanting, its
pitch increasing, matching his song.

O-mah, O-mah, O-mah, O-mah, Nin-o, Nam-muuuu . . .

Then he felt the power lurch beneath him, turn from
a river of fire to a restless snake; the ley line writhed,
as if tortured with fire. It wanted to be free. The Bard
continued his song . . .

> Burning stream of flame beneath,
>> Flowing sunlight underneath.
> Bend and break the spells that keep,
>> Our spirits reigned, our souls asleep.

A ripple of surprise echoed through the group, distracting Alaire. He ventured a glimpse of his surroundings, then opened his eyes wide in surprise. A thunderstorm had formed on the horizon, a tall black anvil of a thunderhead that flickered with threads of angry lightning. A cool breeze swept down from it; then a strong, loud wind smashed into them. Alaire stumbled, regained his footing. *We must continue.* . . .

> *Break the chains, cut the ropes*
> *Turn us loose and let us see.*
> *Freedom for our highest hopes*
> *Transcends the moon of Prophecy.*

A flash of lightning pierced the last phrase of the chant. A long, red glow pulsated from the ground, led up the mountain. His group remained sitting, but he saw their fear; this was what they wanted, this magic, but it still frightened them. Even Konnongur seemed well out of his magical depth.

"Begone! Begone!" Alaire shouted. "Be free!"

The group took up the chorus, repeating the words in a dozen different voices. The wind stopped, and the sky, once clouded with storm, was now clear.

Alaire knew the spell had worked. He felt a drastic shifting of power, falling like broken shackles, mixed with the vague confusion of the Arachnian wizards far up the mountainside, whom he sensed were only now feeling something amiss.

"Back to the village," Alaire shouted, uncertain why they had to be there. The rest of the clan was there, true, but there was something else, some urgent need to be with the others. Halfway there, Alaire knew why. The ground roared beneath his feet. In the quasi-darkness, Alaire saw ripples along the ground, like waves on a pond, moving away from the mountain.

We don't need to be in the village . . . we need to be away from the mountain. . . .

The ground continued to shake and the group started to run. He caught glimpses of their faces, Konnongur's in particular, as they ran across the shifting ground. Exhilarated, not afraid, even the high priest seemed caught up in the moment, this victory of the prophecy.

Kai was waiting for them at the edge of the village, with a hundred or so of the people. Konnongur went through the village, making certain everyone was out of their huts. The shaking ground was certainly going to bring the flimsy structures down.

Someone shouted, then pointed to the sky. A group of wingrats, carrying their Arachnian wizard riders, was beating a hasty retreat away from the mountain. At first Alaire thought the spell was all for nothing, that the wingrats here were clearly imprisoned in the same spell they had been for their entire existence; then one of them began to falter, and the wingrat flew away from the others, flying in wide, crazy circles. Suddenly it turned sideways, then completely over, and the Arachnia, claws and legs flailing, fell free of the wingrat and plunged to the ground below.

A cheer went up as the Arachnia smashed into the ground. The other wingrats began to fly erratically as well, making wide, twisting loops in the sky, moves which their riders were clearly unaccustomed to and unable to negotiate. One by one the Arachnia fell to their deaths, breaking apart on impact, splashing brown on boulders. Nothing living remained below.

The wingrats circled around, swooped in low over the village, then backflapped into an elegant landing. Ten in all, they regarded the group of humans with what looked like wry amusement.

One of them looked directly at Alaire, then mindspoke.

:So you are the bringer of the prophecy,: it said, sounding pleased.

Low Moon felt the ripple of change through the pads of her feet, after watching Alaire and his group walk to the edge of the mountain from a distance. She knew the magic was happening, felt the bindings of the wingrats around her fall. The few Arachnians nearby seemed completely unaware of what was happening.

:Now is the time,: Low Moon spoke to her stablemates, once she sensed their obedience spells had fallen away. *:We must spread out, tell the others to come to Fastur. We are free, and so are the humans. It is time for us to leave this place.:*

They took to the sky exuberantly, flying away in different directions.

After the initial trembling, Alaire felt the ground's shaking diminish somewhat. Still, there was the occasional tremor, and two of the vacant huts had collapsed during the worst of it. He hadn't expected the earth to shake at all, much less for this length of time.

The wingrats who had landed remained where they were for some time. Alaire remembered Low Moon's initial reaction to being free, the transition that she had to undergo. He suspected these creatures were going through the same thing. *Best to let them adjust at their own pace,* he thought.

"The mountain is on fire," someone said calmly, pointing to the horizon.

Indeed it was. Clear in the night sky, Alaire saw a crown of bright orange form at the top of the mountain; from this trickled rivers of light, flowing down the side of the mountain like spilled honey. The Bard hadn't the first clue as to what this substance was, but he didn't like the looks of it one bit.

Kai was watching the mountain too. "Was *that* supposed to happen?" he asked. "Whatever *that* is?" Alaire wished he could answer him. He looked around for Konnongur for answers, but he was nowhere to be seen.

"Alaire," Kai said, pointing to another part of the sky. "What is that?"

At first Alaire thought he was talking about the orange, full moon which had just risen on the horizon, whitening as it ascended into the sky. Then he saw what Kai was pointing at, the flying creatures framed against the full moon. A swarm of what at first looked like birds, then bats; as they drew nearer, he saw what they were, the only thing they could be.

"More wingrats," whispered Alaire.

"How many?" Kai asked.

The Bard shrugged. "Looks like *all* of them."

"The prophecy," someone said, and others took up the chant. "The prophecy, the prophecy, *the prophecy* . . ."

Alaire felt a familiar tugging at the edge of his mind, a voice he knew.

:*Humans. How many?*: she asked, sounding frantic. Alaire glanced around at the crowd of humans.

:*Many. Many. Why?*:

A pause. :*You don't know? The prophecy. We all leave now!*:

"Of course," Alaire said, regarding the others around him triumphantly. "I *knew* that."

Presently, Low Moon flew into view and was the first of the hundreds of wingrats to land. The beating of their wings was loud and windy but did not drown the exalted roar of victory that tore through the crowd. At first, Alaire was puzzled, as he watched the humans slowly approach the wingrats and, one by one, select one and then mount. *They act as if they were born into this,* Alaire thought. Something cold and wet nudged his elbow.

Low Moon. :*On. Now,*: she sent. :*Before the river of fire catches us.*:

The what? Alaire thought, then he saw what she referred to. The trickle of orange that had been dribbling down the mountainside had become a raging river.

Alaire climbed up on his friend and held on tight. Kai had selected his own wingrat and was crawling precariously on top of it. There were still some leather straps left on Low Moon's tack, which he clung to, but as he settled on her back he found that he fit neatly between her wings, as if wingrats had been designed for humans, not Arachnia. The moment they were airborne, Alaire felt the intense heat from the river of fire, and as he looked back at the eerie sight he realized how fortunate they all were to be alive. The river of fire widened quickly, and great pools of bright liquid heat already lapped at the far edge of the village. As if they had been born to ride wingrats, the humans of Fastur quickly mounted and hung on, following Alaire and Low Moon into the night sky. Once they had gained some altitude, Low Moon circled back and made another pass over the village. The river of fire had now consumed half of it, but it looked as though all the humans had made it safely to wingrats and were now airborne. He caught a glimpse of Kai flying in the distance, clinging for dear life to the back of a large female, not even daring to look up.

:*Formation. Now.*: Alaire caught Low Moon's sending to the other wingrats. The Bard saw there were actually many more wingrats than humans, perhaps thousands. Slowly, groups formed in the moonlight, then spread out in a familiar "V" shape. After counting thirty or so formations, he lost track and turned his attention to Low Moon. Her vigorous flapping when they had taken off had settled down into a slow rhythmic beating.

It felt as though this was the bare minimum of effort to keep airborne.

:*We're leaving now,*: Low Moon mindspoke. :*Roksamur is on fire.*:

Alaire glanced down and saw that the entire island seemed to be in flame. In the darkness he hadn't been certain, but from this height he saw there were more mountains spewing the liquid flame. As the fire reached the sea, great hissing geysers erupted as fingers of steam barely visible in the moonlight.

Alaire thought about all the Arachnians down there, now without their flying mounts. *Will anything live through that?* He thought not. He *hoped* not.

The full moon glowed brightly in the night sky, illuminating the formations of wingrats and the occasional human riders. The Bard looked away from the moon's intense glare and tightened the leather straps around his wrists, and settled in for the long ride back to Suinomen.

Chapter Sixteen

King Derek didn't like leaving the cannon behind, not one bit. A wave of thunderstorms had soaked the road ahead of them, making travel by wagon difficult. Some of the heavier artillery sank quickly in the mud, and the lighter pieces made progress slowly, holding the rest of the army back.

"Sire," Captain Romont had said, "we have two choices. Wait until the cannons are freed, which might, I may add, take weeks. Or the rest of the army can proceed and let the artillery catch up later."

The king saw Romont's point. Whatever was happening in Rozinki would not likely be held up by anything, good weather or foul. "Can we spare the men?" the king asked.

"The second company can wrestle with the cannon, while the rest of us move ahead. This is the course of action I recommend."

King Derek had to agree, Romont's plan made sense. The "second company" he referred to were militia, butchers, armorers, carpenters and farmers called up in the emergency.

"So be it," Derek said, and Romont ordered the second company to deal with the cannon and transport them to Rozinki as soon as possible. Wagons carrying powder and shot stayed behind as well, to keep the ordnance with the firepower. Romont conferred briefly with the lieutenant in charge of the second company, to discuss precisely where they should meet.

The merchants who had visited Rozinki from Althea had made excellent maps, to which Derek's army referred. The cannon would be transported to a valley south of the bay the palace overlooked. Here there was thick forest in which to hide, and while strategy involving a flying enemy was new, both Derek and Romont agreed that cover from the air would be important in concealing their heavier pieces of weaponry.

Reykir had continued to ride with the army, but his position, particularly with Romont and the other officers, was unclear. He was not royalty, a soldier, or even a militiaman; yet he was crucial to the mission, for information and insight to this new enemy. King Derek felt a responsibility for him, as he was his brother's apprentice and had gone to great lengths to inform them of the situation in Rozinki, including the near sacrifice of his owl, Rakvel. But he was still a boy, wearing Suinomen clothes and riding a Suinomen dieren; it was easy, even for the king, to forget he was one of their own.

After a short rest, with a water break and brief meal of dried rations, King Derek's army proceeded north along the coastline road, which ran along a ridge overlooking a long expanse of beach. He had little choice in the routes he could take, as to the west was an extensive marsh which was impenetrable, and to the east was ocean. The king had considered sailing to Rozinki, but the merchant ships he would have requisitioned were not available. Later, some of these ships would sail with supplies to aid the army once they had arrived in Rozinki, but that would be days away. The capitol of Suinomen was less than a day's ride away, according to the maps. Knowing their goal was close, the army moved with a new urgency.

Reykir was riding alongside the king when something

off the coast caught his attention. King Derek looked, but saw nothing at sea. It was midday, and the sun overhead was trying to break through a cloud-covered sky, giving the sea and the sky above it a grayish hue.

"What is it?" the king inquired, gazing towards the sea.

Reykir didn't answer right away. Instead, his eyes narrowed, as if he were inspecting a distant cloud.

"It's Alaire," he said, finally. "He's returning from Roksamur."

Derek gazed at the sea. "By ship?" He saw none.

"By rat," he said. "Look, you can see them."

The king saw only a flock of birds off in the distance, flying in a "V" formation. At first this didn't make much sense. Birds migrated from north to south, not east to west. And it was too early in the year for them to return.

"Those aren't birds," Reykir said. "Please, tell your men not to fire. Alaire has escaped from Roksamur. And he's brought some interesting company."

He's in communication with something, the king thought. *He has no reason to lie.* He summoned Captain Romont and told him to hold all fire until further notice.

The contingent of wingrats flew past dawn, and rode an early morning breeze towards their destination. Low Moon nudged Alaire mentally, and told him land was in sight.

A flood of relief came over him as he made out the distant outline of what was probably the Suinomen coast. According to Low Moon, they had not drifted too far south, and they would put down somewhere along the coastline road. The Bard was beginning to wonder if they were all going to make it; some of the wingrats, unfamiliar with such long travel, showed signs of fatigue. Some had even transferred their human riders, with some difficulty, to unencumbered wingrats. The procedure occurred without mishap, but Alaire was glad he wasn't the human who was dangled temporarily in midair while a third wingrat swooped in and deposited him on another mount.

:Humans, ahead: Low Moon sent. *:One is the boy human, Reykir. Many humans, moving towards the palace. Boy human knows we're here.:*

Alaire reached, trying to tune into his apprentice's thoughts. *That must be Derek's army. If not, we might find ourselves in some brand new trouble.* The distraction of flight made contact difficult. Then the distraction of *landing* made it impossible.

Sand and water rose towards them at a frightening rate. Suddenly, they were on the beach. It wasn't until Alaire had flipped over Low Moon's head that he realized they'd landed a bit too roughly; he landed on his back in sand, which knocked a little bit of wind out of him. He turned around to see Low Moon getting to her feet and shaking the sand off her wings.

All around him, wingrats were dropping out of the sky. Some landed on all fours, most not; some tumbled, some rolled. Others misjudged the distance altogether and ditched in the water, just shy of the shoreline. As exhausted as they all must have been at that point, the Bard wasn't surprised to see the awkward landings. Of all the wingrats landing on the beach now, Alaire suspected Low Moon was the only one who had made this trip before.

Hundreds of wingrats continued to drop to the beach, until the entire area was blanketed with frightened humans, beating wings, and the occasional grunt of someone hitting the sand a little too hard. Through the confusion, Konnongur found his way over to Alaire.

"The brothers have made it," Konnongur said. Alaire tried to answer, but he hadn't yet recovered his wind.

The old priest turned and regarded the scene victoriously.

Low Moon slowly looked over the others, in various states of recovery from the landing, then turned her long, rat snout to the sky and let loose with the loudest bellow Alaire had ever heard. It approximated that of an adult dieren, but was deeper and louder.

As if in reply the wingrats nearby began bellowing as well, as Low Moon continued her own song. The phenomenon spread throughout the beach, until the air was filled with wingrat bellows and howls, at times sounding like wolves baying at the moon. Though the sound was frightening, Alaire heard the celebration behind it.

"What are they doing?" Alaire said to Konnongur, after summoning enough wind to form words.

"This is the conclusion of the prophecy," Konnongur said. "I didn't believe it would ever happen, but it has. We are free, as we have never been free before." He looked to Alaire, with a tear running down the side of his face. "And we have you to thank." Saying nothing more, Konnongur took Alaire's hand and kissed it.

While the wingrat howls continued, the humans ran around in circles, hugged each other, rolled in the sand, and kissed the soil they stood on. With the enormous beasts baying at the sky, the humans literally jumping around in ecstasy, the Bard contemplated the strange scene with a detached joy; after the long voyage and the lack of sleep, his mind was having trouble focusing on what was happening. None of it seemed real.

In the chaos, Kai managed to find his way to Alaire, looking winded and considerably pale. "Alaire, do *not* let me get on one of those things again! If I so much as get *near* one, shoot me between the eyes with a crossbow."

"You didn't enjoy our little flight?" Alaire asked,

holding in a laugh. "Would you have rather stayed behind?"

"Well . . ." Kai said. "At least we're home." His eyes wandered across the beach, then up, to the cliffs. "Any idea whose army that is up there?" he said casually.

Beyond the beach was a ridge, along which a sizable army had assembled, and was looking down on them. Alaire scanned the foot soldiers and cavalry, whose uniforms were difficult to see. Then his eyes fell on the banners of the Althean royal family.

"It's my brother," Alaire said, though he didn't really know if Derek was there. "Reykir is up there somewhere."

Gradually the melee on the beach subsided as all eyes turned to the forces gathered above them. An uncomfortable silence fell, but the mood was one of confusion, not fear. *Of course, they're confused. They've never seen a human army before.*

The cavalry ranks parted, allowing three horses and a dieren through; two of the horses were without mounts, and were led down to the beach by the two riders.

The procession felt rather solemn, but when Alaire saw his brother Derek and his apprentice, Reykir, he knew the pomp was for ceremonial purposes only, to show consideration to the new arrivals on the beach. Alaire understood his brother's predicament; here he was, with a well equipped army, confronted by a mob of barbarians. Then he considered his own appearance, then Kai's, the king of this country. Dirty, unshaven, wearing animal skins. *Derek, if you laugh at us, I will kill you!*

Alaire, Kai and Konnongur stepped forward. Derek rode to within speaking range, and stopped.

"Hello, brother," Alaire said sheepishly. "So much for my restful trip to Suinomen, hmmm? May I present Kainemonen, King of Suinomen?"

Derek dismounted and bowed subtly, as a king should to another king, and offered the reigns to one of the horses. "It's my deepest honor to meet you, King Kainemonen. Perhaps it would have been more agreeable under better circumstances." Kai took the reigns of the horse and offered his hand.

"I see you have taken the liberty of bringing your fighting forces to our aid," Kainemonen said. "And I thank you. I trust you know of our predicament in Rozinki?"

"All too well, I'm afraid," Derek replied. "First, Reykir's owl told us. Then Reykir himself, once he arrived."

"This is Konnongur, leader of these people," Alaire said, and Konnongur bowed awkwardly. "He is a descendant of the nephew of King Amber. We are relatives, of a distant sort."

Derek raised an eyebrow at this. "Really? The nephew who was lost at sea?"

"Lost and shipwrecked on Roksamur," Konnongur said. "But I am no longer the leader of these people." He turned to Alaire, and put an arm on his shoulder. "This man is, according to the prophecy."

"Excuse me?" Alaire said. "When did *this* happen?"

But King Derek had started to laugh. "Leave it to Bard Alaire. Sent off on a diplomatic mission, and he returns triumphantly as king of his own people!"

Before the situation had gotten completely out of hand, Alaire had appointed Konnongur temporary ruler of the people of Roksamur, a role in which he had much practice already, and had promised to deal with his new "kingdom" once the situation in Rozinki had been dealt with.

"I still don't believe it," Alaire groaned, urging his horse along the well trod path. Reykir rode beside him, along with King Derek, King Kai and Captain Romont. A full legion of cavalry advanced before them as they made their way to Rozinki, with instructions to Konnongur to follow well behind the army. The people of Roksamur seemed all too willing to lend a hand to the invasion, and had quickly proven much better hunters than the soldiers had been. One of Romont's lieutenants took thirty volunteers back to the mired cannons to help get them through the mud; perhaps, if they hurried, they might eventually catch up to the bulk of the forces.

Around ten wingrats stayed close to the army, governed by Low Moon, while the others left for other regions of Suinomen to gather food. Their dietary needs were considerable, and unless they spread out they would certainly starve. The wingrats staying with them were the older, better trained of the lot, while the rest were young and immature, and would have been more trouble than they were worth in a pitched battle. Kai had given the beasts free run of his kingdom, provided they left farmers' crops and beasts alone when they were scavenging for food. Low Moon assured them that they knew the difference between wild and domesticated food.

"Even as ruler, it sounds as if you might be able to appoint someone else, in your place," Derek said goodnaturedly. "Those are the strangest beasts I have ever seen. Do they think? Are they intelligent?" he added, casting occasional looks back to the wingrats.

"Oh, quite," Alaire replied. "Low Moon, their leader now, in particular." The remaining wingrats chose to march with the army instead of flying. According to Low Moon, their wings were quite tired and they needed to use their legs after the long flight. Once the army was convinced the creatures were on their side, the soldiers were fascinated with them, and no longer seemed to consider them a threat. "We must give them time to adjust to their freedom. It is something they've never had."

Derek nodded, and scratched his beard. "They will make valuable allies, once this battle is over."

"You forget," Alaire said, guiding his horse over a particularly muddy section of road. "The forces we are going to encounter have many more of these beasts than we do, ones trained for war."

Derek frowned deeply at this news. Captain Romont gazed ahead of him, seemingly lost in thought.

"However," Alaire added, "there may be a way around this problem." He explained to his brother how he had first freed Low Moon of the obedience magic, then applied this knowledge to freeing the entire wingrat population of Roksamur. "They will not be expecting a counterspell in Rozinki. I may be able to work the same magic here, with as much success." Alaire wondered if his interference with the ley magic in Roksamur had already weakened the spells on the beasts here. *I won't know anything until I get there. And as it is, I'm about to fall asleep on this horse.*

At sunset, they made camp in a dense forest and sent a scout ahead to determine their proximity to the palace. Kai seemed as dead tired as Alaire felt, and collapsed on a bed of pine needles alongside the Bard. Alaire was vaguely aware of a tent being erected for them, but was also aware they would probably not be using it that night, unless someone carried them to it.

When the first of the wingrats had rebelled against their Arachnian masters, Craig suspected he might have made a very unwise move by throwing in with Su'Villtor.

The incident had taken place the previous evening, when the Arachnian leaders were gathering the wingrats on the hillside for a short scouting expedition into the adjoining farmlands. They did not move with their usual speed and efficiency, and Craig had a strong impression that they had changed. Two wingrats remained in the pasture, and when two Arachnians pursued them, they actually tried to take flight to evade them. But the Arachnians chased them down before they could, and took hold of their reins, the one piece of tack left on when the wingrats were at pasture. They resisted the bugs' attempt to pull them in, and when one actually gnashed at them with those enormous rodent tusks, a company of Arachnians rushed the two and began firing arrows into them, until they bristled with the shafts. They left the carcasses to rot, as warning to the rest. But Craig knew that something was going terribly amiss with the creatures for that to have taken place at all. The Arachnians were visibly rattled by the episode but disclosed nothing to Craig directly.

Then came the discovery of the jeweled leather collar, which he had apparently been wearing for days now all unawares. He had no clue as to why it had been placed on his neck until he removed it. Once he had the collar off he sensed he had done something horribly stupid, but he wasn't certain what it was. With shame turning to rage, he flung the collar at the nearest wall. As the stones shattered, so did his desire to side with the invaders.

He started considering ways he might be able to escape the palace altogether, if the need should ever arise, without the Arachnians' knowledge. Every road leading out of the city was controlled by the Arachnians, and so were the docks. The easiest course of action, he finally decided, was to wait and see what happened. The Arachnians were still in power, and nothing in Rozinki threatened that balance. He'd begun the day's jug of wine and had quickly put thoughts of leaving out of his mind.

Then Su'Villtor had stormed into "his" study a candlemark later. The annoying bug had taken a long look at what Craig was doing and had shaken its bulbous head. Craig resisted an urge to fling the jug at the creature, mostly because it was the last of the stock he had brought up from the cellar and he would have go all the way back down there to retrieve more. Those stairs were getting awfully difficult to negotiate.

"Just as I thought," Su'Villtor said, reprovingly. "The quantity you humans can drink amazes me."

Craig stared at the bug, trying to look fierce, but he was having difficulty focusing.

The Arachnian continued, "Su'Kanguer would like to know what has happened to the crossbows kept in the pantry?"

Craig knew they had gathered up all the weapons they could shortly after the invasion, but had not been told where they were being kept. "How can I possibly know where they have gone if you never told me where they were?"

"Your behavior is becoming suspicious," Su'Villtor continued, as if Craig had said nothing. "The weapons have gone somewhere and, until now, you have had the freedom to move about the palace."

"What about the prisoners?" he asked. An entire company of Arachnians stood guard outside the fighting arena, where Captain Lyam and his men were being kept. *What if they had stolen the weapons?* "Have you checked their quarters carefully?"

Su'Villtor stepped closer and looked down, disapprovingly, at Craig. "Do not insult us, human. They have been closely watched. You have *not*."

Something the bug had said bothered him and it took him a moment to determine what. "What did you say about freedom to move around in the palace?"

"You have *none*," Su'Villtor replied, with a finality that Craig knew was going to be impossible to argue with. The Arachnia noticed the smashed jewels and the limp collar lying on the floor. "Who gave you permission to remove that?"

Craig stood unsteadily, and gazed angrily at the Arachnian. "Permission?" he asked incredulously.

The Arachnia made a noise that resembled laughter. "Yes, permission. Now you have made the decision for us. You are a *hostage* in our game. You will be held for ransom just like your brother!" Su'Villtor turned and walked towards the door with his usual swiftness and agility, then paused. "If you try to leave, we will kill you."

The Arachnia pulled the door closed and something hard slammed across it. Craig looked out his window and saw three Arachnians standing guard. Slowly, ever so slowly, Craig began to suspect that whatever he had done while under the influence of the collar, he was going to start paying for it now.

Chapter Seventeen

Alaire woke to the unfamiliar sounds of an army camp gearing up for war, along with the pleasant aroma of wild game cooking over a fire. Beside him, Kai stirred but showed no immediate signs of coming back to life; the Bard understood, and wasn't certain if his own mind and body were working this morning. The wingrat ride had chafed his legs where the leather bindings had rubbed, and his back was horribly sore from hunching over Low Moon during most of the journey.

He brightened with a cheerful thought. *We have a war to fight today.*

But since this was a battle over possession of Suinomen, he thought it only appropriate that its king be awake for the proceedings. Alaire poked him in the ribs and moved back, narrowly avoiding the wide swing of Kai's right arm as it sought contact with whatever had jabbed him.

"Time to get up. We've got a battle to see to," Alaire said, and Kai managed to sit up. Dressed in the animal skins, with several days of beard and a completely uncivilized look in his eye, Kainemonen looked like his distant cave-dwelling ancestors must have.

"Not dressed like *this* we're not," Kai said resolutely. "I trust there might be some *real* clothes to spare." Yawning once, he climbed slowly to his feet. "You owe me a set, if I recall."

"Ah, yes," Alaire replied, sounding considerably more cheerful than he felt. "It would hardly do to take back your palace dressed like *that.*"

His brother wasn't too difficult to find, as the King of Althea was one of the few in the camp who had a tent. Nearby, Captain Romont was sharpening a sword and gave them a brief nod as they passed. The ten wingrats had gathered under a large oak tree, making Alaire imagine a pack of wolves taking a break. Low Moon was among them, curled up like a cat, asleep. Most of the army had apparently slept in the open on bedrolls and was now lined up for breakfast at the cooks' wagon.

"So you've decided to join the living," Derek greeted them. At his campfire was the game Alaire had smelled earlier, along with the glorious scent of brewed kaffe. "We would have moved you, but you both seemed quite content where you were. We did post a guard throughout the night who, incidentally, is seeing to your horses as we speak. Did you sleep well?"

"As well as can be expected," Alaire replied. "That kaffe is going to save my life."

King Derek had arranged for someone to gather additional clothes for them, and while they changed he briefed them on what he had learned of the situation in Rozinki. "Our scouts returned early this morning with some information you might find interesting," he began. "The Arachnian invaders are quite a curious lot. While it is clear they have looted the city for food, they have actually done very little to incarcerate the citizens, other than imprisoning the military and police forces somewhere on the palace grounds."

Alaire pulled a boot on, frowned at the snugness, and began loosening the straps. "As they are much larger than humans, they may not see the townspeople as a threat."

"There was no militia," Kainemonen said sadly as he

buttoned up a pair of breeches. "After the coup six years ago, we discouraged the possession of swords and daggers. Given the size of the invaders, that they would not put up much resistance is no surprise."

"Their main concern," Alaire said, "seems to be possession of the palace. Were there any of the enemy patrolling the city itself?"

"Few, as we were told. There were a great many at the beginning of the invasion, but a day or two ago most of these pulled back." The king moved to the spit, then plucked the cooked rabbit from the fire for them.

"Interesting," Kai commented. "You don't suppose they're preparing to mobilize?"

The king shook his head, and offered the rabbit on a plate. "If they are, then we would have no way of knowing. The one thing the scouts were able to confirm is that they are guarding the palace gates closely."

"Any information about Craig?" Alaire asked, and Kai looked up inquisitively.

"None," the king said, then looked at Kainemonen directly.

"It appears that our brother might have been involved in this takeover. If this turns out to be true, we will turn Craig over to you when we recapture the palace. In my opinion, he deserves whatever punishment you see fit."

"We don't yet know the extent of his involvement," Kainemonen said, looking uncomfortable. "And as it stands, it is the Arachnians who have invaded, not Althea. I do not hold your kingdom responsible. After all, it was the murder of your ambassador that started this whole thing. It was traitorous forces from within our own court, like the last time, which were primarily responsible for betraying me and the people of Rozinki."

"Su'Villtor," Alaire said.

Kai nodded silent agreement, and looked down at the ground.

"Oh, I forgot something else that might be important," Derek said, ducking into his tent. He returned with a new, cherry wood harp and handed it to Alaire. "This might be useful," he said with a smile, then turned to Kai. "So, Kainemonen, what suggestions have you for taking your palace back?"

"Well, I've had some time to think about this." On the ground Kai drew a design with a stick. Alaire resisted an urge to tune the beautiful instrument immediately and set it down carefully and turned his attention to the diagram. With rocks and pebbles Kai designated various points, the city of Rozinki and the palace. King Derek called Captain Romont, who had evidently finished sharpening his blade.

"The palace is very old, and is built into the side of a hill which is accessible only by one road. If the gate is heavily guarded, we will have considerable trouble getting inside."

"I see," Romont said. "Our cannon should arrive by tomorrow. That is, do we have permission to use them?"

"Well, I prefer to keep my castle intact, but if there is no other way to get to the invaders, then yes, of course you do," Kai said quickly. "We can always rebuild." He glanced back at the army which filled the nearby woods. "What exactly is the makeup of your force?"

"Since we knew we would be fighting an airborne enemy, we brought a large number of archers. A division of mounted men, a thousand archers, and four hundred foot soldiers."

"You mentioned artillery?"

"Fifteen cannons, capable of firing twenty-pound balls," Romont said, not taking his eyes off the crude map. "Each with a crew of five. Then the monster, which may or may not make it this far, it being the one which bogged down the worst. It can discharge hundred-pound balls or a combination of lead shot and rock."

"Which is what we would need to take a wall down," Kai said. "May I make the following recommendation? We may yet achieve the element of surprise. I think we should secure the city, store our supplies out of sight and set up an offensive line here," he said, drawing a line just before the palace. "At the foot of the hill is a good supply of large rocks, with boulders that can conceal cannons. The walls facing the sea are the thickest. Those against the city are rather thin, in places. Also, this is where our roads to the farmland intersect. We may be able to completely resupply your army after taking the city."

"We have supply ships en route," King Derek said. "They will have food and powder, and are scheduled to put in up here," he said, drawing an "X" some distance to the north of Rozinki.

"Why can't we come in from the north?" Alaire asked, between mouthfuls of rabbit. Six years had blurred his memory of the palace grounds. *Was there anything on that side?*

"Unapproachable," Kai said. "A sheer cliff. It's why the palace was built there."

Alaire considered this for a moment. "That route may not be as impossible as you might think," he said. "We do have the means of getting to the top of that hill with very little effort." He gestured towards the wingrats relaxing under the oak tree. "They can take us up there."

"For what purpose?" Derek asked.

"They won't be expecting anything from above. Also, I think it would be an ideal location to cast the spell."

Derek scratched the back of his head, then gave

his brother a doubtful look. "You would be vulnerable."

"Not with archers," he said. "From that vantage point, we would have a good shot at the palace grounds. And at anything that might fly at us."

"Perhaps," Derek said, then turned to Kai. "For the time being, I suggest we make use of King Kainemonen's suggestion that we take the city first."

"We would have the advantage at night," Kainemonen said. "It would be difficult for the flying beasts to attack us in the dark."

"Yes, yes, *yes*," Alaire agreed. It just might work.

"Tonight it is, then," King Derek said.

Throughout the day, King Derek sent out more scouts to determine where in the city the enemy was concentrated. The tavern district seemed to be their favorite haunt.

"Which might," Kai had pointed out, "help us defeat them. I know that maze of streets well. That is, after all, where I once spent a good deal of time."

A scout had also backtracked to check up on the artillery's progress; all but the one large cannon should arrive by sundown. The lieutenant in charge of the operation sent all the powder and ordnance wagons ahead with the rest. Once a crude ramp had been built to roll the large cannon out of a creek bed, which would take another half day, they would have all their artillery.

"By sunrise," Derek said confidently. "We will have what we need."

The Althean army marched at dusk, well rested, well armed, and well versed in the weak spots of Arachnia. All cannons but the one hundred pounder had arrived, with the help of Konnongur's people. Alaire saw that his brother appreciated having the extra hands, even if they weren't that astute in the art of modern war. They seemed more than receptive to orders and obeyed them without question, particularly if backed up by Alaire, their new "king."

Kainemonen led a hundred cavalry and archers directly to the tavern district, taking back streets that the king knew all too well. Alaire rode with him, while Romont and King Derek spread out over the rest of the city looking for the enemy. The penetration happened quickly, quietly, and so far as Alaire could tell, undetected. As expected, very few of the residents were out at night, and the few who saw them cheered the soldiers on. And just as enthusiastically, Kai motioned for them to be silent.

"We should split up," Kainemonen told the company. They did, Alaire taking one half of the forces and Kai the other. The street had an eerie, familiar feel to it. Alaire realized this was the very street he and Kai had been on when they were jumped by assassins. In the summer heat, without the thick layer of snow, the district had a different, volatile feel to it.

One of the scouts, a lad of about seventeen who had been doing a fair amount of running between Rozinki and the Althean army, rushed up to Alaire. "They're in the Dead Dragon Inn, mostly," the boy said, out of breath.

"Do they suspect anything?" Alaire asked.

"They've been doing this every night," the boy said. "At sunset they give up their patrols and head to the inns. The owners try to close up but they just let themselves in and help themselves to the ale."

Wouldn't take much, I suppose, Alaire thought. "Pass the word, keep to the shadows," he whispered to the nearest foot soldier.

Alaire was distracted by a shape coming out of one of the bars. Two Arachnia were walking, none too steadily, down the street. From the shadows, a crossbow went *twang,* then another, and another after that.

One of the Arachnia fell over with an arrow sticking out of its head. The other clutched at a shaft that protruded from its midsection, this one letting out a blood-chilling chitter.

"Watch the doors," Alaire said, but already a fair number of Arachnia, in various states of drunkenness, were rushing out in response to the scream.

"Shoot at will!" Alaire shouted, and the archers quickly advanced and took positions across the street, one row kneeling, another standing. The Bard led a handful of archers to one of the dark alleys, at the end of which was the back door of the Dead Dragon Inn. The moving shadows that fell across their path indicated anything but order inside. The *twang twang twang* of archers and bows from the street played an interesting counterpoint to the sudden clatter of felled tables and gibbering Arachnian.

"Take positions," Alaire said. The archers arranged themselves in the shadows, and when the Arachnians spilled into the alley, they let loose their arrows. At first the insects seemed confused. Then, as if homing in on the arrows' source, they looked directly at Alaire and his group.

The Bard made a chilling discovery. *These bastards can see in the dark!* Too late to move now. The archers continued firing shafts into the charging bugs, striking some in the midsection, others in an eye. One unaffected by the barrage charged directly for Alaire and his line of soldiers.

The Arachnia had no weapon, save for the massive claws which now snapped around the middle of one of the archers; the young man let out a scream, a sound which came to a very abrupt end as the claw closed around him.

Alaire swung with his sword, sinking it halfway into one of the creature's eyes, then began hacking away at the head. The other claw snapped in his general direction, but being smaller and more mobile, Alaire managed to dance clear of it. Once blinded, the Arachnia seemed to lose its will to fight and released its first victim, then staggered free. The archers finished it off and then were busy with two more Arachnians who had charged out of the inn.

It's hard to know when they're dead, Alaire thought, remembering the other Arachnians he'd slain on Roksamur. As with those, there was considerable squirming and writhing, this one making a thin trilling noise as it died. Its blood had leaked all over the alley, making for slick footing.

Alaire checked the fallen soldier, finding him quite dead. He was the only one of their group to have fallen so far, and Alaire hoped Kai was having as much luck.

Once certain all their opponents were slain, Alaire and his group advanced to the rear door of the inn and looked in. Empty. Just beyond the front door he saw fallen Arachnians and, beyond them, flying arrows. *Better not go that way.*

They charged to the end of the alley and turned left. A row of crossbows raised in their direction momentarily, then tracked back to the action on their street. Kainemonen's group was busy finishing up a pair of Arachnians who had made it through that line.

"How do you know when these damned things are *dead*?" Kainemonen shouted when he saw Alaire.

"Blind them," he shouted back. "If they're not dead, they can't do much." Kainemonen followed his suggestion, and began carving away pieces of the creatures' bulbous eyes.

In the middle of the cobblestone street, Alaire counted nineteen fallen Arachnians, and what looked like as many dead Altheans. Not a good ratio, but given the enemy's advantage in size and natural weaponry, he was glad the count wasn't higher. In the gutters, a thin river of Arachnian and human blood mixed and ran down to the sewers. Kai started organizing the men for a tavern by tavern search for more of the enemy.

They swept through several city blocks, finding an Arachnia here and there, but no real concentration. Alaire's impression was that an attack of this nature was the last thing on their enemy's minds; very few Arachnians were actually down here in the city and those who were, were intent on getting drunk. When Alaire and Kai's forces met up with Derek's, they heard the same observation.

"We will send details out to collect the dead at dawn," King Derek said solemnly. "Fifty dead. Fifty more than we should have lost, but still . . ."

Privately, Alaire knew his brother was pleased with the outcome. Now that the city was secured, their work had just begun. Derek turned to Kai. "Show me where you wanted that line drawn up."

Behind him, Alaire heard the rattle of a wagon. When he turned, the biggest cannon he'd ever seen was struggling up a street. A child could climb into its barrel, it was so enormous. Five wingrats pulled at yokes, loosened to fit around their larger heads. Apparently, the dieren had given out.

Kai led the army to the edge of town to a small rise overlooking a bridge, which in turn led to the palace gates. A full moon illuminated the area brightly.

"We'll assemble here," Derek said, and proceeded to divide the artillery into two groups. One, which included the big gun, was aimed toward the part of the wall Kai had insisted was the weakest part of the structure. The other group set up near a row of shops, where it had a clear shot at the main palace gate. The terrain of the entire area was very hilly, not at all favorable to foot travel. This could well prove a problem, Derek confided to Kai and Alaire, but it was nothing they could address now.

"We should attack now," Kainemonen said. "We still have the advantage of surprise."

"I'll have to agree with Kai," Alaire said. "So far, we've been lucky. We've won because, quite frankly, they've been too drunk to fight." He looked up at the palace, a dark monolith devoid of any light or visible life. "We won't be so fortunate at daybreak, when they realize what's happened."

"I tell you, there's something going *on* out there," Erik said desperately, as he shook his father awake. "There was a disturbance at the gate. The Arachnia they let in was wounded."

In the fighting arena, Lyam and his people had been trying to sleep through the night. His son Erik had been pulling double guard duty, watching the palace grounds from the eaves of the arena, where he had an excellent view of the gate.

"Probably just another drunken . . ." Lyam said, as he got up. "Guards out front?"

"They're there, but impatient. There's something going on, they don't get this way in the middle of the night."

Lyam noted his son's youthful excitement and wondered for a brief moment if he ever had that much energy when he was eighteen.

"I'm for the tunnels," Erik said. "There we can hear what's going on."

Captain Lyam had to agree. The disturbance had wakened a fair number of the human prisoners being kept in the building. Lyam held a hand up, which silenced everyone, then selected four men to take with him. Then they descended into the secret passages.

The cache of crossbows and arrows was near the arena entrance. Lyam and his men selected weapons. *If there is something to this, they're likely to be discussing this in the king's chambers,* Lyam thought, as they made their way as quietly as possible through the tunnels.

"Here," Lyam said at a sharp turn, which was as close to the chambers as the tunnels went. A small vent, covered with a grate, led to the other side, where Lyam saw the hint of a candle flame. The captain motioned for the rest to be silent, then held his ear to the vent.

" . . . no way Althea could have made it here," he heard Craig saying. "The people must have rebelled."

"With cannons?" an Arachnia, most likely Su'Villtor, said. "With cavalry? With archers? That soldier died to bring us this information! And you're telling me it was a group of shopkeepers who annihilated our city forces?"

Silence, followed by a long string of Arachnian, all of which sounded quite agitated. Erik's eyes widened at the mention of Althea. *Perhaps we are under attack by Althean forces. We can only hope.*

Su'Villtor continued, "If the king of Althea is at our door with an army, I will personally see to your death."

"You can always use me as a hostage," Craig said, sounding drunk, as usual. "That was the original plan."

"Aie, yes, it was," Su'Villtor replied. Another exchange in Arachnian, then, "There is an army outside, and they are not from the local population."

"Then I must have been mistaken," Craig said. He sounded as though he'd given up and didn't really care what happened.

Good gods, Lyam thought, grinning from ear to ear. *Althea is at our gates!*

"Back to the arena," Lyam whispered. "It's time to start distributing the rest of the crossbows."

When the first light of dawn touched the horizon, Alaire knew that the decision to attack had been made for them.

"If it doesn't work, don't wait for me to come back down. Fire on the palace immediately," Alaire said to his brother. They both looked up at the steep path which, with the lightening horizon behind it, seemed much narrower than Alaire had remembered.

Word arrived from a scout that the enemy was beginning to mobilize within the palace grounds. Arachnians were gathering and arming wingrats, and were in a general state of alert.

"If you're going to do this thing, you'd better do it now," Derek said. "It sounds like you're going to have company up there soon."

Moments later, Alaire was mounted on Low Moon, with his harp slung over his shoulder; on the other nine wingrats were Konnongur and some of the other village elders, with two of Althea's best archers.

:To the top of that hill,: Alaire sent to Low Moon, who in turn passed the direction on to the other wingrats.

Low Moon beat at the air with her huge wings, then took to the sky. Alaire considered making a pass over the grounds, but decided against it; he had a specific job to do, and he had to be on solid ground to do it.

Airborne, Alaire caught the first rays of morning. A light mist blanketed the town. At this height he saw Althea's army in full, laid out in neat, geometric patterns. The cavalry, archers, and artillery made a striking display of force.

Alaire and his mount circled over the hill once; their destination seemed incredibly small, like the head of a nail, before they put down on its flat surface.

Low Moon tucked her wings in and sniffed the air. *:Wingrats,:* she sent. *:Down . . . there:*

The archers quickly dismounted and took up positions on either side of the group. They had a clear view of the palace grounds from up here, partially hidden by the palace itself. Indeed, Arachnians were preparing hundreds of wingrats for battle.

:We must hurry,: Low Moon sent, and Alaire understood her concern. If they didn't break the obedience

spell before the fighting began, the Althean army would be forced to fire upon the wingrats as well as their Arachnian riders. *We must avoid killing the innocent,* Alaire knew. Konnongur's people dismounted, and the wingrats cleared space for them. The magicians sat in a circle, with Konnongur at the opposite side from Alaire.

Again, Alaire reached for the earth power he suspected might lurk in this hill; though it was nothing like the ley lines he'd manipulated in Roksamur, this magic was old, and familiar. This was what the Bard was accustomed to using.

Alaire met Konnongur's eyes, a signal for the others to raise their power. Bard and Fastur magicians fell into the same pattern, and the magicians began to chant.

Nam-mu, *Nam*-mu, *Nam*-mu . . .

From the palace grounds, Arachnians on wingrats rose to the sky. The archers sat poised, arrows nocked and ready. But the Arachnian forces below were ignoring the hill. Instead, they seemed intent on attacking the Althean army.

Then the Bard became aware of another force, the wingrats adding their own power to the spell. The phenomenon surprised him, but when he saw the signatures of their magic, he knew this was going to improve their chances. *The imprisoned wingrats will recognize the source,* he thought.

Now is the time. . . .

Aided with the harp, Alaire began singing the song of Prophecy.

> *Bindings of the thousand born,*
> *Onto this land of Roksamur . . .*

A hundred or so wingrats had taken to the air, and Alaire watched as he sang, weaving the spell, making the magic. Low Moon and the other wingrats continued supplying their own power, with a little more urgency, now that the Arachnian forces were approaching their army.

> *Break the chains, cut the ropes*
> *turn us loose and let us see. . . .*

Finally, an Arachnian spotted Alaire and his group on the hilltop, circled, then flew up towards them.

"Begone! Begone!" the group shouted. "Be *free*."

As on Roksamur, the power shifted suddenly, and all around him Alaire felt a drastic change take place.

The wingrat and rider rose up to them, paused, hovered. The Arachnia was raising a bow; the archers on the hill aimed, but Alaire motioned for them to hold. Then the flying creature began biting at the Arachnia, turning it's long rat snout towards the rider. The Arachnia drew back and the wingrat caught a strap of the leather harness, biting hard, cutting it neatly.

The wingrat flew off a ways and made a long, laborious loop, while the Arachnia tugged ineffectually at the reins. Then the wingrat turned over suddenly, spilling Arachnia and harness.

Just like before, Alaire thought triumphantly. Low Moon turned her snout to the air and howled; the others followed suit.

Alaire dismissed the magic, now that it had clearly worked, and Konnongur stood by him.

"It's happening again," Konnongur said. "The prophecy continues."

Captain Lyam had counted around one hundred prisoners in the fighting arena, and once the forty crossbows had been passed out among them, he instructed the rest of the men to protect the archers with whatever they could find.

Until that time, twenty Arachnians had stood guard

over the arena; now it was starting to look as though the good behavior of Lyam and his men was going to pay off. The number of guards dwindled to ten, then five. Evidently they didn't think the humans were any match for Arachnians.

Unarmed humans were probably not a concern, Lyam considered as he peered through the shutter slats. *Humans with crossbows, now that's a different story.*

Beyond the five Arachnian guards, the rest of the invading army was preparing for war. His son's hunch was proving to be accurate. A group of wingrats had been herded down from the field that had, over the course of the invasion, become their temporary home.

"The bugs are getting ready to fly off," Lyam said to his men. "When the numbers are a little more even we're going to attack."

The guards were getting nervous, as evidenced by their agitated movements. It was clear to Lyam that they were being left to deal with all the remaining prisoners, and it didn't look as though they were comfortable with that.

As well they shouldn't be . . . Lyam thought, then signaled for his men to get ready.

Then from outside the arena, four crossbows released their arrows simultaneously, piercing one guard in head and midsection; before the other guards reacted, Lyam and his men had forced the arena door open and began shooting at the other four. A river of men poured out onto the palace grounds, catching all the Arachnians unprepared.

"To the *gate!*" Lyam shouted, and led a contingent of men in that direction.

The wingrats continued shedding themselves of harnesses and riders, and Arachnians plummeted to certain death on the rocky ground below.

The cheer that swelled up from the army was audible

to Alaire on the hill; within the grounds, wingrats not yet airborne turned on Arachnians, then made their escape. Movement down near the palace caught Alaire's eye. Down near the fighting arena was a commotion.

"What the—" Alaire said, before he saw precisely what was taking place.

"The gate," Alaire muttered. "They're going for the gate. . . ."

A group of Arachnians ran after them, but were soon overrun by their former wingrat slaves. Some men took firing positions; others went for the bar which blocked the gate. Soon the massive gates swung open and the former captives began waving wildly at the forces outside. Their gestures seemed to be saying, *all is clear, enter at will.*

"We should let Derek know about this," Alaire said as he swung a leg over Low Moon. "We may not have to destroy Kai's walls after all!"

Alaire took Low Moon back down to the ground and rejoined his brother, while the other wingrats and their Fasturian riders took refuge behind the front, deep in the city of Rozinki.

"There was a rebellion in the palace! Don't fire!" Alaire shouted as he approached Derek, slinging his harp over his shoulder. "The gates are open."

"Hold your fire," Derek ordered, and the cannon crew extinguished the flame that was about to fire the hundred pounder. Captain Romont assigned a company of archers to follow Kainemonen, Alaire and the king to the palace gate.

After the palace gates swung open, the Althean cavalry charged through. Alaire and Kai stayed close together, looking for a way into the palace.

"Your Majesty!" he heard someone shout, and when he turned he saw Captain Lyam with a group of men, shooting down Arachnians with crossbows.

"Captain," Kainemonen said, as they approached Lyam's group. "Take us to Su'Villtor!"

"Consider it done," the captain said, his men still shooting arrows. The Arachnians were spending as much time fighting their own mounts as they were the humans; most gave up and fled back into the palace, while the newly freed wingrats took to the sky without them.

"They're retreating into the palace," Kai said. "Can we get past the main doors?"

"There's a better way, Your Majesty," Lyam said. "Follow me."

Chapter Eighteen

Lyam led the king, Alaire, and twenty of his men back to the fighting arena, then down into the labyrinth of tunnels connecting it to the palace.

"For six years I have studied these passages," Lyam said as they made their way through the dank underground, holding a single candle for illumination. "The entry points are all in the hallways, not in the rooms themselves, which is one reason they are so hard to find."

He stopped at a wood-paneled corner and put his ear against the wall. "Here. We can enter. It sounds like it's clear."

Lyam pushed a panel, then another; suddenly the wall pivoted open, revealing a palace hallway.

Alaire heard the fighting clearly at the other end of the hallway, but it had yet to reach this far into the palace. Lyam assigned ten archers to cover their rear before pushing forward.

Before they'd gone more than a few paces, three armored Arachnians stepped into view.

"Shoot!" Lyam shouted, and crossbows loosed their arrows. One of the Arachnians fell immediately, while the others staggered momentarily, then charged forward.

Alaire had his sword drawn and swung; a claw grabbed at it, then clamped down once it had gained

purchase. Two arrows whizzed past Alaire's ear before
he stepped back, giving the archers a better shot.

Kai swung at the other one, but his sword glanced
off the hard leather armor. "Lyam, shoot!" he ordered,
and a moment later an arrow pierced the Arachnia's
eye. It let loose a loud, screaming chitter as it stepped
back, and Kainemonen ducked. Arrows continued to
fly, striking Alaire's opponent twice in the midsection,
the shafts burying themselves halfway into the armor.
It released Alaire's sword as it fell backwards; the
Bard retrieved his weapon and proceeded to hack its
eyes out.

The party stepped carefully past the fallen, writhing Arachnians. Alaire didn't know if they were dead,
but they were certainly out of commission.

"The chambers," Alaire said. "Kai—"

They froze the moment they stepped into the
doorway of the king's chambers. Su'Villtor stood against
the far wall, holding Craig with one of his claws at
his throat. Another Arachnia, this one with decorated
armor, a general of some kind, stood next to him.

"You will drop your weapons or this human will
die," Su'Villtor announced. "All of you, now!"

Alaire and Kai exchanged looks. "Do you think we
should do as they say?" Alaire asked.

"Do you?" Kainemonen replied.

Alaire turned to Captain Lyam, "What's your opinion, Captain?"

The captain seemed to consider this seriously for
a moment. "I think they should *all* die," he said finally.

Alaire was prepared to agree, but something stopped
him. He stood there watching his brother strain against
the claw. *I see no obedience collar on him!* he thought
angrily.

"They bespelled me!" Craig shouted. "Look at the
floor!"

"Silence!" the Arachnia shouted.

Alaire saw a strip of leather on the floor, with what looked like shattered stones. One stone was still intact, and Alaire advanced to pick it up. The Bard felt the residue of the broken spell, which was the same as the magic worked on the wingrats. *It worked so well on Craig because he was intoxicated all the time.*

Part of Alaire gave like a thread breaking.

He's still my brother.

"Let them go," Alaire said, laying his sword on the floor. "Killing them will serve no purpose."

"Alaire, *what are you doing*?" Kai asked. "This man is a traitor!"

Alaire decided to approach this from a different angle. "Why did the Arachnians of Roksamur invade Suinomen? What do your people want?"

"Your kingdoms," Su'Villtor said. "Which we will yet take for our own, even if we fail today."

"If you fail today, you'll have nowhere to go," Alaire said evenly, taking a step forward.

"We have Roksamur and we will take Althea, too!" Su'Villtor said.

Alaire shook his head. "Roksamur is no more. The island was covered by fire. Do you not know of the prophecy?"

"All lies," Su'Villtor said. "We will return to what was ours, and we will rebuild our forces and take this land for our own!"

"Alaire, step back!" Lyam shouted.

An arrow shot past Alaire's right ear, and the Bard ducked instinctively. The arrow buried itself in Su'Villtor's right eye, and the Arachnia screamed as it pulled the sharp tip of its claw over Craig's neck, cutting it open.

"Craig!" Alaire shouted, as he ducked and rolled out of the line of fire. His harp fell off his shoulder and clattered against the wall. Lyam's archers rained arrows on the remaining Arachnia, reloaded, and fired

again. In moments, the bug bristled with arrow shafts
and was pinned against the wall.

Alaire rushed over to Craig, who was now lying in
a pool of his own blood. The Bard pulled him clear
of the writhing Arachnia, then leaned over to examine the wound.

The cut was deep, down to the windpipe. An artery
had been severed. Craig lay limply in Alaire's arms,
dead, or nearly so.

Kainemonen stood over his friend and his dying
brother. Alaire looked up, not sure what to say, or
feel, right then.

Instead, Kainemonen did the talking. "You're not
going to give up now, are you?" the King of Suinomen
said, holding Alaire's harp out to him.

For a moment, the Bard didn't know what he was
talking about. Then he remembered the time he had
saved Kainemonen's life by performing Bardic magic.
The king's wounds had been far more severe than
his brother's. He had not performed that particular
Bardic spell since that day in winter, but as his
brother's blood leaked over his hands, he remembered
the spell, every word, every nuance, in detail.

With red hands, he took the harp. Then, taking a
deep breath, he reached deep into his soul and started
to play.

The song returned to him easily, though he hadn't
practiced it in years. The music conjured memories of
Kainemonen lying in a snowbank, crimson with blood.
Alaire hoped he wasn't too late to save Craig.

The song ended, and his brother continued to lie
motionless.

"Again," Kai whispered. "Try it again."

Alaire went through the song again, this time putting a little more enthusiasm into the music. He
hadn't slept much in too many days and was bone
weary, but it had become important to save his

brother, traitor or not. The song ended with no sign of life from Craig.

What am I doing wrong? Alaire thought desperately. Then his master's words echoed in his mind.

The essence of Bardic magic is the ability to make, and unmake.

Closing his eyes, he began the song again, this time finding the power he needed; he imagined his brother's wounds closing, healing. He opened his eyes, and saw a cloud of light encircling his brother's neck. When the cloud disappeared, the neck wound had healed.

"Brother . . . " Alaire whispered, leaning back against the wall. "Are you . . . ?"

Craig coughed, once, before Alaire's vision turned to black.

The sleep Alaire lapsed into felt as though it lasted an eternity. Memories of his master, Naitachal, of his childhood, of his father, Reynard, drifted in, then out. He became aware of pain throughout his body as his eyes flickered open.

His vision wavered momentarily, before he was able to focus. He was lying in a large bed with a white canopy. Others were in the room, but the pain was too much to allow him to turn his head.

"He's awake," he heard Kainemonen say. Then Kai leaned over him. "How are you doing, Alaire?"

"Horribly," he said, struggling to at least sit up. Propped up on an elbow, he took in the room, which was the very room Kai had assigned them on their arrival. "The invasion?"

"Crushed," Kai said solemnly. "The Arachnians, they didn't want to surrender. They forced us to kill every last one of them."

The Bard felt neither relief nor regret. He felt little of anything, except confusion.

"You went into shock," Kainemonen told him as he helped him arrange a feather pillow behind his back.

"How long?" he asked, in a whisper.

"Four days," Kai replied.

Alaire stared at him, uncertain if he'd heard him correctly. "Konnongur came in to help you heal, on the first night. That was when you . . . died."

Finally, something he understood. Death. This explained why he felt the way he did. *I died. I sure feel like it.*

"Physically, you were exhausted. You hadn't slept enough in days. Then, you worked the spell, the prophecy spell. All those wingrats, suddenly free. That power went through you, whether you realized it or not. Then you did the healing spell, which saved your brother. It was too much, we were told. Your body and soul gave out."

"My compliments to Konnongur," Alaire said weakly. "He's more advanced in the healing arts than I gave him credit for."

"Uh, Alaire. Konnongur didn't heal you. He said you were too far gone. He gave up, that first night."

Alaire rubbed his eyes, massaging the sleep out of them. "Shame on him, then," he said in jest. "Evidently he gave up too soon. Then tell me, friend, who did the honors?"

"Reykir."

Alaire's apprentice stepped into sight, on his left holding his flute triumphantly. "Didn't do me much good," he said, with a smile. "You hadn't shown me how to protect myself. Very nearly did us both in."

"Understandable," Alaire said. *Reykir worked the magic? Bardic magic, that saved my life? With that damned flute?* "I wasn't aware you were that far along, Bard."

"I wasn't aware either," Reykir said, then his eyes met Alaire's. "Bard?"

"Yes, Bard," Alaire said. "Only a Bard could have pulled *this* off."

"But I'm . . ."

"Don't argue. You graduated," Alaire said, sounding irritated despite his best efforts not to.

"Yes, sir!" Reykir said, with a smile that threatened to split his head open. "Is there anything I can get you?"

Alaire considered this for only a brief moment. "Yes, there is. Would you *please* fetch me a cup of kaffe?"